COULD IT BE?

After Water Tower Place, Anita decided to cross Michigan Avenue to hit the stores on the west side of the street and then head south back to the hotel.

As Anita stood on the corner among a growing throng of stopped pedestrians, waiting for the light to change, a city bus pulled into view. The doors hissed open, a line of people climbed out, and then a line of people climbed aboard. The doors slapped shut, and the bus loudly lurched forward.

Anita saw the succession of faces in the bus windows roll past her. For a moment, her eyes locked with the sad eyes of a young passenger staring out. A frozen image, like a snapshot, then he was gone.

A little boy, maybe four years old.

A little boy with an uncanny resemblance to Tim....

BRIAN PINKERTON

ABDUCTED

LEISURE BOOKS NEW YORK CITY

A LEISURE BOOK®

March 2004

Published by

Dorchester Publishing Co., Inc.
200 Madison Avenue
New York, NY 10016

ISBN 0-8439-5331-4

Printed in the United States of America.

Visit us on the web at www.dorchesterpub.com.

ABDUCTED

Part One

Chapter One

Anita felt years of stress lift off her body as Dennis drove the Jeep across the Bay Bridge, leaving Digital Learnings behind in a galaxy of skyline lights. The magnetic pull of motherhood had drawn her out of her San Francisco office to return home to Rockridge for good. There was no going back.

It wasn't that she disliked Digital Learnings. Far from it—she enjoyed the camaraderie of her coworkers, the challenges of her clients, the kudos that came after she mastered another polished piece of product from rough thoughts. But it was work. A job. A 9-to-5 gig that had stretched unfairly to eclipse the daylight.

With a growing certainty, she had come to realize that the paychecks and ego fulfillment were holding her captive from what was truly the most important thing in her life: an amazing two-year-old boy with blond hair, curious eyes, and fast feet. A son named Tim.

Her boss, Maggie, and five coworkers all understood. At least they said they understood. There was encouragement, but some of it felt hollow. Could they really identify with her? Only two had children—one of them being Maggie, saddled with a teenage girl who (at least in anecdotes) existed only to defy her mother and flirt with every known illegal substance and forbidden activity. Maggie tossed out the latest family melodramas for morning coffee conversation, reciting arguments with bitter amusement and weary aggravation, but no real resolve. The stories were usually cut short by, "Well, I better get back to work." Priorities.

I'm not going to let that happen to me, Anita had told herself. But there had been some days where she saw it coming. Like the day when the nanny called and Tim was running a high temperature and a parent was required to sign him into the hospital. Dennis was unreachable. Anita was needed. Her first reaction: *Damn it, I have a presentation this afternoon.*

But it hadn't taken long to snap out of her work mode, cancel the client, exit the office, and speed home. Tonight was not much different, except this time the retreat was permanent.

"This is the right decision," Maggie had said earlier, "for *you.*" She said it in a slightly barbed way that meant, "but not for me." They were having a "good-bye Anita" dinner on Fisherman's Wharf. Dennis had looked up from his crab cakes and locked eyes with Anita; he never cared for Maggie's tone. She was shrill, she lacked tact, and she was a charging bull packed into a child-like five-foot-two frame. Dennis would be happy to see her fade away and never disrupt the household calm with another client crisis.

Over the years, Dennis had done his best to sidestep his wife's coworkers and she didn't really blame him. They were a knot of high-strung, high-maintenance women—not a male in sight—who dug into every detail of their work with a life-or-death importance. They mainly knew Dennis from the pleasant voice that answered the phone at home. They probably didn't know that he often told them she wasn't there—out shopping—when in reality, she was reading a bedtime story to Tim, or bathing him, or just holding him in the big family-room chair, watching his soft face drift off to sleep. She didn't mind when Dennis did this. But she always called back. And when she did, it almost always guaranteed that the next few hours belonged to Digital Learnings.

Not anymore.

Dennis already seemed happier with the new arrangement. Tonight at dinner he was more talkative than usual, even charming to her co-workers. At thirty-two, he had retained a youthful handsomeness and stayed in shape, even as his face sagged a little, drooped even, and his fabulous head of hair thinned with slow-motion menace. His new glasses gave him the look of a thoughtful professor—she had picked them out and convinced him they were hip. Originally, he wasn't looking for hip. He wanted something similar to the wide frames he had worn ever since high school.

Anita knew he was nervous about his new responsibilities as sole provider. She knew it would cut into his CD shopping sprees and box seats at Pac Bell Park. But he would be getting a lot more in return.

Anita looked forward to cooking real dinners, surprising Dennis with exotic recipes—no more carryout, microwave meals, or frozen pizzas. She would make sure he appreciated her stay-at-home status, even if her coworkers made her feel guilty.

"I would like to propose a toast," Maggie declared during dinner, "to Anita's early retirement." Chuckles, smiles, clinking glasses. As the wine flowed, the words became sloppier and more sentimental.

"I just want to thank you for being an amazing person," Liz told her, following up with such a laundry list of glowing qualities that Anita wondered if it was part of a scheme to make her feel bad for leaving.

"I will miss your tenaciousness and incredible focus," said Mita. "But most of all, I will miss your sense of humor. Who's going to crack us up? You were the one that could always cut through the crap. You put things in perspective."

The group promised to stay in touch. How can you go from spending sixty hours a week together to zero? Come and visit when you're in the area, they implored her. We promise not to give you any work.

Their joking was laced with apprehension. "I want to thank you for increasing my client load," Mita remarked. "You know, there were still those four hours of sleep that I could turn into billable hours."

Anita had given Maggie six weeks' notice and Maggie had promised the others that someone would be brought on board to replace her, but— no surprise—it hadn't happened yet. Not even a single interview. If it took away from client time, it was hard to find a slot in Maggie's overstuffed calendar.

"To replace Anita, we're going to have to hire two or three people," Maggie had said. It wasn't a bad idea—the small company was seriously understaffed, and not because of money. Digital Learnings was bringing in more revenue every month, making its name well-known in the interactive textbook field, winning its first slew of industry awards and getting great write-ups in technical publications. Maggie just couldn't get around to expanding the staff—and her staff suffered for it.

If it was suffering. Some of them appeared to feed off the chaos and crushing workload. It made them feel important. But not Anita. *Tim* made her feel important.

Tim always made her day. His little reactions to her—the way Anita could bring out a smile, the giggles, the wide-eyed wonder. She wanted to be the center of his universe again, like the weeks she had stayed home with him after he was born.

In recent months, Anita had become worried that Tim was growing up thinking the nanny, Pam, was his mommy. He certainly saw more of Pam than anyone else. Lately, Anita had been more like an occasional visitor, some lady who shared time with him on the weekends, but otherwise appeared as a sporadic glimpse in the morning or at bedtime.

On some nights, being careful not to wake him, Anita brought Tim into her bed in a feeble effort to spend more time with him. Now more than ever, she wanted to be part of his days. His personality was developing, his curiosity was expanding, his vocabulary was growing. He wasn't the passive, anonymous sleep/cry/poop machine anymore. He was quickly becoming a little person.

It still hurt Anita that Tim's first steps took place in front of Pam. Pam had sent a text message via cell phone. When Anita glanced at it during a meeting, she almost broke down in tears in front of everybody.

TIM HAS A SURPRISE FOR YOU, said the message. HE WALKED! HE TOOK FOUR STEPS IN THE LIVING ROOM. HE IS SO PROUD.

Anita felt crushing guilt and the ball began rolling that would lead to her decision to quit.

When the Jeep Liberty finished crossing the bay and reached solid ground, the departure from Digital Learnings somehow became permanent. Anita felt no regret in the pit of her stomach. No anxiety. No sadness. Just a warm, light feeling. And stronger affirmation that this was the right thing to do. Maybe in a few years, when Tim was in preschool, she would do some part-time consulting.

Maybe. And maybe not.

Anita had grown up with all the benefits and baggage of a stay-at-home mom, and she couldn't imagine anything less for Tim. There was a strong, invisible bond with her mother that always maintained a presence, no matter how far apart they lived or how much time separated phone calls or visits. She wanted that for her relationship with her own child.

As a stay-at-homer, what would every day be like? Anita tried to imagine. For one, she looked forward to ditching the business suits, the nylons, and the makeup for sweats, sneakers, and a cheap hair clip. Maybe she'd grow out her black hair, and let it go loose and tumble. And it wouldn't be a bad idea to join Dennis's health club—maybe going three nights a week to keep in shape. She wanted to keep the fat banished from her five-foot-eight frame. One good thing about Digital Learnings: the job stress and missed lunches kept her lean and mean.

Tomorrow morning was going to feel refreshing, like a hot shower. Nowhere to rush off to, no horrific to-do list piling up in her head moments after the alarm clock buzz. No commuter crawl from Oakland to San Francisco. No panicky clients filling up her voice mail. No computer freeze-ups, no printer breakdowns. No piles of half-finished or barely started work serving other people.

Sorry Mita, sorry Liz, sorry Maggie. Sorry Jenna and Yvette. It's all in your hands now.

They would carry on. It was arrogant to think that her absence would somehow collapse the company. Others had left before, and despite all the hand wringing, things worked themselves out.

No, thought Anita, I'm not worried about my friends at Digital Learnings. I don't feel sorry for them. But I do feel sorry for Pam.

Sweet, shy, and incredibly devoted Pam. Two days after submitting her resignation, Anita delicately broke the news to her. Dennis stood nearby, silent. Pam, a quiet and homely woman in her late thirties, took it hard. She didn't respond for several minutes. Anita could tell that Pam was holding back a cracked voice and tears.

Anita had felt awful—but then again, why should she? They both loved Tim. And this was best for Tim.

Pam didn't appear to have much of a life outside of her nanny routine. She was obviously someone who never quite figured out what she wanted to do. Or perhaps she was waiting for someone to hand her the answer. In any case, her love for children had defaulted into a career. Pam's simplicity and sweetness seemed more suited to dealing with children than other adults. And she was great with Tim. Tim loved her. It was a perfect match.

Upset, but swallowing back the hurt, Pam had said she understood. Anita and Dennis promised her that babysitting opportunities would come up. They didn't want Pam to feel cut off from Tim's life. And they didn't want Tim to face an abrupt separation from Pam.

Tonight, Pam was at the house with Tim, her last official day as Tim's nanny. Earlier in the evening, when Anita and Dennis were backing out of the driveway on the way to dinner, Dennis had suddenly stopped the Jeep, swearing, realizing that he had forgotten his wallet inside the house. When Dennis returned, he had unsettling news.

Dennis told Anita how he entered the house and caught Pam off guard. She was picking up some of Tim's toys in the kitchen. And she was crying.

"She seems distraught," Dennis told Anita. "Now I feel like crap."

"You shouldn't," Anita said.

"I know."

"She just loves Tim, that's all," said Anita. "I don't blame her. They've spent so much time together . . ."

"I think he's her best friend," Dennis remarked. It sounded like a joke. But in a way, it wasn't.

Soon, Pam would have to leave the house for her apartment knowing that she would not return the following morning. Oh God, thought Anita to herself. I hope Pam doesn't fall apart in front of us. There had already been enough drama for one day.

The traffic on Interstate 580 was light, and Dennis was darting around anyone in his path. It was a chilly, colorless February evening. As they advanced through the familiar succession of East Bay neighborhoods, Dennis played his favorite CD by The Who. Gradually, he had been inching up the volume. Now it was too loud, like the neighborhood teenagers who blasted rap until their cars vibrated and looked ready to shed parts.

Anita reached over and brought down the volume.

Dennis looked at her. Anita said, "Pam's check. The bonus."

Dennis nodded, shrugged. An indication that he wasn't in the mood to turn the topic into a discussion. They had considered giving Pam a final bonus check to say thank-you for everything.

"How about three hundred dollars?" asked Anita.

Dennis made a small grimace. "We're letting her keep the cell phone."

That was a decision made earlier in the week. The cell phone was originally provided to her so she could reach Anita or Dennis—and vice versa—at all times. She carried it with her when she took Tim to the park, her apartment, Mc-Donald's. But it was a lame gift; Anita felt Pam deserved more.

"Come on, we can afford it," she nudged him about the check. "I know it's not in the budget, but . . ."

"OK," said Dennis flatly. "Sure." End of discussion.

He just wants to turn the music back up, thought Anita.

"We need to remember to get the baby's car seat out of her car," she told him.

"Right," said Dennis. "She can't keep that."

"Relax," she told him. She put her hand in his hair, stroked it. They were both apprehensive about the reduced money flow of going down to one salary. On paper, it looked doable. Dennis was seeing a healthy spike in commissions from his real estate dealings. In fact, the company recently rewarded his third quarter sales performance with a San Francisco Giants golf bag and a complete set of clubs. It was a thoughtful gift that blended two of Dennis's favorite pastimes: golf and baseball.

Dennis had stumbled a bit in the early days of his career, and for a long stretch Anita had been bringing home the lion's share of the bacon. The reason was simple and complicated: alcohol. When sales hit the skids, Dennis hit the bottle, and ultimately his alcohol problem outlasted the downturn in the economy.

Despite the girls' generous consumption of

wine at dinner, Anita was pleased to see that Dennis had no problem staying on the wagon. He appeared disinterested in drinking. Some of the others knew about his alcoholism, and no one urged him to share in a glass.

The alcohol period definitely strained the early years of their marriage. Fortunately, he quit when she was pregnant with Tim. She had convinced him that the stress of it all would hurt the baby—and she even floated the concept of leaving to avoid bringing up the baby in a home with an alcoholic father.

Dennis sobered up. He got his act together. At work and at home, he mended broken fences. And he didn't look back.

It had been a narrow victory. A ninth inning, bases-loaded, game-winning catch. The recovery rejuvenated the marriage.

Anita felt confident that her decision to quit working would also strengthen the marriage. In the past year, she knew she could be a bitch. He wasn't the only one who brought distractions into the marriage. If he was an alcoholic, she was a workaholic. She had been working late a lot, often bringing projects home, even bringing the laptop into their bed, which annoyed him to no end.

She had become distracted and detached. Tim wasn't the only one neglected. The whole family was affected.

Now everything was falling into place. The more she thought about it, the more it made her prickle with good feelings. *It's all coming together now.*

The Who screamed from faraway inside the car speakers. "Can I turn it back up?" Dennis asked, in a mocking voice suggesting a little boy asking his mother for permission.

"Go ahead." She nestled close to him.

He returned the volume to something near the maximum level.

Now in Rockridge, the Jeep pulled onto tree-lined Vernon Road, just moments away from their split-level house in one of Oakland's most desirable neighborhoods. The homes, shingle-sided bungalows with wide lawns, were mostly dark and blank with occasional windows illuminated like restless eyes.

Anita felt a sudden surge of joy. This is really it. The future is here.

She couldn't wait to slip upstairs, peek in on Tim, touch his hair, adjust his blanket, and kiss his delicate face.

Mommy's here. I'm home for good.

At 11:15 P.M., Dennis pulled the Jeep into the driveway. Anita saw a troubled look cross his face. Then she felt something, too—something was strange, something was out of place.

Pam's Toyota was gone from its traditional spot alongside the curb in front of the house.

"Where's her car?" asked Dennis.

The first sensation, Anita would remember over and over in the years to come, was nothing more than curiosity.

And then her world came crashing down.

Chapter Two

Anita and Dennis opened the front door and entered stillness. Usually, Pam showed up with a greeting. There would be the traditional exchange of "How's Tim?," "Tim's great," "Did he give you any trouble?," "Oh, no, not Tim." Even if Tim gave her trouble, they doubted Pam would say anything—it would encourage too much conversation. Pam didn't like to make waves. She didn't like to make *ripples.* If the hour was early, Tim would run to the door at the sound of the latch. There would be the pitter-patter of tiny feet followed by a delighted squeal.

Tonight: silence. Without taking off his coat, Dennis turned left and headed down the short corridor that led to the family room. When Tim was asleep in his crib, Pam would typically perch herself in front of the television, watching miscellaneous sitcoms with eyes glued but no laughter. But tonight the set was off. The family room was empty, undisturbed.

"Hello? Pam?" called Dennis. It sounded weird—as if he was calling somebody out of hiding.

Anita dropped her coat on a chair. She headed upstairs, picking up the pace with every step. She hurried through a dark corridor—not stopping for a light switch—and entered Tim's bedroom.

"Dennis, he's gone!"

Tim's crib was empty. Someone had removed him. He couldn't climb out by himself—not unless he had learned a new trick today. Anita touched the mattress. It was cold. Tim's favorite stuffed bear was gone.

Tim had been in a deep sleep before they left. Anita had kissed him and he stirred. The little fingers moved, grasped air . . .

"*Tim*," cried out Anita, alarmed.

Dennis was behind her in an instant. He threw on the lights. He looked into the crib, glanced around the room, then left.

"Maybe she left a note," said Dennis, quickly heading for the kitchen.

Anita followed. "I'll check my cell phone." She grabbed her purse, fumbled for the phone, checked it. No voice mail. No text messages.

"I don't see a note," Dennis said from the kitchen. "There aren't any messages on the answering machine."

Anita dialed Pam's cell phone. "Where the hell did she go?" she said, punching the numbers.

"Without telling us," said Dennis, angry, the lines in his face tightening. He stepped alongside his wife, and together they waited for the call to go through. . . .

"Voice mail," said Anita.

Dennis rolled his eyes, tossed up his hands.

"Pam, it's Anita," Anita said after the tone. "Listen, where are—we just got home, it's after eleven, where are you? Is Tim OK? Please call us right away. Call us as soon as you get this message. Pam—" She really wanted to break into a shout, something like *what the hell is going on,* but simply ended with a limp "Thanks."

She hung up and Dennis was staring at her. "I guess I'll check outside," he said. It was too late, too cold to be a logical place for a two-year-old, but it did remain unchecked.

Anita opened the closet in the foyer. Pam's coat was gone.

Pam's purse was nowhere to be found, either.

Anita could see Dennis in the backyard. She watched him through the dining room window, under the exterior lights that were rarely turned on. He walked to one corner of the backyard, then to another. He glanced around some bushes. He looked up a tree.

It was almost funny, but Anita didn't feel amused. Maybe after they found Tim it would be funny, an anecdote. Dennis looked up a tree.

The silence inside the house was awful—no

noise aside from the gurgle of the large, saltwater fish tank in the living room. The collection of exotic fish zigged and zagged indifferently.

Anita checked her watch, even though she knew the time would just send more stingers into her heart. *Pam should be calling any minute,* she told herself, taking a deep breath. *Stay calm. If Pam doesn't have a good reason for all this, she will never set foot in this house again.*

She heard Dennis return to the family room. She hurried to meet him. He was already checking the garage, which connected to the family room through a door. Anita's Volkswagen Jetta sat in silence. Dennis examined it and left the garage.

"We didn't check the basement!" he said.

". . . or the closets," shrugged Anita.

Dennis scrambled down the basement, disappeared for a few minutes, then came back up.

"Dennis, this isn't hide and go seek. They obviously went somewhere," she said. "I just don't . . . I can't imagine where they would go at this hour unless . . . unless something happened to Tim."

Dennis' eyes lit up. "Call the hospital."

His words sent shivers through Anita. What if Tim was hurt?

When they had left for dinner, Tim had been asleep in his crib. What could possibly happen? He choked on something? Pam took him out and dropped him? A high fever? But why wouldn't she call? The cell phone had been turned on all night. The batteries were recharged. *Why the silence?*

Anita dialed information, got the number she needed, and called the hospital.

"Yes, I'm calling to see if my little boy was—he was with his babysitter—his nanny, tonight—they're not here and I want to check—" Despite Anita's broken speech, the person on the other end knew exactly what she was asking.

Anita spelled the names. She described Tim. She described Pam. After a long delay, the voice on the other end asked if Tim was Asian and about sixty pounds.

"No!" thundered Anita. "I told you—he's . . . he's only two years old. Blond hair . . ."

"I'm sorry, ma'am, we haven't admitted anyone fitting your description," said the voice, unperturbed.

Anita hung up. OK, she told herself, think hard. People don't just disappear. They go someplace. Has this ever happened before? Coming home to an empty house? No, never this late. But there was one time . . . when Anita came home from work . . . early, around six o'clock . . . and Pam and Tim were gone . . . Where were they? . . . They were at Pam's apartment. They had gone to close windows prior to a storm and wound up staying late when Pam's elderly neighbors crowded around Tim like a celebrity.

After returning to the house, Pam had apologized profusely. Anita had said it was no big deal, she knew he was safe with her.

I never should have said *no big deal*, she thought.

"I'm calling Pam's apartment," she told Dennis.

Dennis just nodded.

Anita dialed. After five rings, the answering machine picked up.

"Shit," said Anita.

"Hello," said Pam underneath a layer of tape hiss. "You have reached . . . Pam Beckert." Her voice was fragile, measured, self-conscious. No doubt, recording this message had been a multi-take affair. "I'm not home right now . . . But please leave a message . . . And I will call you back . . . Have a nice day."

Beep.

"Pam, it's Anita," said Anita in a harsher tone than the message she left for the cell phone. "Where is Tim? Where have you taken him? It's going on midnight. Call me *right away*. I don't know where you are. I want Tim home." She hung up. No bye, no thanks.

"This is unbelievable," muttered Anita. Dennis stood next to her, staring out the front window, looking for car headlights.

He could probably use a drink, Anita thought. I could use a drink. I am going to drink when all this is over.

Anita dialed Pam's cell phone again. Voice mail. She hung up.

"You don't think they went next door?" said Dennis. "I mean, sometimes she takes him next door to play with the beagle."

Anita pushed aside the kitchen window curtains. The Simons's house was dark. They were asleep and not entertaining visitors. It was a ridiculous thought. It was desperate.

Anita truly felt that at any minute, the phone would ring. Or Pam's car would pull up to the house. And there would be some kind of logical explanation. She just didn't know what it would be. But Pam was a responsible person. She was cautious. She wasn't some reckless teenager who had dragged Tim along to a keg party or a boyfriend's pad.

"Sometimes she rents videos. Maybe she realized she had to return a tape by midnight . . . Or that we were out of milk. Or . . ." Dennis shrugged.

"You're really searching," said Anita.

"Well, then Goddamn it, you tell me where he is," snapped Dennis.

"We're not going to get in a fight over this," Anita responded, feeling the tension tighten the muscles in her neck. "That won't solve anything."

"Then don't make cracks. I'm trying to figure out where our son might be."

"I know, I know," said Anita. "I'll call the hospital again."

"They could be at another hospital in the area," said Dennis.

She dug out the metro phone book from a cabinet. More calls to hospitals followed, each ending the same way. No Tim. One nice woman on the other end placidly suggested they contact the police.

"We probably should," said Dennis.

"I don't know," Anita said, feeling increasingly helpless. In her work and home life, she was used to crises she could control or at least influence in some way. But this was something that she couldn't get her hands around . . .

Anita grabbed her cell phone. She called Pam's cell phone and again got dumped into voice mail. She called Pam's apartment and the excruciating unanswered rings led back to the answering machine.

"Does she have any friends in the area?" asked Dennis.

"Nobody she talks about," said Anita. But then it triggered a thought.

"Roy," said Anita. "Her brother Roy. He doesn't live far. I'll call him."

Anita had met Roy exactly once. But it had been a fairly memorable event. One evening, she came home to find an unfamiliar, rusted Chevy in the driveway. When she walked in the front door, she discovered a large, unshaven stranger seated in the living room. He was drinking a bottle of her Heineken and watching the fish in the aquarium.

If it was an intruder, he was being remarkably casual about it.

The man had a crooked nose and long sideburns. He wore jeans, cowboy boots, and a faded flannel shirt. He quickly rose and approached her with his hand stuck out. "Hi, I'm Roy."

Anita just as quickly backed up toward the front door. Pam, carrying Tim, then stepped into view, coming down the stairs. She looked equally startled, although she at least had the benefit of knowing all the players.

"I'm sorry," she told Anita. "I was changing Tim. I—I didn't tell you—Roy came over to help me. Roy's my brother. I lost my ring."

"Down the sink," Roy explained.

Then the full story came out. After lunch, while Tim napped, Pam had been scrubbing macaroni and cheese residue out of a pot. She had taken off her ring and placed it on the kitchen counter, near the edge of the sink. Somehow, the ring got bumped, slid into the sink, and down the drain.

She had contacted Roy for help. Roy drove a bread truck, and when his shift ended late in the afternoon, he came over to help.

The ring, Anita observed, was a cheap piece of costume jewelry. But it held great sentimental value to Pam—having belonged to a favorite aunt, now dead.

So Roy came over, dismantled the pipes under the sink, and rescued the ring.

He was a broad-shouldered man, about the same size as Dennis, and probably four or five years younger. His voice was rough, and his speech was grammatically challenged.

He also ogled Anita's body in a direct, unapologetic manner. Anita distinctly remembered that she was wearing her provocative red business suit that day, embellishing an afternoon PowerPoint presentation with a dose of leg and cleavage, a shameless but effective marketing move to secure a male client.

After catching Roy—twice—staring through her clothes, she quickly turned away from him and faced Pam.

Gently, as if talking to a child, Anita said, "You should have told me your brother was coming over. He scared me—startled me, I mean."

Pam apologized more than was necessary, and Roy departed within a few minutes. Anita had never given the encounter another thought—until now.

Maybe Roy could provide some insight?

She called information. Roy Beckert. Got the number. She dialed. It rang eight times, she knew she was waking him up.

The receiver on the other end rattled and clunked a bit before a voice came on. "Hmmgh . . . Hello?"

"Roy, I'm sorry to bother you at this late hour. It's Anita Sherwood. Your sister is our nanny . . ."

"Yeah?" he said simply, thickly; she wondered if he was even awake yet.

"We came home from dinner, and she was suppose to be here with Tim, our son, our two-year-old, but they're both gone. Do you—?"

"They're not here," he said without a trace of empathy. "She doesn't bring him here. I'm sleeping."

"Do you know where they might be?"

"I have no idea."

"Where do you think she took him?"

"I told you, I have no idea. Listen, I'm sorry. You woke me up. I just don't know."

"OK . . ." Anita wished he could at least offer a clue or suggestion, anything. "If you hear from her, or you think of a place she might go, please call me. Let me give you my number. Do you have a pencil?"

"Just a sec." Lots of fumbling. "OK. Shoot."

She gave it to him, thanked him, and the call ended. She was right back where she started. Nowhere.

She tried Pam again on the cell phone and at home and got the same nonresponse.

"Who else can we call?" said Anita. "This is crazy."

"What about the Roebers?" suggested Dennis. The Roebers were the family down the block where Pam had once served as a part-time nanny. The Roebers had recommended Pam.

"They're not listed," said Anita. "But I have the number in my address book. It's in the nightstand."

"I'll get it," said Dennis, itching for something to do, somewhere to go, after standing at her side for what seemed like a dozen phone calls.

Dennis hurried upstairs.

Anita went to the front door and opened it wide, as if the action would encourage Tim home. She looked down the dark street for any sign of headlights. It was remarkably easy to imagine. Pam and Tim returning home. Pulling into the driveway. Anita would dash to the car to retrieve Tim. Check him for bumps and bruises. He would smile at her, unharmed and unaware of her panic. Pam would explain what happened in a breathless, frightened voice. It would begin with "I'm so sorry, Mrs. Sherwood, but" and then the rest would spill out: whatever the reason was for their absence. And it had better be a damn good one for scaring her half to death.

And if it was an unacceptable reason, well, Pam was banished from Tim forever.

"Anita!"

She jumped. Dennis was yelling from upstairs. She turned around, but didn't have to go to him. He was already coming down the steps two at a time.

Dennis looked frightened, and that sent fear racing through her veins.

"Anita," said Dennis. "The money is missing. A lot of money. The drawer in the dresser . . . where the cash is . . . under the shirts. It's gone. All of it."

Anita immediately knew what he was talking about. Their secret "cash stash."

Bewildered, Anita said, "We've been robbed?"

Dennis continued. "Pam saw me take money out when I was paying back some expenses. I didn't think anything of it. I figured, she'd never . . . you know. But she knew that we kept money—a lot of money—in that drawer. No one else did. Anita, she has Tim, she took our money."

"Dennis," said Anita, voice trembling, hands shaking, "we have to call the police."

Dennis charged into the kitchen, snatched the phone, and dialed 911.

Anita listened. His words sounded unreal, like some kind of play. Some kind of melodrama she was watching, but not participating in.

"This is an emergency," said Dennis. The words came out of his throat in an eerie, frightened tone she had never heard before.

"Our son has been kidnapped, abducted. We think we know who did it."

Anita looked at the clock. Ten minutes after midnight. It had almost been an hour since they returned home.

Did it take us a whole hour to call the police?

Dennis hung up the phone.

"The police are on their way," he said. There was nothing more to say. They went to the front door and waited. Within minutes, the darkness of night was disrupted by flashing red and blue lights.

Chapter Three

Two patrol officers stood at the front door, young men with identical buzz cuts, bland expressions, and tidy uniforms with Oakland Police Department patches sewn on the shoulder. The only distinction was race: one black, one white.

Anita admitted them inside. They were big men and filled the foyer—add Dennis to the mix, and Anita felt miniature. Anita saw the guns in their holsters, the handcuffs hanging from their utility belts. For a split second she could imagine them drawing weapons on Pam's frail figure, slapping cuffs on her skinny wrists. It was such a bizarre picture, it didn't make sense. But none of this made sense.

The officers introduced themselves. Improbably, the black one was Sandburg, the white one was Johnson.

"Our son is missing," Dennis began. "His name is Tim, he's two years old." Johnson had already pulled out a pen and started filling out a report. "He was here with the nanny and now they're both gone."

"When did you last see them?" asked Sandburg.

"Around 8:00, 8:10. Before we left for dinner," answered Anita. "Tim was asleep in his crib." She remembered pulling the blanket down over his bare feet, which had a habit of poking out defiantly.

"When we came back from dinner, the house was empty," said Dennis. "Her car was gone. Her name is Pam Beckert."

"When did you return to the house?" asked Sandburg.

"About an hour ago," said Anita.

Sandburg raised an eyebrow. "An hour ago?" he said, and she immediately understood his tone to imply *Why did you wait so long to notify the police?*

"We thought she just . . . took him somewhere . . . had a reason," said Anita. "She's never done this before. She's been our nanny for a year and a half. We trusted her."

"We realized something was wrong when I found the money missing," said Dennis. "We had some cash upstairs in a drawer that she knew about."

"How much?" asked Sandburg.

"Five, six hundred. I kept it under some shirts," said Dennis. "In an envelope."

"I take it you've searched the house for your son?" asked Sandburg. Apparently, he was the talker and Johnson was the one who wrote everything down.

"Inside and out," said Dennis.

"And this nanny, she didn't leave a note?"

"Nothing," said Dennis.

"She has a cell phone," said Anita. "We've been calling every ten minutes. But I don't think she has it turned on. We tried her apartment, too."

Sandburg asked, "Do either of you have any relatives that may have come by and picked them up for any reason?"

Anita and Dennis shook their heads.

"Has she ever disappeared with your son like this before?"

"Never," said Dennis.

"Well, once, sort of," corrected Anita. "I came home and they weren't here, but they were at her apartment, and it was like six o'clock in the evening, not like this."

Anita looked down at her watch. 12:30 A.M. It was a new jolt to her heart. There could be no harmless, innocent reason for their disappearance at this hour. No trip to the park or walk for ice cream. This was serious and bad. Where the hell were they?

More than anything in the universe, she wanted Tim in her arms right now. She wanted to feel his warm, soft little body, safe and sound.

"Do you know if your nanny has any criminal background?" Johnson spoke up this time.

"No. I don't think so. I mean, we ran a background check when we hired her," replied Anita.

Sandburg said, "We'll run a check."

Johnson flipped to a new sheet on his clipboard. "Here's what I need," he said. "I need a description of your son, and the nanny, and the nanny's vehicle, that we can send out over the police radio. Let's start with your son."

Anita and Dennis detailed Tim's every statistic. There was something chilling and clinical about Tim being reduced to numbers and colors. Thirty-six inches . . . 28 pounds . . . blue eyes . . . blondish hair . . . green one-piece pajamas.

"And his bear," Anita added, choking on the words, suddenly seeing an image of Tim being dragged off somewhere, confused and cold, clutching his bear for security, when what he really needed was his mother. . . .

The police read Tim's description back to her, adding "male Caucasian," which sounded strange, like an object.

While Dennis went upstairs to retrieve photos of Tim and Pam for the officers, Anita described Pam Beckert to the best of her ability. Age about thirty-eight. Hair auburn, straight, usually pulled back, lots of forehead. Thick glasses. Height maybe five-three? Weight . . . 110? What was Pam wearing? Jesus, what was it? Something drab, always something drab. A plaid sweater vest over a white blouse. Grey polyester slacks. Or was that yesterday?

When Dennis returned, he helped describe Pam's car—a blue Toyota Corolla at least ten years old—but neither one of them knew her license plate number. Jesus, thought Anita, I don't even have my own license plate number memorized.

"It's OK," said Johnson. "We'll get it through the DMV."

Anita heard a car door slam. "Oh, thank God!" she exclaimed, moving swiftly.

But out front was a car she did not recognize, a white sedan. Two men climbed out.

"Our detectives are going to take it from here," said Sandburg. "Like I said, I'm going to put the information out on the radio. I will also contact the California Highway Patrol."

"OK, thank you," said Anita. "Thank you so much."

Sandburg left the house with Johnson. On the way to the patrol car, they stopped to talk to the detectives on the lawn.

Anita put her arms around Dennis and held tight. She could feel his heart pounding. She could feel her own sweat sticking to her clothes.

"I can't take this," said Anita. "I'm going to be sick." The pleasant, soft buzz she had during the car ride home from three glasses of wine was gone, obliterated by adrenaline. Her stomach felt knotted.

"We'll find him," said Dennis, but his voice wavered.

When we get Tim back and he is sleeping in our bed, Anita told herself, I'm never going to let him go. And I will never let Pam near him again.

The detectives entered the house slowly, wearing dark, plain clothes. They introduced themselves as belonging to the Oakland Police Bureau of Investigation. They were older guys, which somehow reassured Anita. The patrol officers had looked too young . . . too disinterested . . . too something. They probably didn't have kids of their own yet. How could they relate to the terror of a missing child?

Lieutenant Mike Calcina was probably fifty, his age mostly revealed by the gray in his hair that was balanced equally against the brown. He had warm eyes and a tight, square jaw that worked over some chewing gum. His partner, Sam Segar, was a leaner, balding man with a thick black mustache and large bags under his eyes. The exaggerated mustache made him look like a foil in an old silent comedy.

Sam's eyes began probing the house, like a bloodhound sniffing for clues, and it was apparent that his feet were anxious to follow.

"If it's all right with you, Sam's going to take a look around the house," said Calcina.

"Fine, fine," said Dennis.

Sandburg returned inside the house with the police report. Calcina took it, studied it.

Dennis nudged Anita. "Try her again on the cell phone."

Anita had forgotten the phone was still gripped in her hand. She quickly dialed and got an immediate voice mail message. No change. She punched a button to end the call. "She's shutting us out."

Calcina looked up from the police report. "She has a cell phone?"

"Yes, we bought one for her," said Anita.

"What's the number?" he asked.

She told him, he wrote it down. There were new police faces in the house. He went over to one of the men, gave him the number and instructions. When Calcina returned, he said, "Do you have someplace we can sit and talk?"

"Any place," said Anita. "The living room?"

They went into the living room and found seats. Anita and Dennis sat together on the couch.

The conversation began by covering much of the same ground as their dialogue with Sandburg and Johnson, but probing deeper. Dennis told Calcina about the missing money, and Calcina started asking about Pam's financial state. It became apparent that he was expecting a ransom.

"I don't think she did it for money," Anita finally said. "She wants Tim. She doesn't want to be separated from him. It's like she thinks she earned him."

Dennis told Calcina about returning to the house for his wallet and finding Pam in tears in the kitchen. They talked about Pam's strong bond with Tim, the termination of the nanny arrangement, her lack of any outside social life.

"Has she ever alluded to taking Tim like this? Even facetiously?" asked Calcina.

"God no," Anita said.

"Is she on any medication that you know of?"

Anita looked at Dennis, shrugged, then shook her head.

"Does she drink?" asked Calcina. "A heavy drinker?"

"I don't believe so," said Dennis.

"Any strange or unusual friends?"

"Not that I know about," replied Anita.

"Has she ever . . ." Calcina paused. It was the first time he had broken the pace in his rapid-fire questioning. "Has she ever acted in an inappropriate way toward Tim?"

"She's not a molester," said Dennis firmly.

"How do we know?" shot back Anita. "Did we ever think she'd steal him?"

Dennis just looked at the floor. "This was probably an impulsive action. She freaked out. I have to think she'll come to her senses. She's not insane."

Calcina said, "We take a missing child report very, very seriously. These first few hours are critical. I want you to think hard, identify every possible place they might go, anyone they might visit, anywhere they may have gone in the past. Your nanny must have left here with some kind of destination in mind."

"Well, there's her apartment," said Anita. "We called—"

"We have a patrol car heading there," answered Calcina. "Does she have family in the area?"

"Yes, a brother." Anita relayed the information, describing her recent call to Roy, and added, "I don't think they're all that close, but he is . . . a little odd, I guess."

Calcina stood up, crossed the room, and spoke to one of the new police officer faces. When he returned, he said, "OK, we've got an officer going over to talk with the brother. Anybody else? Her parents?"

"Her parents are in Florida," said Anita.

"Do you know where in Florida?" asked Calcina. "Do you know their names?"

"No, but the brother could tell you. She didn't really talk about them."

"Anybody else? Aunts, uncles, anything? Friends?"

Dennis just shrugged.

"What about enemies?"

Anita thought it over. "I never heard anyone say anything bad about her."

Segar walked over. "There's no sign of forced entry," he said. He looked at Dennis and Anita. "Have you looked throughout the house to see if there's anything unusual or out of place?"

"I did," said Dennis. "The only thing I noticed was the missing money."

"You didn't find any doors unlocked, windows open, that kind of thing?"

Dennis shook his head.

"Do you have an attic?" asked Segar.

Dennis and Anita exchanged glances. "Yes," said Dennis.

"Can you show me where it is?"

"Sure," said Dennis. "But I don't think—"

"We just want to make a clean sweep of the house. If you could come with me . . ."

Dennis looked at Calcina. Calcina nodded in agreement. Dennis rose and left with Segar.

What could be in the attic? wondered Anita. Pam and Tim hiding? Playing hide-and-seek?

She checked her watch. 1:17 A.M. It sent shockwaves through her body. *Don't look at the time anymore,* she told herself.

"Mrs. Sherwood," said Calcina. "Where did you say you went to dinner tonight?"

"Fisherman's Wharf."

"No, I mean the name of the restaurant."

"Sea Breeze."

He wrote it down. Why was that relevant?

"What time did you arrive there?"

She told him.

"What time did you leave?"

She told him, her voice gaining an edge.

"And who were you having dinner with?" asked Calcina, pen poised to record every name.

She gave him the names of her coworkers, the name of the company they worked for. In a sudden instant, she realized: *He's going to check into my story.* He had isolated her from Dennis. Dennis would probably have to answer these same questions . . . and Calcina would check for in-consistencies.

"Am I a suspect?" blurted Anita.

"This is standard procedure," said Calcina.

"So I am? We are?"

"We always look at the family as possible suspects. You don't want us to rule anything out, do you?"

She shook with disbelief. "What is this? You think I killed my son and stashed him in the attic?" The Jon Bonet Ramsey news stories flashed before her.

"Please," said Calcina. "Don't get alarmed. Just answer the questions to the best of your ability. Did you call home from the restaurant, or did the nanny contact you?"

"No," Anita said, slumping back into the sofa. "Tim was in bed when we left, we figured everything was fine. We had no reason to—"

"You arrived home at quarter past eleven, and you contacted the police after midnight," said Calcina. "Why the delay?"

Anita felt dizzy. The world was spinning out of control. On top of everything, they wanted to accuse her of doing something sinister to Tim? Why was he doing this? Why wasn't he out looking for him? Tim was out there, somewhere, lost and confused. These questions about her dinner were a waste of time.

But she knew if she protested, it would just make her look guilty, like she had something to hide. Did she need an attorney?

Anita heard the front door opening and closing. More investigators.

"Do you have family in the area?" asked Calcina.

"No," said Anita.

"What about your husband?"

"His parents live in Kansas City. Why?"

"Any brothers, sisters, aunts, or uncles?"

"I want to call my father," said Anita abruptly.

Calcina softened his tone. "We need to keep the phone line open in case someone tries to reach us about Tim." His eyes were gentle, but serious. "Don't be offended by the questioning. We just want to rule out the possibility that you or Dennis had anything to do with this. We want to get that out of the way."

"OK," said Anita. "Call the restaurant. Call my coworkers. You're just wasting time."

A policeman with a round gut approached them. "We interviewed the neighbors on either side and two across the street," he said. "There's a Mrs. Bowman at 1732 who thinks she saw the nanny's car leave about 8:30."

You woke up my neighbors? thought Anita. She started to look at her watch, then stopped herself. She pictured her bewildered neighbors coming to the door in their pajamas and robes.

She could hear the heavy footsteps of police roaming the house. She wanted all of them out; she wanted Tim inside. This madness had been going on for much too long and she was coming unglued.

"We've contacted the FBI," said the cop with the gut.

Anita looked up. The FBI? Was it this serious already? On a level with terrorism?

Calcina could sense her concern. "This is a requirement in cases like this," he told her. "We have what appears to be a kidnapping."

"Oh, God."

"Don't you want every possible resource at your disposal?" asked Calcina.

Anita rose from her chair. Her throat was dry, tightening up. "I need a glass of water," she said. Calcina said nothing.

Anita moved through the various strangers in her house. They barely even looked at her, as if she was not even relevant to the case. She felt the weight of her body hanging off her frame. She was exhausted, limp with shock.

In the kitchen, heading for the sink, Anita caught a glimpse of one of Tim's fingerpaintings stuck to the refrigerator door with alphabet magnets. Cheery rainbow colors splashed across the paper. She could recall his proud, beaming face as he gave it to her. Like a gate bursting open under pressure, an avalanche of emotions spilled out.

Anita dropped to her knees and started sobbing.

Chapter Four

"Pam's great," said Barbara Roeber, standing in the frozen foods aisle of the Albertson's grocery store.

Tim was six months old and Anita, feeling the pressure to return to work from both Maggie and the Sherwood bank account, had officially started her nanny search. She had made the leap from considering the concept to accepting it: She was researching nanny agencies, au pair services, reviewing the local classifieds, and spreading the word among her friends.

Talking to Barbara Roeber had been near the top of her list. Bumping into her in the grocery store just made it happen sooner. Barbara, who lived down the block, had a nanny. Maybe Barbara could share some advice? Maybe her nanny knew other nannies?

"Even better," Barbara told her. "My nanny is available."

The nanny's name was Pam Beckert. Barbara had hired her about a year ago, when she was pregnant with her third child, Charlie. Charlie was going to be a big baby and created havoc on Barbara's spine, ultimately causing a herniated disk in her back.

Mostly bedridden, with a three-year-old girl and one-year-old boy gleefully tearing up the house, Barbara had hired a nanny to help with the kids and housework.

The arrangement had worked extremely well, but now, with Charlie a few months old and the back healing, Barbara was ready to go solo again. Pam would be concluding her nanny term at the end of the month.

Barbara first heard about Pam through a woman at her church who used her to babysit and had sung her praises.

"Pam has been a godsend," said Barbara in her mile-a-minute baby voice. "She couldn't have been nicer to the kids. She's real quiet, but she's reliable and we never had any trouble with her. The kids love her and she'll do anything to help out. She was doing the laundry, the cooking."

From what Anita had heard on the neighborhood grapevine, Barbara's kids could be a handful. Barbara looked perpetually tired, never wore makeup, yet remained attractive. Her husband was a dentist with a storefront office slotted between a submarine sandwich joint and a laundromat at a nearby strip mall. Anita and Dennis saw them at the yearly block party barbecue, and they waved at one another from passing vehicles from time to time. Barbara had the best garden on the block; God knows where she found the time. Anita didn't know her extremely well, but well enough to trust her. Despite the baby voice, she was serious and seemed smart.

In fact, her shopping cart was heavy with healthy food: fruits, vegetables, grains. Embarrassed, Anita stood strategically in front of the junk food selections that mingled with baby jars of rice cereal, squash, and sweet potato in her cart.

Tim cooed. He was snuggled into his detachable car seat, which was snapped securely into the front of the shopping cart. The coo was Barbara's cue to come closer and take a look.

"What a beautiful little boy," said Barbara. "Look at those lashes and that hair. How old is he?"

"Six months," said Anita, sharing in the opportunity to beam over Tim.

"Sleeping through the night?"

"Yes, he's a real sweetheart."

Tim's eyes were alert, taking in the two friendly faces, and he smiled back at them.

"What a great smile," remarked Barbara.

Anita delicately pulled down Tim's lower lip to show off his first tooth and the bump in his gum that would soon be tooth number two. "He's been drooling up a storm lately."

"I'll bet it's going to break your heart to leave him," said Barbara, tickling lightly under his chin, encouraging the smiles to continue. "When do you have to go back to work?"

"Well, fortunately I'm good friends with the person I work for, so they've kept it flexible. But it's been a long time, and they're getting impatient. Business is booming, for better or worse."

Barbara nodded. "I admire moms who can juggle it all, working and the kids. Sometimes, as much as I love my kids, I feel they've robbed me of some of my identity. You know, in some ways, your career is who you are. You're Sam the dentist, or Jerry the lawyer, or Anita who makes educational CD-ROMs. I'm Barbara the housewife."

Anita nodded, didn't know what to say. Tell her that she had made the right decision when it was the direct opposite of her own choice?

Fortunately, Tim diverted attention from the conversation with a burp, followed by a truly boyish grin of pride.

"I better let you go," said Barbara. "But call me and I'll give you Pam's number. She'll be so excited."

"Don't tell her anything definite," said Anita. "I haven't discussed this with my husband. We're going to want to meet her first, and start with some babysitting, to test her out." I hope it doesn't sound like we don't trust her recommendation, thought Anita. "We want to make sure she clicks with Tim."

"Who wouldn't click with such an adorable, sweet boy," smiled Barbara, looking at him again. Tim's eyes were taking in all the colors and lights of the grocery store. He reached out, as if to grab at something on one of the towering shelves.

Barbara's number was unlisted, so Anita wrote it on the back of an expired coupon in her purse.

They said their good-byes. Anita advanced to her next destination, the most familiar spot in the store: diapers and wipes.

Stocking up, she couldn't stop thinking of the odd concept of having a stranger in her house taking care of her baby—somebody else would be doing most of this diapering and wiping while she returned to computers and meetings across the Bay. Was it really the right thing to do?

She couldn't help but recall Barbara's tone of despair and defeat when calling herself a "housewife." Did people take housewives less seriously than working mothers? Was a housewife somehow a lower class of being? The quality of daytime TV seemed to cater to that thought.

Later that afternoon, Anita sat in the rocking chair in the baby's room, breastfeeding Tim in the semidarkness while fresh spring air rolled in through the windows. His eyes were closed, mouth moving, little hands pressed against her chest. His face was so achingly precious, his features still so tiny, right down to his miniature square fingernails. Anita felt horrible pangs of sadness. She stroked his hair.

She knew she would have to rent a breast pump to pump milk at work at regular intervals . . . so someone else could feed it to him. How weird was that?

I'm going to leave him with a stranger . . .

But I know so many people who have done it . . .

Does it make it the right thing to do . . .

I never told Maggie I wasn't coming back, it wouldn't be fair, she has bent over backwards . . .

Dennis can't support us yet, he's close, but . . .

She watched Tim feed and wished she could feel his utter relaxation and contentment. *Timothy, I wish you could give me some advice.*

For several days, she put off calling Barbara for Pam Beckert's phone number. Then, once she had it, she delayed calling Pam for several more days, hoping that the added time would cause her to change her mind or reevaluate the game plan.

It didn't.

"We've got to make a decision one way or another," huffed Dennis, and, for once, his sentiment paralleled Maggie's.

"I just need to know, hon," said the latest Maggie message on the answering machine.

Anita called Pam on a Saturday. According to

Barbara, she lived in a small apartment building about ten minutes away.

A thin, uneven voice answered. Anita couldn't help starting to conduct her evaluation immediately. Pam sounded simple, but articulate. Uncomfortable but mature.

Pam said that Barbara had already told her to expect the call, so she was familiar with the situation.

"We're still weighing our options," said Anita. "But if you're available, we'd like to start with some babysitting."

"That would be great," Pam responded, a rise in her voice.

The first "trial-sit," as Dennis called it, took place the following Thursday. This was no ordinary babysitting gig. It was contrived to the hilt.

Anita and Dennis made plans to go into Berkeley for dinner and a movie, any movie. Pam was supposed to arrive at six. But Dennis would be "running late," allowing Anita to observe Pam and Tim's interactions for an extended period.

When Pam arrived, she had just completed a full day with the Roeber kids, so she was rumpled, but smiling eagerly. Pam had a mousy, slight built, and her plain face was dominated by her thick glasses, the type of Coke-bottle lenses you didn't see much anymore as most people turned to contact lenses or laser eye surgery.

Her clothes were colorless and her hair was flat and straight and indifferently styled. *Frumpy* was the word that leapt to Anita's mind.

Anita was actually encouraged that Pam wasn't a great young beauty. Part of it may have been selfish—not wanting a prettier woman under her roof—but most of it had to do with securing a nanny with minimal distractions, that is, boyfriends.

She had heard too many horror stories about babysitters who neglected the child while entertaining long phone conversations—or worse, secret visits—from boyfriends. The last thing Anita wanted was some chick grinding away with a young stud on the sofa while Tim cried with poopy diapers in his crib.

Pam looked a few years older than Anita and had a maternal aura about her. She was awkward during the initial chitchat, obviously shy, or "reserved" as Barbara had put it, but sweet. And capable?

Anita led Pam to the living room to meet Tim. He was on a blanket on the floor, rolling a little bit, grabbing at the scattered circle of toys around him.

Pam knelt before him and broke out of her shell with a big, genuine smile. As if tapped by a magic wand, Pam became animated and vibrant. She brought her finger forward and Tim grasped it. "Hello big boy," she said.

Anita watched the interaction closely. Tim's face was uncertain at first, but quickly warmed to Pam's gentle, soft-spoken greetings.

Before long, Pam had him giggling.

Anita felt waves of relief. Tim felt good, so she felt good.

Tim was trying to sit up, clumsily. "Go ahead, pick him up," said Anita. Pam looked like she had just won the lottery. "Thank you," she said. She was careful, and held him correctly, safely, motherly.

Pam carried Tim as Anita gave her a tour of the house. Anita ran through the list in her head of all the essentials—changing table, diapers and wipes, food, bottles, bouncy seat, phone numbers "just in case."

Anita asked Pam to feed Tim in his high chair while she got ready for going out. Anita retreated upstairs, but moved around a lot to catch glimpses and eavesdrop on the interaction.

Tim was making happy noises.

Pam appeared to know what she was doing. She was experienced with small children.

Both of them were happy.

What great luck, thought Anita. She had anticipated a long and grueling nanny search—she didn't expect to find a good one so quickly.

Still, the audition wasn't over.

Pam returned for another babysitting turn three days later. This one included a bath. Plus, a brief Timmy tantrum. Pam handled it well. She soothed Tim quickly and distracted away the tears. From everything Anita observed, Pam was very attentive to Tim and intuitive to his needs. She wasn't just some flake looking for steady cash. She was truly motherly. A pro.

"I like her, I guess," said Dennis at dinner during babysitting night number two. They sat in their favorite Chinese restaurant. "I mean, I don't see anything wrong with her. You're the better judge of these mommy things."

"She knows her stuff," said Anita. "I know she doesn't have much of a personality. She's not full of sparkling conversation—"

Dennis chuckled in agreement.

"—but she really likes Tim and I feel I can trust her."

To get a more complete picture of Pam, they began filling in the details of her past. Some if it, Pam provided. A lot of it they researched on their own.

Maggie had been the one to suggest contacting an independent investigative service to run a background check. Anita thought it felt sneaky, but agreed that it was worth doing, if only to secure peace of mind. Since they weren't going through a nanny agency, they had to do their own screening.

For two hundred dollars, a company called I Spy conducted an extensive search to dig up dirt on Pam. They checked the records of counties where she had lived to see if there was any criminal history—any felonies or misdemeanors. They ran a civil records search for lawsuits, verified her education, looked at her driver's record, and ran a credit report to find any defaulted loans or car repossessions. Nothing showed up that would indicate irresponsibility or dishonesty. In fact, the search turned up so little, it was as if she didn't even exist. She was barely a blip.

While the investigation service did their work, Anita checked the references. She and Dennis had dinner with the Roebers, who did nothing but speak about Pam in glowing terms. It was obvious they were both rooting for Anita and Dennis to hire her. Anita speculated that part of their motivation was guilt from letting her go. Barbara said that when Pam was told her services would no longer be needed, she took the news very hard. "She acted like somebody died," said Barbara.

Anita also called Pam's prior employers, the Savios, a couple Barbara knew from church.

Susan Savio was equally complimentary. She worked part-time for the city, and all her kids were now in school. Susan said she was especially impressed by the extra work Pam did around the house. "She did everything but vacuum the front yard," she told Anita. "The kids just loved her, she never grew impatient with them, even when they were brats. You know, I actually felt bad for her. I got the feeling she always wanted kids of her own."

Anita also checked some of the other references. She tracked down other babysitting clients in the neighborhood. She also spoke with former employers, including a small company where Pam worked as a receptionist and a bank where she once held a clerical job.

In those cases, where kids weren't involved,

Pam was barely a memory. "Quiet . . . shy . . . hard worker" were some of the descriptions. "She kept to herself."

Throughout all of the research and investigating, Anita did not encounter any red flags. Nothing that would indicate a lack of maturity or responsibility.

The decision was becoming clearer and clearer.

Finally, Dennis and Anita invited Pam over for dinner. But it was really a job interview. A chance to evaluate her directly. Anita was mostly interested in what Dennis would have to say afterward, since she was already pretty certain of her decision.

Pam sat across from them. Anita served pasta and salad. Tim played in the bassinet, occasionally tossing out a toy for attention.

Pam did not look comfortable. She was restless. She kept looking in Tim's direction. She definitely preferred his company. And tonight, he even appeared to recognize her when he smiled at her. Pam had kissed him on the cheek.

How can I *not* hire her? Anita wondered.

The interrogation was as unintimidating as possible. Anita had a list of questions in her head, some of which she had found in a "nanny handbook" from the library. Dennis gently drilled her with hypothetical situations focused on discipline and emergencies. They were both impressed that Pam was CPR and first-aid certified.

Anita asked about her educational background and Pam candidly discussed several short-lived attempts to get a teaching degree at community college. The interruptions were financially driven.

Pam had no real hobbies or special interests, and that disappointed Anita. At least make something up, she thought. Say you like basket weaving or bowling or belong to the Barry Manilow fan club.

The only serious flaw Anita could identify was Pam's lack of ambition to do anything other than sit with someone else's children and care for someone else's home. Maybe I'm being a snob, Anita thought. Who says she has to hold lofty ambitions if this is all that makes her happy?

After the job-related questions were exhausted, Anita turned the conversation over to more innocuous things like Pam's family background and growing up. But the topic didn't seem to relax Pam any further.

She said her parents lived in Florida and she visited every Christmas. But she didn't appear particularly close to them. Pam's brother Roy, a truck driver, lived in the area, but she didn't have much to say about him either.

Anita couldn't resist asking about a boyfriend. It caused Pam to blush deep red, and Anita immediately regretted it. "Nobody right now," she said. Anita wondered if there had been anybody ever. She started to feel pity then, and quickly changed the subject to the job. Pam seemed agreeable to the proposed salary terms, hours, and vacation time. She was happy to help out with housekeeping duties.

At the end of the meal, Anita invited Pam to go visit with Tim, and a look of total relief washed over her face, as if she had been sprung free from the slammer. As Anita and Dennis cleared the dishes, Dennis wordlessly pointed to the crumpled wad on Pam's chair—during dinner she had quietly shredded the napkin in her lap.

As Pam played with Tim in the living room, Anita and Dennis quietly conferred under the steady splash of the kitchen sink.

"She's so introverted," said Dennis.

"It's not us. I don't think she's comfortable around adults in general," replied Anita.

"That's probably why she can't work in the adult world," mused Dennis.

"I know, she's nervous," said Anita. "I think she's very conscientious. I think she's good for Tim. What do you think?"

"I trust your judgment," said Dennis.

"No really, what do *you* think?"

"I think she's fine."

"Then we're . . . decided?" said Anita, suddenly feeling frightened. "Should we . . . ?"

Anita thought back to her mother's advice during a phone call the day before. "Trust your gut instinct," said her mother.

Anita's gut instinct said *Pam's the one.*

She took a deep breath. "Well, then . . . let's tell her."

They joined Pam and Tim in the living room.

Pam was holding Tim close to her chest.

"We'd like to make you an offer," said Anita.

Pam broke out in a wide smile. "Oh, wonderful. Thank you." Her grip on Tim tightened.

They discussed the terms of the agreement. The first two months would be a probationary period to allow everybody an out if the match was not a good one. Anita handed over a work agreement contract for Pam to take home and review. The template had come from a Web site run by a parenting magazine. It detailed the job conditions, work hours, amount per week, and so on. They also talked about the handling of taxes and health benefits. And then there were the logistics of securing a baby car seat for the backseat of Pam's Toyota, giving her house keys, and meeting the neighbors.

Throughout it all, Pam was full of smiles, lighter, as if a great weight had been lifted off her small shoulders. Her joy was unmistakable. *She really wanted this,* Anita recognized, and good feelings pumped through her veins. *She really loves Tim. This is going to work out just great.*

When Pam left later that evening, Tim even looked sad.

Chapter Five

Anita felt lost somewhere in the zone between the very late and very early hours. It was still dark, probably 3 A.M., possibly later. She could see police cars, marked and unmarked, crowding the street and driveway. There were officers talking to one another in pockets on the lawn.

She also noticed a woman in a long coat with a pad and pen, wandering, trying to engage in conversation with investigators. Anita felt her chest tighten, her breathing hurt. A reporter.

Another hard reminder that this was big, this was not right, this was horrible, no matter how hard she tried to come up with a rational explanation that assured Tim's safe return.

Inside the house, the police had set up a table and plugged in a different phone, one connected to a recording device, caller ID, and small speaker. There was other equipment, including a police radio that crackled with constant voices. Calcina called the set-up a command center to stay in touch with headquarters and the precinct, and to take any calls that might come in from the state police or other departments and agencies. The Missing Child bulletin was spreading fast and furiously. An AMBER Alert had been activated.

Calcina had bragged about the number of resources at their disposal: emergency networks, experts, various databases. There was something the FBI ran called The Child Abduction and Serial Murder Investigative Resource Center. Anita didn't want to hear any more after that.

Anita's feet ached, but she couldn't sit—she had tried many times, and continually bounced back up, anxious. Standing in a corner of the living room, out of the way of everybody, she watched Calcina converse with one of the investigators. He looked committed, sympathetic, gentle even, for a cop. She wanted so bad to believe that he would orchestrate a fantastic rescue and return Tim to her arms.

When Calcina disengaged from the investigator, he walked over to her.

"How are you holding up?" he asked.

"Are we going to find him?" Anita blurted. Her words came out slurred, punch-drunk from exhaustion.

Calcina smiled for the first time. In fact, it was the first time she had seen any of the police smile.

"You have a lot of reasons to feel optimistic, Mrs. Sherwood. We have a pretty strong idea of who took him and why. As far as we know, we're not dealing with a professional criminal or a sexual predator. Just someone who likes your son too much. So he's going to be safe. And we're going to get him back."

Anita still gripped her cell phone; she hadn't let go for hours, somehow it was the only connection—however remote—to her son's whereabouts. "I just wish we could get through," she said.

"I think we'll hear from her," Calcina responded. "I have a feeling she's going to want to call you, if nothing else, to say Tim is safe. I don't believe her motive is to hurt you."

"Well, she's doing a great job of it," Anita muttered.

"If she calls, you're going to have to keep her on the line as long as possible," instructed Calcina. "Don't say anything that will make her mad—and I know you want to let her have it. But stay calm, engage in conversation, and don't let her hang up. We might be able to triangulate her location through cell phone towers."

Anita nodded. Dennis silently appeared at her side.

"We have the state troopers on alert to watch the main highways and state borders," said Calcina. "They have a detailed description of Pam's car. Everyone is very committed. Everybody wants to be the hero who finds your son."

Dennis remained quiet. He took off his glasses and rubbed his tired face. His words had dwindled over the hours and he looked sick, gray. Anita knew she looked just as bad, probably worse.

Calcina continued his update, and while the fury of activity was impressive, the lack of leads or clues from all this activity simply made Anita feel worse. Calcina informed them that detectives were already interviewing Pam's brother Roy and Pam's former employers the Roebers and the Savios. Also an undercover car was camped outside Pam's apartment. An officer was going to talk to Pam's neighbors.

Anita remembered meeting a few of the neighbors—mostly senior citizens. Pam's social life certainly wasn't helped by living in a building that was one step removed from a nursing home. The building itself was drab and smelled bad. The corridors were very dim to hide the stains in the decades-old carpet.

Anita had dropped by to pick up Tim one day when Pam needed to stay home to wait for a serviceman to repair her electric stove.

Anita had been struck by two things about the apartment: It was unbearably plain, and the only personal touches revolved around Tim. There was a small, framed picture of Tim on top of the television, of all places; and then two snapshots under magnets on the refrigerator. Several scribbly drawings by Tim—including an attempt at spelling his name that looked like "WIT"—were laid neatly on an end table, alongside stale editions of *TV Guide* and *People*.

In the center of the room, there was a blue plastic laundry basket filled with children's toys. Anita had figured they were things accumulated over years of babysitting, but then realized that many of them looked new, focused on Tim's age group.

At the time, it made her feel sad. Pam spending her own money on toys for a child who didn't belong to her.

Now, tonight, that basket felt like a big blue warning that she had ignored. Pam wasn't just affectionate, she was obsessed. She was crazy.

How did I misread her? Anita asked herself. What's wrong with me? Was I so wrapped up in my career—

"Anita," cried a voice.

Anita turned to see Barbara Roeber rushing toward her. She had just walked right into the house, like everybody else.

Barbara grabbed Anita, giving her a big hug. Maybe it made Barbara feel better, but it was just awkward to Anita.

"I'm so sorry," said Barbara, face puffy and eyes bloodshot. Her hair was tied in a tight ponytail and she wore a USC sweatshirt, blue jeans, and pink slippers. "The police told me what happened. I wish I could help. Oh God, I feel so responsible."

"It's not your fault," said Anita.

"I'm the one who told you to use her. I swear, I

never thought in a million years she'd do something like this. I don't understand."

"I know, I know."

"She would never hurt him," said Barbara, eyes big and sad. "Wherever he is, Tim is safe. I remember when Scott ran into a doorknob and had this big welt, Pam freaked out more than anybody. She's sensitive."

"Yeah," said Anita. "I don't know. This is just— madness."

"I hope you don't blame me," said Barbara.

Oh, that's all you're worried about? thought Anita. Then kindly go to hell.

Instead, Anita said, "I don't blame you or anybody. I just want . . . I want Tim back." She felt her throat tighten, the tears begin to surface.

A policeman with big ears and a disinterested face showed up, stepping between them. "Ma'am," he said. "There's a reporter from the *Oakland Tribune* . . ."

Anita nodded, she could guess the rest.

"She wants to talk with you."

"Who told her to come here?" asked Anita, not even covering the bitterness in her voice.

"She probably heard about it through a police scanner. They usually monitor—"

"No. I don't want to talk to her. Tim's only been gone a few hours. He'll be back soon. This is not a news story."

"She's probably going to write about it either way."

"Then fuck her," said Anita. Barbara's face lit

up with surprise. Maybe she had never heard the word before.

"You might want to reconsider if this continues," said Big Ears. "The publicity will help. If you have a picture—"

"There are pictures all over the house!" snapped Anita. "Which one do you want? Tim at the beach, or at the zoo, or Santa's lap or what?" Anita felt ready to burst into tears again. Around the room, people were catching glimpses of her and then quickly turning away. Big Ears just looked at her, stoic, well trained to sidestep a tirade.

Anita moved away from Barbara and the cop. She saw Dennis still talking to Calcina, blank expressions on both sides, so no news there.

What she really wanted to do was take a shower. She knew she probably smelled, her dinner clothes were sticky with sweat, her skin felt clammy all the way up to her scalp. She wanted to tear everything off . . . kick everybody out . . . pull out her hair . . .

Anita wondered if she was going crazy. If this was how insane people felt every minute. Maybe when dawn arrived, it would wipe away all this madness and the new day would be a return to normalcy. It was all just a long, sick dream . . .

Anita headed into the kitchen for another glass of water. She wasn't really thirsty, but it was something to do. She had just entered the kitchen when it happened:

The cell phone rang.

She had forgotten it was still gripped in her hand. She almost dropped it, as if shocked by electricity.

The entire house—which had been buzzing with conversation and footsteps—went silent in a heartbeat.

It rang a second time, the familiar electronic tones singing out, crystal clear.

Hands shaking, she jabbed at the little button that said YES. She started to bring the phone up to her ear, but quickly realized—

—there wasn't a voice waiting on the other end.

A small icon appeared on the cell phone display. An envelope.

Anita felt the swell of bodies around her now, eyes watching her. Someone hissed, "Answer it!"

"There's no one there," replied Anita, staring at the symbol, as if in a trance. "It's a text message."

Dennis was practically on top of her now. "Open it!" he exclaimed.

Her hand was shaking so violently that she didn't know if she could do it properly. But no one else was going to take the phone from her.

Anita opened the text message. As she read, her eyes filled with tears, blurring her sight, but not until she absorbed all the words:

I LOVE TIMMY. I AM MORE OF A MOTHER TO HIM THAN YOU EVER WERE. YOU CAN NEVER UNDERSTAND. HE WILL ALWAYS BE WITH ME.

"What does it say?" asked one of the investigators. Calcina moved in closer and the others parted to let him through.

Anita turned and shoved the phone at Dennis. She left the kitchen. She wanted to get away from all of them. She wanted to scream.

The voices in the kitchen began erupting, one after another.

"It's her . . ."

"It's the nanny."

"What's it say?"

" 'I love Timmy . . .' "

"Can we trace . . . ?"

" 'I am more of a mother . . .' "

"God damn it . . ."

" ' . . . never understand. He will always be with . . .' "

". . . you can't . . ."

"See if she's still on the line."

"This confirms it. We have a kidnapping."

". . . try calling her."

"Call her . . ."

Dennis now: "I AM!"

"This is evidence. Save the message!"

"This is admission of guilt . . ."

Then Dennis: "Shit!" Followed by: "She's disconnected."

"She sent the message and hung up."

"Can we still trace—"

"I don't think so. There's no signal."

"She's no dummy."

"Let's contact the carrier's SMS technicians—"

"There won't be anyone . . ."

Anita felt overwhelmed by dizziness. The words to the message were burned into her mind in capital letters: I AM MORE OF A MOTHER . . .

How dare she?

. . . MORE OF A MOTHER TO HIM . . .

She's nobody's mother!

Still, Anita couldn't help feeling gripped by guilt. She caused this to happen. She had left Tim with a nanny since he was six months old. Who was the mother if the mother was never home? In reality, she abandoned Tim a long time ago. They were already apart . . . What did this change?

Her thoughts began to torment her. She wanted to rip them out of her skull.

She saw Barbara Roeber coming toward her. The grating baby voice. "Aw, Anita . . ."

"I c-can't," Anita said simply, holding up her hands to ward off another hug. "I can't talk about this right now. Please."

Barbara nodded vigorously, wide-eyed, and the concern on her face looked very legit, and Anita felt bad, but she didn't want somebody to climb aboard her grief. Dennis was chatting away with the investigators in the kitchen, suddenly reanimated. His voice sounded more hopeful. At least the unknown had been replaced by a clearer picture and maybe some clues. That should be a reason to feel better, right?

Anita didn't feel better. Calcina came out of the kitchen. He looked her straight in the eye.

"Anita, we'll find him," he said with firmer reassurance than she had heard before.

"Put her in jail," Anita responded. "I'm not a

vindictive person . . . but . . . if you don't put her in jail . . . I might . . . get a gun and shoot her or something."

Great thing to tell a policeman, she immediately thought to herself, followed by *Who cares, who cares?* There were too many thoughts swimming in her head. She was drowning in them.

"I want to call my parents," she said then.

Calcina started to reply when—

The telephone rang. Not the chirp of the cell phone—this was the louder, longer ring of the house phone. It cut into Anita like a knife.

"Answer it!" she shouted, as if the thought hadn't crossed anyone else's mind.

Dennis grabbed the receiver and she heard him say: "Hello?"

The voice on the other end could be heard amplified on a speaker in the living room. "My name is Sandra Moran with NewsRadio—"

Calcina was on the call in a flash. He took the receiver from Dennis. "Don't call on this line, Sandy," he said. "I'll give you another number."

Anita looked over at Barbara, who stood in mute obedience. "I guess this'll be all over the news tomorrow," said Anita.

Barbara nodded, shrugged.

"I mean today. It's already tomorrow . . ." Anita's voice trailed. She couldn't think straight. The house felt crowded and claustrophobic. Some of the investigators were investigating, while others just sort of stood around, as if waiting for something to happen, staring blankly at one another or watching the fish in the aquarium. The floor was littered with dirty footprints. In the living room, the carpet was wet from where someone must have spilled something.

Calcina walked up to Anita, Dennis at his side. "Anita. Here's what I recommend. I know you probably don't like the idea of getting the media involved, but they can be a major ally. Let's find a recent picture, a good one, and a picture of Pam for the early morning TV newscasts. It's too late for the newspapers, but the sooner we get their faces out there, the sooner we can have the whole state of California on the lookout. There are only so many police . . . but think of the power of having every citizen—"

"OK, OK," interrupted Anita, resigned. "Dennis can help you, I—"

Two new faces, WASPy men with well-groomed hair and sour expressions entered the house. Calcina exchanged some words with them, and then introduced them to Anita and Dennis. They were FBI agents from the field office. One of them started talking about fingerprints: Tim's fingerprints, Pam's fingerprints . . .

"I'm going upstairs," said Anita.

Calcina shot her a look. "Don't touch anything."

Anita nodded. I'll just float through the house like a ghost, said the delirious voice in her head. My feet won't even touch the carpet.

She moved up the steps, slow and painful as if climbing Mount Everest. She went into the bathroom and turned on the faucet. Avoiding her reflection in the mirror, she splashed cold water on her face. The shock felt good. She dried herself off. *I'll touch anything I please. It's my house.*

Anita didn't want to return to the activity downstairs. Tim's door was open, the light had been left on by one of the investigators. Currently, it was empty.

Anita stepped into the room cautiously, as if it might swallow her up in horrible emotions. Tim's shelves were untouched, toys and baby pictures pleasantly lined up. The curtains were drawn. The toy chest and closet were closed. The room was clean and tidy, without menace.

Tim's crib was empty, but didn't look unusual. She stared into the crib, gazing over the humps and curves in the blue blanket in the corner, examing every little wrinkle in the mattress cover, as if somewhere they offered a clue. Maybe if she stared long enough, she could somehow connect with him, read his thoughts, become telepathic. It was possible, right? It was just a frequency, like a radio frequency, except for brain waves.

God, Anita, you are losing it, she told herself.

She touched his blanket with the back of her hand, imagined him reappearing, curled up in a comfortable ball, little hands touching his hair, which is often how she found him. She wanted to bring the blanket up to her face and inhale, basking in the familiar sweet smells.

"Tim, we're going to bring you home," she said. It was just a matter of time, the tortured passing of some hours, and then everything would be back in place.

Anita returned downstairs. She found Dennis slumped against a wall, a deep frown etched into his face. His eyes were tired behind the glasses. She walked up to him and their arms came out and she held him and he held her. Neither one of them said a word.

In the living room, there was a sudden buzz of voices and excitement. Dennis and Anita pulled apart and started to move toward the commotion, but Calcina was already on his way to them.

"We have some information," he started.

Anita gasped. Good or bad? Good or bad?

"Do you want to sit down?" he asked.

"No," said Dennis.

"Please, what is it?" asked Anita.

"A state trooper found the car."

"Thank God!" exclaimed Dennis.

"The vehicle is parked near Highway 101, a couple hundred miles north . . . just south of the Del-Norte/Humboldt border, near the coast."

"Is my baby OK?" said Anita; that was all that mattered.

"There's nobody in the vehicle," continued Calcina. "It's in a wooded area, off the main roads. A search is already under way. We have a lot of men going there from various law enforcement agencies."

"So he's okay?" said Anita.

"We don't know," Dennis told her.

"You think they're just walking around in the woods?" asked Anita.

"Well, we don't know," said Calcina. "There's the possibility that she ditched the car and she's in another vehicle. She probably knows we're looking for her Toyota."

"This is good news, though, right?" asked Dennis.

Calcina responded, "Every clue helps."

In the swirl of voices coming from the other room, Anita heard: ". . . they're getting the Coast Guard . . ."

"Coast Guard?" said Anita. She stared hard at Calcina. Immediately, her heart began thundering in her chest.

Calcina winced. It was probably something he didn't want her to hear. He spoke carefully. "The car is parked near the ocean. We have to act quick just in case . . ."

He didn't have to continue the thought. Anita exchanged a mortified glance with Dennis.

"Worst-case scenario," said Calcina. "We have to look into every possible scenario. You know that."

Several investigators were leaving the house. Calcina watched them go, then turned back to Dennis and Anita. "I'm going to the site."

"I'll follow," said Dennis quickly.

"It's a long drive," said Calcina. "You're in no shape. Why don't you ride with one of us."

"I'm going, too," said Anita.

Calcina shook his head. "No. I'm sorry. I need

one of you to stay here in case she calls."

"I want to go where Tim is," said Anita. "If I stay here I'll go crazy." But Calcina just gave her a stern look.

Dennis headed upstairs to change his clothes. He was still wearing his slacks and polo shirt from dinner. Anita followed.

They both changed in the bedroom, quick and sloppy, into jeans and sweaters.

"I'm going with you," said Anita.

"Honey, you heard the lieutenant," responded Dennis. "They need you to stay."

"I don't care. We're going to get Tim. I'm not waiting around the house, *it's torture.*"

Dennis gave her a long look, then nodded. "OK. I'll get directions. We'll take the Jeep. We've got to move fast."

Dennis got directions from one of the investigators. Then Anita joined him as he left the house. They walked swiftly across the lawn to the Jeep Liberty. No one seemed to notice—except for a TV news reporter and cameraman.

"Can't talk," said Dennis quickly. "Going to get my son."

"Why do you think your nanny took him?" shouted a red-haired woman, soaked in makeup and waving a microphone.

Anita slammed the car door on her. "Let's go," she said.

The Jeep backed into the street, careful to avoid the investigators, reporters, and curious onlookers who were scattered everywhere, hovering around the house and moving slowly in the dark, like a scene from *Night of the Living Dead*.

The Jeep accelerated down the street.

"I didn't lock the front door," said Anita.

"Is that a joke?" said Dennis. "We have the Oakland Police Department in our house."

Anita smiled, almost laughed. Suddenly, breaking free from the house and its chaos, she somehow felt better. She could breathe again. They had a destination now, and things were clearer. Early daylight was moving across the sky.

"We're going to get Tim back," said Anita.

"Yes, we are," said Dennis. His voice wasn't just hopeful, it was affirmative. "Yes, we are."

Chapter Six

The Jeep soared north, tearing past car after truck after car. Anita caught blurred glimpses of ordinary faces going about their ordinary routines. She wished she was one of them.

The drive would take most of the morning. Dennis and Anita had planned to take turns driving, but so far it was all Dennis, gripping the wheel with white-knuckled intensity, eyes glaring ahead.

While he drove, Anita was supposed to catch up on sleep—impossible. Fear and adrenaline kept her wide-awake. A planned stop to grab coffee never materialized. Anita merely sat silently, watching to see that Dennis didn't suddenly nod off and veer off the highway.

Dawn spilled out over the northern California coast, filling in life and color to the area surrounding Highway 101. The daylight brought another layer of cold reality to the night's surreal turn of events.

Aside from the hum of the Jeep, Anita and Dennis were sealed in a vacuum of silence. Ordinarily, when Dennis drove, there was loud music from his favorite rock-and-roll CDs, The Who, The Rolling Stones. At one point, they did try the radio but snapped it off when a newscast began with a reference to "every parent's nightmare."

Early on, there was an attempt at some conversation. It looped in circles of anger, disbelief, and helplessness, before fading altogether when words couldn't match the horror. Without conversation, Anita was left with images. As much as she tried to stare at the landscape outside her window, she kept seeing Tim.

Moments of Tim, like film clips. Achingly vivid recollections of his touch, his smell, his warbling little voice. Snippets of dialogue from the past week played in her head. Tim was learning to put his new vocabulary into phrases and sentences. He was learning how to walk up and down the stairs rather than slide and climb. He was more focused on favorite books and games. Overnight, he had started to brim with curiosity about everything around him. His range of expressions was growing, each one a delight. Of course, there were moments where the "terrible twos" emerged, flashes of defiance and temper, but they were usually short-lived. He was always on to something else.

She recalled their last encounter. She had come home early from her last day of work, loaded with boxes of belongings from Digital Learnings. She rarely, if ever, came home early, so he was wild with delight, bare feet running in circles around her. She gave him a goofy key chain from one of the boxes—something a vendor had given her. He had gripped it tight for the next hour. A gift from *Mommy*.

She gave him a juice box with a straw and told him not to squeeze it. He did, red fruit juice squirted on his shirt, and she had shouted at him and scolded him—

Oh no, Anita thought. The memory stung. He had cried. But briefly. Pam had changed his shirt, soothed him. The thought of scolding him suddenly filled Anita with guilt, although it was really nothing harsh, nothing out of the ordinary, nothing that any other mother wouldn't have done. But now it was his lasting memory . . .

Pam had fed Tim while Anita changed clothes. Pam didn't act unusual, perhaps quieter than usual. Dennis arrived home somewhere around seven, as Tim was being prepared for bed. Pam handled the diaper change, the face washing, getting rice out of his hair. In fact, realized Anita, she had seen Tim very little in the final hour before she left with Dennis for dinner.

I didn't even read him a story, realized Anita, followed by *Why am I torturing myself like this?*

Tim was asleep in his crib when Anita and Dennis left for dinner. She had checked on him once, touched him gently, he stirred, and it was good-bye. See you later. Not even the tiniest thought that he wouldn't be there when they returned. It seemed so long ago, years ago.

Now this. This madness. She tried again to affix her focus emotionlessly on the scenery outside the car. The trees waved in the cold. At various times she could see the ocean. As the highway rolled beneath the car, Anita couldn't help but wonder about Tim's state of mind when he traveled this same route hours ago: Was he awake? Was he scared? Was he warm?

Tim trusted Pam. For better or worse, he was probably not fearful. Just tired and confused. And hungry? He would be hungry by now. What did Pam have to feed him? Had she even thought that far ahead?

Maybe he was being fed right now. Maybe Tim had already been rescued and all this worrying was unnecessary. In their rush to leave the house, they had left the cell phone behind with the police, so there was no way for anyone to reach them. She considered checking the radio for news, but decided that was not how she wanted to receive her progress reports. God forbid, what if . . . ? She squelched the thought.

The drive was starting to hypnotize her. She wished it would numb her. Or at least settle the buzzing, gnawing tension in her chest and stomach.

"Oh God," she finally said out loud, the first words in a long time to pierce the silence.

Dennis didn't react. He continued staring ahead, eyes sunken and bloodshot, face dark with stubble. He was barely moving, aside from small adjustments to the steering. Finally, when she didn't expect it, he spoke aloud in a cold, flat tone.

"I'm going to fucking kill her."

The directions took them off Highway 101 and into Prairie Creek Redwoods State Park, about thirty miles south of the Oregon state border. Dennis took a wandering, unpaved road along a rugged stretch of coast, under a dense canopy of redwoods, seeing very little traffic or signs of civilization. The trees practically blocked out the sun; it felt eerie, like the day was already coming to a close.

At this point, the information vacuum was truly driving her crazy, along with the thick tension that threatened to implode the Jeep.

"I see something," said Dennis, his voice cracked and murky from remaining silent for hours.

Then Anita saw it, too. There, tucked deep among the redwoods, was a police car, then a second police car, and then . . .

An explosion of activity. They had entered the hornet's nest. Police, emergency vehicles, television vans, men in FBI windbreakers, all mixed up and moving around.

In the midst of everything, Anita spotted Pam's parked Toyota, surrounded by yellow police tape.

She felt a thunderbolt of both terror and relief.

Dennis parked on the grass. He leapt out of the Jeep; Anita followed, out of the stale car air and into the harsh winter chill.

"It's so cold," she said, and she wanted to cry, but wouldn't, didn't.

She followed Dennis to Pam's car.

"Don't touch anything!" shouted an FBI agent.

Anita looked in the window. She saw the baby car seat they had bought for Pam so long ago . . . the cell phone . . . Pam's purse. She left without her purse?

"Are you the mother?" asked a slick, Clark Kent lookalike with a rich voice. A television voice.

"No," said Anita. More reporters began closing in, armed with microphones, notepads, cameramen.

Dennis scanned the crowd. "Where's Calcina?"

Anita looked, too. She found him fifty feet away talking with a group of investigators. She moved to get in his line of sight. He saw her, grimaced at the sight of both of them, and held up a finger to indicate "one minute."

"Have you ever experienced trouble with your nanny before?" asked a perky blonde with big hair, accompanied by a young photographer.

"Not now," Dennis said firmly.

The photographer took pictures anyway. Anita did her best to ignore him.

"Dogs," said Dennis.

"Dogs?" Anita repeated, not knowing what he was talking about, until she followed his gaze into the forest, where several investigators held bloodhounds on leashes. The canines were muzzled, moving quickly and crookedly between the trees.

Earlier in the evening, one of the investigators had asked for Tim's blue blanket "to pick up the scent." It was another surreal moment at the house, lost in the commotion of everything else. Now it was another ugly reality.

"I don't think they've found them yet," said Dennis.

"No," said Anita. Her attention became distracted from the dogs to a steady, growing noise in her ears. The sound had started a few minutes ago as a faraway hum and now reached the level of a rapid, forceful pounding that bounced off the trees.

Dennis jerked his head. "What the hell is that?"

Anita turned around in a complete circle, searching for the source, and found nothing, even as the sound intensified. The ground shook beneath their feet, yet no one paid it any attention.

Whump-whump-whump-whump.

The pounding amplified dramatically until it drowned out all other sounds, blasting through the trees. It felt like a fast, hammering heartbeat in Anita's chest. She followed the direction of the noise, taking several steps, breaking into a jog, then running. She ran deeper into the woods, past faceless investigators and through the maze of giant redwoods. She almost stumbled, but didn't slow down her momentum. The noise continued to grow louder, assaulting her, vibrating her bones.

WHUMP-WHUMP-WHUMP-WHUMP.

All of a sudden, the forest vanished.

The trees and brush stopped coming, the bright daylight returned, and there was a wall of blue. Blue sky and blue ocean for as far as she could see. Her feet stopped abruptly, because if they had continued, she would have gone soaring into space.

The ground ended and plunged hundreds of feet into a faraway swirl of rocks and sea. Anita screamed, but the scream was lost in the gigantic *ROAR.*

A helicopter charged into view, big and orange like a monstrous insect, hugging the coast. The blades sliced through the air, deafening, hammering her ears until she thought her head would burst. The force sent her staggering backward.

Strong hands grabbed Anita and pulled her back. It was Dennis.

She was mere feet from the edge of a cliff. A driving wind cut across the horizon, chilling her flesh. Down below, she could see Coast Guard boats appearing tiny in the waters.

Anita knew that no one could survive a fall into the violent, freezing waters below. They would be pulverized by the rocks, pulled into the ferocious spirals of sea. It looked like the mouth of a monster.

The helicopter made a sharp turn and started to circle back. Anita pulled loose from Dennis's hold and retreated back into the woods. Her tears felt cold on her face. Dennis came after her.

"Anita!"

"Don't talk to me—"

"He's not down there."

"How do you know?"

"You can't think this way."

"Everybody else obviously is."

"Everybody who?"

She didn't want to engage in a conversation with him. It was all too much to bear. She returned to the mob of people at the site of Pam's car, waving away reporters with both hands.

Almost immediately, Calcina was in front of her.

"Where's Tim?" said Anita, out of breath, starting to choke on her own words. "Where is he? *Where is he?*"

Calcina waited for Dennis to catch up.

Anita saw the reporter watching, but keeping a distance. Video cameras were rolling.

"We don't know," said Calcina. "Here's what we do know: She left everything behind in the car. The phone, her purse, the money. All she took was Tim. She hasn't made any more calls."

"Why are they looking in the ocean?" asked Anita, pushing the words out painfully.

"We are searching the ocean, the woods, the highways, everywhere. There's a good possibility she switched cars."

"Are there any footprints?" asked Anita.

Calcina shook his head. "We had a heavy rain here earlier that's made it very difficult. We haven't had any luck so far, but you never know—"

"I'm tired of not knowing!" snapped Anita.

Calcina said nothing. His eyes looked tired and sad, and she immediately felt bad. He was the last person to take her anger out on. He was doing everything he could.

"What can we do to help?" asked Dennis.

"Help us check the woods. But don't get lost. Stay in sight. We're scouring the area for clues. It could be anything."

In that instant, Anita saw Roy Beckert. He was nearby in a flannel shirt and jeans, talking to an investigator. She couldn't detect any emotion in their faces, any significant exchange of information.

Then, for a moment, Roy noticed Anita. Their eyes locked. She didn't look away. Finally, he did. There was no sympathy, no apology in his eyes.

Just the sight of Roy filled Anita with rage. She couldn't bear to see anyone associated with Pam in any way. She felt sick.

The roar of the helicopter kept rising and falling as it circled the area. After a while, it no longer filled her with dread, it became white noise. Someone with the state police gave her a donut. She took several bites and promptly threw it up.

The investigators all had similar expressions:

frustrated and grim. When one of them broke from the norm and showed an inexplicable smile or bored yawn, it angered her.

Anita and Dennis joined the search of the woods, silently going off in random directions and circling back, undoubtedly covering ground that was already covered.

Throughout it all, Anita tried to comfort herself with a series of potential scenarios.

Maybe they'll be discovered hiding out in the woods . . .

Or the highway patrol will catch them in another vehicle . . .

Maybe some campers or hikers found them and took them somewhere . . .

As the feeling of hopelessness continued to grow, Anita finally gave in to Calcina's persistence that she and Dennis talk to reporters. "If you're on camera, if the public can see and feel what you are experiencing, they will be moved to help," insisted Calcina.

The first interview was horribly awkward, but by the third one she was doing better, less aware of the camera, more prepared with statements. Dennis chimed in here and there, but the media seemed more interested in her. The mother's grief was more dramatic. Better ratings. Whatever. *Just get me back my son.*

Cold and exhausted to the point of delirium, she finally returned to the Jeep and locked herself in the backseat. She curled herself into a ball. No matter how difficult it was, she needed some sleep. She needed a clearer mind. Maybe a clearer mind would provide her with the clue that would solve the mystery. I'm not abandoning him if I sleep, she told herself. I'm making myself stronger so I can rescue him.

She slept for about an hour and a half, awakening occasionally with a disoriented jolt, a few seconds of *Where am I? What's going on?* followed by the brutal return to reality.

She was sleeping fairly deeply when a tapping on the window woke her up. It was Dennis and Lieutenant Calcina. Their faces were serious, not happy "we rescued him" faces.

She nearly fell out of the car in her haste to hear what they had to say.

"It's not Tim, but it's not good," said Dennis quickly, his voice thin and breathless. He then looked at Calcina to deliver the news.

"The Coast Guard found a body," said Calcina. "Adult female, drowned. She's been dead for less than twelve hours."

"No," said Anita, grabbing at her hair. "No no no no no."

"It's probably her," said Dennis. "Roy is . . . he's identifying the body."

"Where's Tim?" asked Anita, hysteria washing over her. "Please tell me he's all right. Please. Please."

"We'll continue to search for Tim," said Calcina. "There's a chance that he's in these woods—that she abandoned him and then took her life. He could be lost. We're increasing the numbers of investigators. We're expanding our search."

"He's going to be so cold," said Anita.

Dennis stepped forward and hugged her. She wrapped her arms around him tight. More than ever before, she needed his strength. They held onto one another until they could barely remain standing.

When the reporters started closing in on them again, Dennis and Anita retreated into the back of one of the police vehicles, where they could hear the buzz of activity on the police radio.

Anita held her face in her hands and cried.

The next two hours brought only one piece of news: confirmation that the drowned body belonged to Pam Beckert. She probably died very quickly, said an investigator, either from drowning or from the battering against the rocks. *Died very quickly*, thought Anita. *Should that make me feel better?*

She had never, ever been seized by terror that gripped so hard.

This must be what it's like for relatives after a plane crash, she thought. The waiting, the hoping, the praying for a miracle.

The afternoon gave way to the shroud of nightfall. As the darkness deepened, the temperature dropped. Someone distributed flashlights. Someone else brought bags of fast food. Anita ate part of a hamburger, very slowly, tiny bites. It tasted like nothing. But she kept it down.

With all her remaining strength, she forced

positive thoughts into her head. She envisioned a storyline where Pam left Tim sleeping in the car, killed herself, and then some campers found Tim and took him someplace safe and warm. They were feeding him, being gentle and kind, and trying to locate the proper authorities. Tim would be back in her arms by bedtime. They would all go home together.

Just before sunset, Anita and Dennis saw a handful of investigators pull together. Anita had been watching faces all day, most of them stoic, but these expressions were different. They were alarmed. She tried to lip-read. One of them appeared to say "Oh, shit," in reaction to the words of another.

The investigators began to spread out, meeting in twos and threes with others who started coming in from the forest.

Anita and Dennis quickly climbed out of the police car.

"What's happening?" shouted Anita; but no one wanted to look at her. Only one person stepped forward.

Lieutenant Michael Calcina, shoulders sagging, walked up to them slowly. His mouth moved, but he was still searching for words.

Then Anita saw the tears in his eyes.

She closed her own eyes. She closed them as tight as she could. But she could not shut out his words.

The Coast Guard had discovered an object bobbing in the waves. A small, brown stuffed toy.

It was Tim's bear.

Chapter Seven

All through the memorial service, Anita didn't let go. She stood between her father and Dennis, clutching their hands as if they supplied the sustenance that kept her from crumbling. She needed to feel their life because she felt none inside. The tiny coffin at the front of the church contained more than the symbolic loss of Tim. It contained a huge portion of herself, removed and killed off, forever.

She felt like a shell, or an alien, surrounded by two hundred human beings inside St. Mary's Cathedral. They were sympathetic. They cried. But they could never identify with her. She existed in another world now.

The service was beautiful. She knew it objectively, even if she didn't feel it penetrate her or provide comfort. Maggie had offered to supply her with tranquilizers to get through this day, but it wasn't necessary. Anita was already numb.

While everyone was dressed in a mournful black, the church itself was alive with colors. Flower arrangements spilled out in every direction. The April sun lit up the stained glass windows with an almost fluorescent intensity. Even the organ painted colors with its rich, thundering tones.

Anita remembered Tim's fascination with the church. He was always good here, attentive. Other children would let out shrieks of boredom, or wriggle and cry, or kick the pews with intermittent thuds, but not Tim. His eyes used to roam the elaborate woodwork, the dramatic figures in the stained glass, the long rafters and expansive arched ceiling. He looked for the source of every curious sound: the choir, the organ, the singing that spun a web around him. He even seemed to pay attention to the sermons, drawn in to the gentle, Mr. Rogers-like articulation of Father Hammil.

Now God had him for good.

Anita fought it at first. Without a body, she would not accept Tim's death. Even after the police declared him dead and closed the case, she refused to hold a service. At the very least, she wanted to postpone the funeral until a body was recovered. But the pressure for closure mounted until she felt she would crack apart.

Calcina had explained that they were fortunate to even find Pam's body, the way the powerful tides along the coastal rock churned and pulled everything back to sea. The search for Tim in the water and in the woods lasted a long time, and involved a lot of manpower. But the hope grew dimmer every day.

Anita prayed that the police would find a reason or piece of evidence to breathe new energy into the search. But there was none.

The text message Pam had sent now became an all-too-clear suicide note tinged with defiance and the revelation of Tim's fate. "He will always be with me."

In true nonconfrontational fashion, Pam didn't leave the world with a conversation, no adult interaction. Just a cowardly note.

"He will always be with me."

The words were burned into Anita's consciousness. He's not with you, she wanted to shout. He's with God. And you are burning in Hell.

Dennis admitted that his hopes of finding Tim alive died when the stuffed bear was discovered. It looked so soaked and gruesome that neither one of them could look at it for more than a few seconds—it provoked another level of horrible images they did not want to contemplate.

For several weeks after the bear's discovery, Anita dashed aside its implications. She hounded Calcina mercilessly every day for any news, any clues, *anything.* Wherever she went, Anita kept an eye out for Tim. It was crazy and compulsive, but she couldn't stop.

And it got her in trouble. On several occasions,

in crowds on the sidewalk, in school yards, at the mall, she would see Tim out of the corner of her eye. The jolting discovery—followed by the quick realization that it was not Tim, not even close— would nearly send her into hysteria.

When Dennis was with her, it would infuriate him. "Why are you doing this to us?" he demanded once, loudly, outside the restaurant where they were picking up another carryout dinner. People stared, people knew them like local celebrities now. "I can't take much more of this, Anita."

But she couldn't help it. And it wasn't always her fault. There were the sick crazies who called and left ominous messages: "I saw your son. He was at the zoo with a fat man wearing women's makeup." Or "My neighbor Frank has your son locked up in his basement. Here's his address . . ."

She passed the leads on to Calcina, who barely reacted, his voice remaining steady, while hers swelled with panic and hope.

"Yeah, we get those calls at the station, too," he said. "Unfortunately, this happens. You get disturbed individuals who want attention, or they want to cause trouble for someone by implicating them for a crime they had nothing to do with."

But he always promised to look into it. Then, about six weeks after the abduction, when the search was all but over, she created headlines at Sears.

She hated shopping now because she hated

appearing in public, but she was simply picking up some dull necessities—undergarments, mostly—when she saw an elderly man and a little boy getting into the elevator off the children's department.

The boy, from a distance, seen from behind, looked like Tim.

The elevator doors shut. Anita dropped everything and screamed. She told a clerk: "That man stole my son."

The staff responded with lightning fast efficiency—she later discovered that they were well trained to follow a strict procedure. In a matter of minutes, the entire store was in lockdown. Gates rolled down to seal off anyone from disappearing into the adjacent mall. Doors to the outside were locked and guarded by security. Scores of police materialized out of nowhere. Every customer was trapped inside, buzzing with excitement, as the store was thoroughly searched: every restroom, every storage space, underneath every clothing rack, behind every counter.

When police apprehended the elderly man of Anita's description, the two-year-old boy in his possession only had a vague similarity to Tim. Both looked terrified. The elderly man was befuddled and pale, repeating over and over, "It's my grandson. He's my grandson."

The little boy looked ready to cry.

When Calcina showed up—sweaty, chest

heaving from running—the look on his face sent a chill through Anita.

Without a fault, through the investigation, he had been warm, patient, compassionate, and controlled. Now he was just one pissed-off cop. She could tell he was holding back from chewing her out.

She felt sick. She apologized to everyone over and over, automatically, until she didn't even hear her own words.

"Look," said Calcina. "I understand how traumatic this has been. I know how important it is to still have hope. But, when you're under this kind of stress, your mind can go into overdrive and play tricks. It's like a hallucination or mirage. You see what you want to see. I'm just saying this because you need to be aware that it happens."

"He looked like Tim," said Anita simply, flatly.

Calcina nodded. He promised to set her up with a grief counselor.

I don't need a grief counselor, she wanted to tell him. He won't make me feel better. Only one person can make me feel better. And he's gone.

Anita knew that she would keep seeing Tim until there was closure. The funeral would be closure. But it would also be the death of hope.

As the weeks continued to pile up without progress, with rapidly dwindling resources devoted to the search, Dennis started the conversation about a funeral service. When the police closed the investigation, she knew it was time to put Tim to rest.

Still, she pushed it away for more weeks, until it loomed so big and heavy that she could no longer push.

She then faced the reality of Tim's funeral, knowing it would be the worst day of her life.

She now knew why relatives of plane crash victims wanted remains—any remains—for a burial. The absence of a body tormented her. He needed to return to her, come home, even in the worst possible state.

In the end, there was only a lock of hair, saved from his first haircut. During funeral preparations, she had the option of a memorial board with pictures or a casket to fill with mementos. She chose the latter.

The casket held the hair snippets, good-bye letters, family pictures, favorite toys, drawings— every item bringing wrenching tears as it was added to the collection.

At the funeral service, her brother, her father, Dennis, and his father carried the casket up the aisle. Father Hammil delivered a homily that tried to make sense of a life cut so short and something he called the "disruption of the orderliness of the universe." Her father delivered a eulogy. Despite being an engineer, he was a polished speaker, and brought tears out of everyone's eyes. He spoke about the little boy who touched so many lives.

Originally, Anita had planned to deliver a eulogy, and even wrote one out, but she couldn't say the words out loud without a complete breakdown. Finally, she put the handwritten eulogy into Tim's casket. Afterall, it was for him, not the crowd at the funeral service.

Dennis had considered speaking as well, but simply could not articulate his thoughts, and probably couldn't bear to try. His survival technique seemed to be silence, and he spoke very little during the worst weeks, blank-faced with an emptiness in his eyes.

Anita knew Dennis was hurting tremendously. He had taken to fatherhood very strongly, with even more devotion than she ever imagined. Tim brought out a warm and wonderful side of Dennis and he relished the time they spent together. Now he was just vacant and detached, like someone pulled the plug.

When the mass ended, the pallbearers regrouped to accompany the casket out of the church. As Anita turned to leave the church, she could finally see the rows of faces that she had felt behind her, looming like one large being. There wasn't much to distinguish them. Uniformed in black, red eyes, red noses, long faces. Everyone was sniffling, shuffling, looking away from her. A few individuals came up to her and offered words that she barely heard and hugs that she barely felt.

Outside the church, reporters had gathered. She refused to acknowledge them. A woman waving a microphone tried to find a willing sound bite. A TV station needed some compelling footage to sell advertising space around. Would they ever leave her alone? Weeks ago, one had the nerve to ask if she was going to attend Pam's funeral. She had just glared in response.

After the funeral, Anita gathered her remaining stamina to attend a luncheon with a small group of friends and relatives at the home of her neighbor Gilda. Gilda and her husband had moved into the area around the same time as Dennis and Anita, and they had become fairly close over the years. Gilda had a young daughter about Tim's age—she was wisely absent from the house.

The gathering was well meaning, but awkward. There was only one subject to talk about, and no one dared show disrespect by straying to something else. Everyone took a turn coming up to offer their deepest, most heartfelt condolences. They all had good intentions, but they simply could not soothe her or reach her pain. They were on the outside, looking in.

And when they weren't coming up to say how sorry they were, they were staring at her from across the room with sorry, pitying eyes.

Barbara Roeber still looked shell-shocked, feeling the burden of responsibility for recommending Pam. Anita didn't know whether she should harbor animosity toward her or not. Surely Barbara could have offered up something about Pam's obsessiveness or possessiveness around children. Unfortunately, the truth was that Anita missed it, too. No one could have seen this coming.

Maggie was there, along with all her cohorts from Digital Learnings. Maggie kept saying, "Please let me know what I can do to help," although there was nothing. Nothing.

Several people offered meals—what night would be good to deliver dinner? Anita did her best to be appreciative while turning them down. She had built up a collection of stock comments and replies.

The exhaustion was quickly settling in. She wanted to leave and be alone, but too many people had driven or flown from out of town. In fact, she had not seen such a comprehensive gathering of family and friends since her wedding.

One of Anita's least favorite people, Dennis's mother, was here, inevitably. She spent most of her time hovering near Dennis. She always treated Anita with an artificial cheer, never failing to contradict or undermine her. Shriveled, frowning, blue-haired Myrtle Sherwood still wanted to be the number one woman in Dennis's life, and Anita was still and forever the competition. Not an unusual scenario, Anita understood, but irksome all the same, especially when her parents treated Dennis like a prince.

Maggie, bless her, injected the one and only moment of humor into the day when she provided Anita with a quick, snarling impersonation of Myrtle Sherwood's loud displeasure over the lack of ice for her vodka and 7-Up. Anita had shared many "in-law" tales with Maggie, who didn't even speak to her mother-in-law anymore. They had a falling out more than a decade ago over who would host Thanksgiving dinner.

Anita's family, up from Nevada, hovered around her, peppering her with questions, examining her delicately. "Do you want something to eat?" "Do you want to sit down?" "Do you need to go home?"

Anita's brother Peter tried to make her feel better with an affectionate, long-winded remembrance of his encounters with Tim, but it only brought tears to her eyes. Finally, Peter simply told Anita that he loved her very much, which he had never said before, and possibly didn't mean. It was her cue to tell her brother that she loved him, too, but she merely nodded.

If there was any relief to be found, it was the presence of her parents. Perhaps it was the simple fact that they had always been her protectors and guiding lights. Now she felt like a little girl again, needing them to make everything all better.

Her father was as pragmatic as they came— precise with his words and actions and always right, if not very emotional. Her mother was a heavyset, cheerful woman who could find the silver lining in almost anything. It was strange to see her today without a smile. She looked much older.

Both were retired, and they were prepared to stay with her and Dennis for an indefinite period after the funeral. Even if Dennis did not favor the arrangement, he did not object. He probably knew she wouldn't let him.

Dennis was simply too shattered to be a pillar of strength right now. Anita knew that her parents would help keep her from going off the deep end. They would also help fill out the haunting emptiness at home.

The luncheon broke up in the midafternoon. Once a few people started leaving, the rest followed quickly. Anita could not blame them. They needed to reconnect with their own safe and secure lives. She wished she could leave the gloom behind as well, but it was going to travel with her, like a rain cloud following a cartoon character.

Gilda wrapped up the leftovers and passed them out to the reduced group that was going home with Anita and Dennis. Anita thanked Gilda for everything. Gilda cried. Myrtle Sherwood quickly downed her third vodka and 7-Up.

Dennis helped Anita with her coat and then, unexpectedly, kissed her on the cheek.

"How are you feeling?" he asked.

She thought about it, and then replied truthfully, "I'm not."

The silence chilled her. No melodic babble, no squeaks and beeps and silly voices from toys, no little feet banging across the floor. The house was lifeless. She kept the television on—tuned to the inoffensive chatter of the Weather Channel—just for voices to stir the air.

Dennis didn't say much in the days after the funeral. Most of the time, he slept or fussed around the house with long-neglected projects like fixing the leaky toilet. At least he hadn't returned to drinking, a fear that stayed at the back of her mind.

Eventually, Dennis returned to work. He seemed to find solace in the routine of his job, and it probably did him good. His absence made the presence of her parents all the more crucial. She couldn't bear the thought of being left alone in the house.

Tim remained in every room, touching every object with memories. He was everywhere and nowhere.

Anita knew she could not find comfort, but hoped to coast on some kind of passive neutrality. She needed to relax her mind. One afternoon, for hours, she sat in a chair in the living room and simply stared at the aquarium. She hypnotized herself with the motion of the fish and the gurgle of the tank. As time passed, she noticed that one of the fish was missing. One of the clown fish. Tim loved the clown fish and had helped pick them out at the pet store.

That night, she asked Dennis about the missing fish, and he muttered that a clown fish had died.

Something snapped when she heard that. Anita broke down in sobs all over again. Certainly Dennis thought she was crazy, but no, she was just terribly, horribly fragile.

"It's just a fish," said Dennis.

"You don't understand," she responded, and they didn't discuss it again. She avoided the fish tank. Just another object that stung her with pain.

Soon after, Anita's father purchased several new fish for the aquarium. New life. Maybe it was meant to be some kind of a symbolic gesture. If so, it didn't soothe her.

While the days were bad, the nights were worst. Every night was a reminder of "the night" that her world fell apart. She frequently awoke with a start, thrown into immediate confusion and fear. Then she would stay awake in the dark, her mind sadistically wondering about his final minutes. Did he suffer? Was it quick? The cold water, the suffocating, the waves, the rocks—she couldn't chase it out of her head.

Just as bad, however, were the good dreams where she interacted with Tim—and then woke up to rediscover his absence all over again. It caused her to relive the agony of feeling him slip away.

In the mornings, she felt relief when her parents joined her. Her parents provided a steady stream of dialogue—most of it trivial banter to distract and fill the silence. They hung around the house and helped out with cooking and housework. Often it was invaluable—like the time her mother tended to the basket of Tim's dirty clothes that had remained in the basement ever since he disappeared.

"What are you going to do about his room?" her mother asked carefully one morning over sandwiches in the kitchen.

"I don't want to change anything," she replied. The clothes were still neatly folded in the drawers, his toys on shelves, and his picture on the walls. "I want to keep it as is. Like a museum or memorial. I can't just throw it all away. . . ."

"Not throw it away, but pack it away," her mother suggested. "Maybe it's doing more harm than good."

Anita knew that her mother had caught her crying in Tim's room on several occasions, sobbing over a small sock or toy truck or book with chew marks.

"I'm just not ready yet," said Anita.

"I understand."

"Even though it makes me cry, sometimes the only thing I can do to hold myself together is to remember the good things. It brings him near to me. It's better than just pushing the memories away, isn't it?"

Earlier in the week, Anita had even gone to a nearby park, Tim's favorite place, and soaked in the vivid images of prior visits. She could see his looks of glee as he scrambled on and around the equipment, pausing frequently to seek her out, and beaming when he caught sight of her.

"Have you called the counselor yet?" her mother asked.

The grief counselor recommended by Lieutenant Calcina. The card was still on the dining room table, jumbled with unread mail. "No."

"It's worth a try. You know, I've been reading about traumatic stress disorder . . ."

"Mom, I'm okay. I'm not a mental patient."

"Of course not, but there is help available that goes above and beyond what your father and I can—"

"If it means that much to you, I'll go," said Anita. "I'll call. But if I don't like it, I'm not going back."

Anita set up an appointment for the following Tuesday, which turned out to be perfect timing. She had been avoiding the newspapers, but on Tuesday she caught a glimpse of the *Oakland Times* that her father had brought into the house.

Anita had thought that the media would stop after the funeral, but no, they were still milking it. Today there was a feature on "Can You Trust Your Nanny?" with a sidebar "Signs to Watch For," as if killer nannies were an epidemic. It caught her so off guard, she went to the kitchen sink and threw up.

The media coverage had been sensationalistic ever since Tim disappeared, but she kept thinking it would come to a halt when there was nothing new to report. She and Dennis had granted only a few interviews after the discovery of Pam's body, and Anita had regretted them. She either broke down in tears or appeared too robotic in an effort to avoid breaking down. Spreading her grief across everyone's television screen for the nightly news was just another horrible layer of angst that she didn't need right now.

The press continually displayed a lack of tact, like the time a photographer camped out on the front lawn waiting for them to come out the front door to acknowledge the garish heaps of sympathy that total strangers had dumped on their doorstep: cards, flowers, toys, and balloons, as if there was a birthday party inside. Worse yet, people were leaving teddy bears similar to the one discovered in the ocean. Sure, it was well meaning, but it was creepy beyond belief. And now a photographer wanted them framed in a shot with all this junk. Dennis had gone out through the back door and circled around to the photographer, threatening to smash his camera. The photographer scampered away, promising, "I'll be back. The sidewalk is public property."

The media became her first topic of conversation with the counselor, Dr. Andrew. She had barely sat down in his office when she began to rant. "I'm going through the worst, most horrible thing anyone can imagine, and I can't suffer in peace. It has to be in the newspapers and on TV and in *People* for the whole world to stare at, like my misery is some kind of entertainment or freak show. I feel like I'm in a cage at the zoo."

Before long, her sessions with Dr. Andrew became the only thing she looked forward to. They actually made her feel good. And it wasn't anything he said, really. It was her own words.

She realized that with Dennis, with her parents, with Maggie, with all of them, she was cen-sored, she was behaving the way she was expected to behave, playing a role. But with Dr. Andrew—in his sterile office, with the door closed, staring into his dull fat face—she could unleash. Everything spilled out. Her rage, her sorrow, her incomplete thoughts, her confusion.

She upped the visits to three times a week. Dennis groaned at the expense, but she begged him to let her do it.

She spent hours and hours with Dr. Andrew, often addressing one simple question:

Why?

Over and over, she tried to fathom what was going on in Pam's head. What would cause a woman to love a child so much that she would steal him from his family and then kill him—and herself?

Dr. Andrew talked about how an emotionally vulnerable person could be driven to irrational acts by intense rage or sorrow. They talked about much publicized cases where a loving parent—in the throes of a divorce—murders the children, much to the disbelief of everyone who knew the family.

"It's my belief that when Pam took off with Tim, it was an impulsive action, without much plan-ning or forethought," said Dr. Andrew. "And then, eventually, the sun comes up, things be-come clearer and it dawns on her that she can never carry off such a crime. She reaches a dead end. She realizes that the police will catch up with her and take Tim back to his parents and put her away in jail. The only solution, in her mind, is to jump. She takes Tim with her. It's the only action left. The only option to keep from losing him."

Understanding Pam's psychosis did not erase Anita's escalating feeling of rage toward her. And Pam's death did not satisfy her as punishment. Instead, it felt like Pam's escape.

Anita scrubbed every remnant of Pam from her house. She destroyed every photo, every document relating to her employment, and everything Pam had ever given to Tim.

Still, it didn't make her feel better. Sometimes, it only heightened the intensity of her anger.

One afternoon, after her parents had returned home to Nevada, Anita saw Roy at the local pharmacy. She was filling a small basket with various medicines to relieve the punishing effects of stress on her head and stomach. Roy was dressed sloppily and flipping through a sports magazine. There was something so casual, so unaffected about his appearance that she couldn't stop staring. She felt her veins fill with anger. Involuntarily, she stepped toward him.

Roy glanced up. Their eyes met for a moment. Then he quickly returned his attention to the magazine. Wordlessly. As if she was a stranger. Or a phantom. A nothing.

That set her off.

Anita lost control, screaming at him. It could have been gibberish, she didn't care, as long as he got the full blast of her fury. In front of the whole store, she hollered in his face, at his ugly crooked nose, as if *he* was the guilty one.

He absorbed the profanity silently—to a point—and then his face turned deep red. He threw down the magazine and rushed toward her.

Oh my God, he's going to kill me, thought Anita.

Roy grabbed Anita by the wrists and shoved her backward, into a shelf, spilling items to the floor.

He was yelling, his eyes ablaze, staring into her so hard that she thought her head would explode.

"You think it doesn't hurt me?" he screamed. "You think I don't care? I lost my sister. I lost my sister and my entire family is ruined by what happened. This is a lot bigger than just what happened to you."

He let go of her, tossing her arms away. Her wrists hurt. Her back hurt from hitting the shelf.

She watched him storm off, past the silent store manager, out of the aisle, gone from sight.

Anita started shaking uncontrollably. Her basket of medicine was on the floor.

"Are you . . . OK?" asked the store manager, and she could see that he was probably twenty-five years old, tops. And terrified.

"Yes," she nodded. She started to cry. She stood there for a few minutes, wanted to make sure Roy was long gone, and then she left the store, the basket remaining on the floor.

She nearly hit a pedestrian on the drive home, her mind was racing off in so many different directions. Her heart was pounding out of her chest, her breathing so rapid that she was gagging.

At home, she stripped out of her clothes and climbed into bed, head throbbing. Like a little girl, she wanted to go under the sheets for protection.

She couldn't sleep, so she simply held herself, waiting for Dennis to get home so she could tell him about the encounter with Roy. What would Dennis do? Go beat him up? She probably deserved the response Roy gave her. What did Roy ever do wrong? Other than grow up with a piece of trash sister.

Anita waited and waited. Dennis didn't come home on time. And he didn't call. Something was not right. Then again, the world was no longer right.

It was after nine o'clock when Dennis entered the house and climbed the stairs. When he entered the bedroom, she knew immediately. It felt like a punch in the face.

For the first time in years, Dennis was stinking drunk.

Chapter Eight

"You do everything you can to protect your child," said Anita, staring into the blackness of her coffee. "You babyproof the house. You cover the electric sockets, you tie up the cords to the blinds. You take away toys that could make them choke. You put up fences at the top of the stairs. You spend all night listening to them through the baby monitor. You check on them when they make a noise, you check when they don't make a noise. You keep them out of the street. But you never think to protect them from the nanny. The nanny is suppose to protect *them*."

She sat with Maggie in a coffeehouse on College Avenue. After repeated tries, Maggie had successfully lured her out of the house. For many weeks, Anita resisted social interaction. Her answering machine recorded a lot of sympathy, but she just couldn't call anyone back. After a while, every message sounded the same, offerings of food or conversation "if you just want to talk."

She didn't just want to talk. She hoped no one would take offense. But they really didn't want to enter her world. It would drag down their day, and it wouldn't improve hers.

Maggie's legendary pushiness, however, finally broke through. "C'mon, I know you're there!" she would announce when the machine kicked in. "If you don't pick up, I'm going to come over. I'll bring meatloaf!"

The humor helped. Mainly because no one else dared with wisecracks.

And sitting here now with Maggie in downtown Rockridge wasn't nearly as frightful or painful as she expected. No one stared, although sunglasses and a baseball cap helped. The coffee was doing a nice job of propping her awake, countering the steady diet of sleeping pills that got her through the night. The caffeine didn't infuse her with energy by any means. But it did bring her to a pleasing, floating state of neutrality.

"You never could have anticipated this," said Maggie gently. "She didn't have a criminal record. No history of mental illness. There's no nanny agency in the world that would have caught it. The bitch just snapped."

"I know. But I still feel responsible in so many ways. I'm the one who hired her. I'm the one who brought a stranger into my house. She really didn't have many references. And I always thought she was a little odd. Shouldn't that have been a warning sign? She was so awkward around me and Dennis . . . and obsessed with Tim. You could see it in her eyes. If only—"

"If only if only!" retorted Maggie. "You can write a whole book of if onlys. The simple fact of the matter is *none of this was your fault.*"

She was practically shouting now, and Anita didn't want the attention, so she nodded and waved a hand at Maggie to lower her voice.

Anita spared Maggie her biggest *if only*: If only I hadn't chosen to return to work.

That was the one that haunted her the most. *If only I had chosen my child over my career.*

Instead, Anita murmured, "Peas."

Maggie raised her eyebrows. "Excuse me?"

"It's all because of peas."

Maggie nodded with a smirk that said yes, go on.

"No, really," said Anita, and this was actually something she had thought about a few hundred times. "When I ran into Barbara Roeber at the grocery store, I was looking for frozen peas. If I had picked up the peas earlier, or later, or not bought peas at all, it's very possible I wouldn't have run into her and asked about her nanny. The store was crowded, I had Tim, I was trying to hurry. If Barbara Roeber wasn't in that aisle the exact same minute that I was, none of this would have happened. I probably would have started with the nanny agency, found someone decent, and never had a reason to contact her. It was peas. It was Goddamned peas. And I don't even like peas that much. They were on sale."

Maggie gave her a no-holds-barred "you're crazy" look.

"Let me tell you something," Maggie said. "Whether we like it or not, life is a game of inches. A little movement one way or another, and the whole ball game changes. There's no way we can control it. You bump into Barbara at the grocery store and a whole chain of events unfolds. That's the way it is every second of your life, you just never think about it. You wouldn't even exist if it wasn't for the chance encounter between your parents, and then their parents and their parents . . . an inch here, an inch there, and the whole world is different. There's no script to follow. We're at the mercy of random chaos."

Anita almost laughed. "Since when did you get so philosophical?"

Maggie flicked away crumbs from the muffin she had finished an hour ago. "When I was seven years old, living in L.A., my parents took me to a dollhouse museum. We parked, it was across the road, and I was so excited, I pulled away from my father. I just broke free. And I ran straight into the path of a car. It was a big red Cadillac and it was going really fast. It would have *creamed* me, Anita. That car missed me by maybe two inches. I could feel it go past, the breeze, the exhaust, I could practically taste the chrome on the bumper. Two inches closer, two seconds earlier, and there would be no more Maggie Marks."

An uncharacteristic look of vulnerability crossed her face. "Growing up, I used to obsess on that. For years, if I thought about it at night, I couldn't sleep. Then you realize that you can't obsess. It'll paralyze you. Because every day brings more moments like that. Most of them aren't life and death. But everything is a game of inches. Even now, your decision to come out. Maybe it's the nudge that puts you on the path to recovery."

"God I hope so," said Anita. Maggie, bless her, *was* making her feel better. "I need something in front of me; all I can do is look back on what's happened. I don't see a future."

Maggie looked for Anita's eyes behind the dark lenses of her sunglasses.

"Come back to work," she said.

Anita looked away.

"It'll cleanse your mind," said Maggie.

"I don't know if I'm ready."

"What else are you going to do?"

Anita didn't have an answer. Every day was a big zero, indistinguishable from the next. She was lucky if she accomplished minimal housework. It took great effort just to wash the laundry, buy groceries, and feed the fish. Sometimes she didn't even shower. Inside the house, time passed, horrible thoughts rolled around in her head, the sun went up, the sun went down, that was about it. The house hurt, but it took enormous effort to get outside.

"You need to be with people," said Maggie. "You

can't be alone every day. Aren't you lonely?"

Anita nodded. She usually woke up after Dennis left for work. She went to bed, sleeping pills in her belly, before he came home. He was nothing to wait up for. Half the time he was late and drunk. They found no solace in each other.

She needed conversation in her life. But she didn't want to talk endlessly about Tim. It was too painful. She didn't want people pitying her. Maybe working would force her mind onto new things.

This coffee with Maggie had been a surprising lift to her spirits. Maybe returning to work would be another boost.

"OK," said Anita. "I'll give it a try."

Maggie's face lit up as if she wasn't expecting an affirmative response. "That's great! I'll start setting up your office tomorrow. When do you want to return? How do you like your bagels?"

Anita felt something like good feelings start to move throughout her body, prompting a small smile. Maybe it was the caffeine, or maybe she was really feeling life stirring inside again.

Anita reached out and put her hand on Maggie's hand. "Thank you for getting me out of the house. I needed this."

The following Monday, cleaned up and back in makeup and a business suit, she commuted into San Francisco. The blue suit hung loosely on her frame; she hadn't realized how much weight she had lost since the last time she wore it.

There was some comfort in entering the familiar surroundings of the job, as if she were stepping back into the world that existed pretragedy. Everyone greeted her with a hug and heartfelt encouragement. It did feel good.

There was not a whole lot to do during the first week. Everyone was in the midst of something, but no one asked her to assist yet. Maggie gave her a summary of the latest clients and activity. She also introduced Anita to Beth Lewis.

Beth was new, an attractive young kid out of UCLA. She was hired after Anita left. Anita quickly learned that Beth was already a star performer, charming the clients, putting in monster hours, and even finding time to do innovative things with software templates Anita had designed years ago. Beth was fresh-faced, peppy, perfect.

During week two, the realization hit Anita: They don't need me. They have Beth. Why am I here?

Is it charity?

There simply wasn't enough work for Anita to do. At times, she felt as though the others were holding back. Mita still juggled multiple accounts and worked evenings. Maggie continued to groan about being understaffed. Were they afraid to approach her? Were they isolating her from the clients?

Anita tried not to be a downer, forcing out smiles, engaging in pleasant chitchat that used to come effortlessly but now required great energy and focus. She didn't want to be doom and gloom. Sure, she felt like doom and gloom, but she didn't want it to surface on the outside and keep people away.

The work for Anita picked up during week three, bringing a new realization: She didn't give a shit.

The presentations, the strategies, the stuffy, academic clients, the hours of programming to add a little bit of multimedia razzle-dazzle to dry text . . . Was it always this dull? Or were they just giving her the unwanted scraps?

Or had her perspective changed? What used to be challenging, fulfilling, meaningful . . . was it now just a heap of trivial bullshit?

Anita found her mind wandering all the time. And not just to Tim. She could get fixated on a cloud outside her window. A car horn. The numbers on her clock. The murmur of conversation through office walls.

As her attitude toward work became indifferent, the days became gruesomely slow. At the same time, she fell behind, slogging through projects as if she was underwater. When she tried to push herself, the only outcome was a killer headache.

Then there was the always aggravating commute between San Francisco and Oakland. Every bad driver, every logjam, every red light set her off. She ground her teeth until her jaws ached. She had no patience.

And she found no satisfaction in reaching her destinations. Not work. And certainly not home.

She barely communicated with Dennis anymore. He was just a tall, slouched figure moving through the house. They avoided conversation and eye contact, as if each other was a constant, dark reminder of the trauma they jointly experienced. Dennis had never been a big talker, but now their exchanges were even more sparse, fragments left hanging in the air.

He brooded. He drank beers until the recycling bin overflowed. And he played his rock CDs at a volume that prohibited conversation. Early on, she bitched at him to turn it down, but he would pretend not to hear and she had no energy to fight. So The Who assaulted their drums and guitars, The Rolling Stones snarled and riffed, and Van Halen screeched and soared. Maybe he can bury his depression in noise, thought Anita, but it doesn't work for me.

Their sex life was all but over. They had tried a few times after Tim's death, but it felt alien, remote. The passion was diminished, the emotions flattened, the arousal missing.

She wished he would open up to her, so that she, in turn, could unleash her own built-up thoughts and words. But Dennis, true to his nature, kept everything bottled up inside. There was no outlet.

My husband can offer no strength or comfort, she realized.

If this was the ultimate test of their marriage, they were failing.

At work, the relationship with her coworkers

also felt damaged. People simply didn't talk to her the same way. Everything felt forced, phony, brief. While Anita still hurt, the sympathy and sensitivity her friends had shown at the time of Tim's murder dissipated like yesterday's news. And nothing took its place.

Then Maggie bought a dog. A small yappy terrier that she insisted on bringing to the office and calling "baby." Anita's nerves were far too jittery for this high-strung animal that scampered restlessly from office to office. Anita started closing her office door, an antisocial move to be sure. But she still became preoccupied with the sound of the dog's jingling tags, its panting, its toenails scratching the carpet.

Returning to work had provided a brief lift, but now it was over. She felt just as gloomy as before, except now she had to hide it. After six weeks, she could no longer hide it.

The others pretty much ignored her, but Maggie gave her strange looks as if to say "C'mon. Cheer up."

Finally, she said it directly.

She came into Anita's office and closed the door. Anita knew what was coming. And she was in no mood.

"You can't be down in the dumps like this for the rest of your life," said Maggie.

Often, with Maggie, the best approach was to just nod and let her go. But this time Anita couldn't.

"You—" Anita said in a tone that was more personal than she meant, but there was no turning back. "You think I have a choice in this. Like I forgot to turn on a light. You don't understand. You don't know what I'm going through. Even if you did almost get hit by a car thirty years ago, you don't understand. You don't understand."

"I am trying to help you," Maggie responded forcefully. "You are wallowing in this. You can't bring Tim back by wallowing."

Anita didn't even want Maggie to say Tim's name. Somehow, it angered her. "Leave him out of this."

"I want to!" Maggie was almost shouting now. "But you won't. You can't. Anita, look to the future, or you will never get out of the past. It doesn't have to be like this. You can always have another child, right?"

That did it. The insensitivity of the remark— implying that Tim could easily be replaced by another child—was the last straw. Anita resigned the following day.

Her return to Digital Learnings had lasted less than two months.

"I tried to reconnect," she told Dr. Andrew during one of their final sessions. She was only seeing him sporadically now. It was getting too expensive, with diminishing returns. "I really made an effort, but I'm just not ready yet. I don't know when I will be able to connect with anything anymore. I'm just floating around like a ghost that can't pick up anything or touch or feel."

Only her parents could offer any small semblance of comfort. But they were far away. They were aging, and she hated to drag them down into her darkness. Meanwhile, her friends were scattering.

Dennis, too, seemed to lose touch with his friends. He continued to disappear with his San Francisco Giants golf bag on Saturdays, like always, but admitted one night that he rarely played with others. Instead, he went to the driving range and smacked bucket after bucket of balls. She could imagine him taking out all his aggression on the little white golf ball, pounding it as hard and as far as he could. One after another after another, for hours.

Whenever he left the house, he usually came back drunk. She berated him one night. "Doesn't it even bother you that you're driving drunk, that you could kill someone, and send another family into the same kind of grief that we are feeling?"

Dennis just shrugged.

"Is that your response to everything?" she said.

"Yes," he stated. He headed for the family room.

"And now you're going to drown everything out with the stereo."

He turned to face her. "Do you have a problem with that?"

"Yes, I do."

"Then what would you rather I do?" he said, placing emphasis on every word.

"Talk to me."

"About what? What is there to talk about?"

"I don't care. Anything!"

"Today was a beautiful day," he said in a mock tone. "Temperature in the seventies, clear skies. Not a hint of rain. The Giants beat the Cardinals 6–4. Barry Bonds was two for five with a home run."

"Go play your fucking music," she spat back at him. He was nonsense, she lived in a crazy house. They were now twisted, ugly, distorted caricatures of the people they used to be.

Dennis cranked his music and drank his beer. Anita took two sleeping pills, put on her nightgown, and climbed into bed.

This isn't the way we really are, she told herself. We are not these people.

She reached deep for memories of the man she married. The good times seemed decades ago. Who was the real Dennis Sherwood?

They had met five years ago when he fell off his bike.

In college at Berkeley, she jogged a lot. She thrived on it. She was very conscientious and protective of her appearance. She wanted to look good. She wanted to look hot.

Boy, how things had changed since then.

The jogging burned away the starchy cafeteria food, kept the butt firm and the thighs taut. When she worked up a good sweat, she imagined that the sweat was actually pounds dripping off her body. It gave her energy, a buzz, and cleared her head when the homework and classes clogged her brain.

If she missed a day of jogging, it bummed her out, as if she were going to instantly grow blubber and lose focus.

In college, she was fairly striking: willowy, lively dark eyes, square-jawed, with black hair that shined. She always sat alert in her seat, her back straight, articulate and outspoken. The boys gravitated toward her. The brave ones, anyway. She later discovered that some classmates thought she was too serious or pretentious, not approachable. They didn't know that she had a sly wit and could get silly with the best of them. She could let slip with a case of the giggles, usually a sign that she had been won over, because she didn't offer it up undeserved.

She was running in place, off the curb, waiting for a light to change, when she met Dennis. He was whipping around a curve on his bicycle and didn't see her until it was too late. To avoid hitting her, he wiped out on the pavement.

She gasped.

He sat up and smiled, straightening his glasses. "I meant to do that," he said. He was handsome, athletic, and already scoring points for wit.

"Are you OK?" She came near, and he quickly rose, indestructible macho, but couldn't hold back a grimace. Then she noticed a torn hole in his jeans, a bloody knee.

"Maybe we should exchange insurance information," he said. Chalk up another point for humor.

They got out of the street and wound up talking through dozens of light changes, oblivious to the traffic around them. He was an economics major, a junior to her sophomore. She found him charming and confident. He looked a little familiar—and they realized she had once dated someone in his fraternity. A guy named Ernie who spent two dates complaining about his girlfriend back home before Anita cut him loose.

The day after the collision, Anita sent Dennis a care package: gauze, bandages, Bactine, and a note begging him not to sue.

It cracked him up. And accomplished exactly what she wanted: a date was set for that weekend. Inside a month, they were inseparable. She spent a lot of money on movie tickets for her roommate, to send her off when Dennis came by. The top bunk saw a lot of wild activity. Fortunately, no one ever rolled off.

After two years, they realized they must be pretty serious, and the marriage talk began. It seemed like a natural progression and they set a date, timed to follow his graduation. She didn't want him escaping into the real world without her. They were both in love, fresh with enthusiasm to jointly take on the future.

In college, Dennis was a heavy drinker. It never seemed to hurt his grades and, in fact, fit in nicely with his fun-loving, frat-boy persona. Outside of college, however, it quickly lost its youthful charm. In the second year of marriage, the drinking got in the way. It jeopardized his job. It tainted his mood and ignited rage. It earned him a DUI. And, worst of all, it led to an ugly incident where he struck Anita during an argument.

Although she later regretted doing it, Anita picked up the phone and called the police to report domestic battery. Assault was something she would never take lightly.

"If you ever hit me again, I will divorce you," she had told him. The police came, and there were cooled tempers and tears. Dennis actually cried. He begged her forgiveness. She forgave him.

The following day, Dennis cleared out the liquor cabinet and announced he was going cold turkey. And he did.

Dennis attended a few AA meetings but mostly conquered the booze by himself. The marriage strengthened, and when Tim arrived, Dennis became a wonderfully responsible, doting father. She was impressed and proud. Tim brought out the best in him.

After Dennis defeated the bottle, Anita remembered thinking, "That's it. We hit rock bottom and survived." Little did she know, it was nowhere near the rock bottom she would later experience.

The death of Tim brought back the old demons. In the chaos, a doorway slipped open to allow them in. Now she couldn't chase them away. Arguing with Dennis about drinking was more difficult than ever because she knew firsthand the horrors that fueled it. In a way, it was hard to blame him, especially when she was leaning on pills to sleep through the night and provide a fog for the days.

She was lost in her own stupor now. She couldn't connect to Dennis, her job, her neighbors. Unable to draw comfort from familiar people, Anita turned to strangers. She went online.

At various times, she had been encouraged to join support groups, including one specifically for parents of killed children, but just couldn't do it. And Dennis refused to join her.

But on the Internet, faceless and anonymous, from inside her home, she found it easier to communicate with others who had suffered a similar tragedy. There were chat rooms, Web sites, newsgroups, and she became hooked on them, surfing and exchanging dialogue until the late hours.

It was well after midnight when she came across one particular piece of information that sent shockwaves through her body. It was just too believable.

Eighty percent of couples who suffered a murdered child subsequently divorced.

Anita wondered, are we going to be part of the eighty . . . or part of the twenty?

One afternoon, Dennis came home early, unexpectedly. He had trouble walking; he had to lean into everything. He was very drunk, even for him.

She came downstairs, and he told her the news in a single sentence.

The real estate company had fired him.

Anita lost it. She exploded. She tore into him. "You have done nothing but make this whole experience worse. You have used it as an excuse to get drunk and screw up, and now you've ruined your career, the only thing that was still standing."

"I don't see you working," he shot back.

"I'm not stinking drunk, either."

"Just shut up." His sloppy inebriation quickly turned to hard rage. "You're in no position to talk."

"I've kept quiet long enough. And now you're going to listen to me, and you're going to *talk* to me."

"I have nothing to say to you." He headed for the kitchen, and she knew he was going for the liquor cabinet.

"So drink and puke and pass out!" she screamed.

He grabbed the gin bottle. No beer this time. Hard stuff. He poured it into a glass.

"Why don't you just suck it out of the bottle?"

He looked at her, dopey-eyed and pathetic. "You think I like this life?"

"You think I do?"

"Why don't you leave me alone, and we can both be happy."

Anita felt a swirl of rage and sadness. She didn't know whether to scream or burst into tears. As Dennis finished the glass, she said, "You are destroying us."

Dennis allowed the gin to seep into his system. He put the empty glass on the counter. She could see his chest moving. He was breathing hard. He replied.

"No. *You* destroyed us, Anita. If you had stayed home and been a mother, none of this ever would have happened. I could sense all along that there was something weird about her, and I said things, on many occasions, which you ignored. You turned a blind eye to it because all you cared about was preserving your career. Tim was the *last* thing on your mind."

Anita felt a surge of rage. "How dare you say that," she spat in her harshest tone, words dripping with hatred. "You know that isn't true. You are a weak, desperate piece of *shit*."

Dennis hit her.

He smacked her across the face with his hand, a sudden jolt, and she felt the sting, stumbled backward, almost fell, but grabbed the refrigerator door handle for balance.

"Get out!" she screamed.

He stared at her.

"I mean it! *Get out! Get out!*"

Dennis turned and left the kitchen.

He left the house.

He drove away.

Anita locked the doors. She was hyperventilating. She wanted to run from room to room, smashing things. She paced wildly.

When Dennis called fifteen minutes later, he was crying, apologizing.

She didn't care.

"I want a divorce," she said simply.

He murmured drunken words that were so entangled that she couldn't understand him. She hoped, at the very least, that he could understand her.

"I . . . want . . . a . . . divorce," she repeated, crisp and clean, and then disconnected. She slammed the receiver back into its cradle.

Eighty percent.

She felt overcome by dizziness.

All your fault.

She wanted to throw up, but there was nothing to throw up, no food in her stomach, nothing since breakfast. Was there breakfast?

Tim's bear.

She climbed the stairs. They seemed to move, swim, like an escalator from hell.

I am more of a mother.

She staggered into the bedroom, barely able to move in the right direction, slamming into the doorframe.

You can always have another child.

She tore through the clothes in her closet, going deep into items long buried and forgotten.

Pam's great!

She found her old blue sweat suit from college. Not really fashionable anymore, wrinkled and faded, but still there, faithfully.

Damn it, Tim, you spilled your juice!

She peeled out of her jeans and turtleneck and pulled on the sweat suit. She dug out her gym shoes and stuffed them on her feet.

They're getting the Coast Guard!

Anita burst out of the house. She jogged across the lawn, reached the sidewalk, then followed it in one direction: away.

She jogged past her neighbors, left them behind, advanced to a new block, and then another. Perhaps she could outrun the crashing storm that lived above her head. The world moved past her.

Her head hurt. Her limbs hurt. She could feel the shin splints sending shock waves up her legs with every step. But she couldn't stop. Physical pain was trivial. She let her rage combust throughout her body and fuel her momentum.

She seethed with anger for Dennis. For Maggie. For Roy. For the reporters who hounded her. For the police who gave up hope. Everybody was her enemy now.

But as she continued to run, leaving behind a lot of junk from an overflowing mind, her anger at the world receded.

Some focus returned. Anita knew that more than anything, she needed someone to lash out at, but the only person who truly deserved it was dead.

She could not touch Pam.

Finally, after a long run, Anita stopped jogging. She collapsed to the grass. Her destination stood before her, all red brick and indifference.

Pam's apartment building. Anita could see Pam's windows. They were dark and empty.

Anita remained sitting on the grass, catching her breath, lungs aching, staring at the building as if it could somehow cough up an explanation for the evil that once lived inside.

In several windows, elderly faces began to peer out at her. Who was this stranger on the grass, casing the joint? The faces looked worried. Gray-haired grannies with big glasses. Frowning old men with droopy jowls.

Anita felt very old herself, just like one of these withered seniors, retreating from the world in their tiny apartments, idly killing time before the grim reaper pressed the buzzer. Every day, slipping a little further into irrelevance, watching the days grow dimmer, less focused.

Two weeks earlier, Anita had stared into a palmful of sleeping pills and weighed the pros and cons of ending her life. Ultimately, she couldn't commit the act. While she no longer had enthusiasm for life, she couldn't muster the energy to die. And what would it achieve, really, aside from giving her own parents the same kind of sorrow she now suffered. Pointless.

I don't need to die, Anita told herself, watching one of the old ladies get on the phone, probably calling the police, or the funny farm, to come drag her away.

I don't need to die because I'm already dead.

Part Two

Chapter Nine

Anita sat in a ten-by-ten-foot booth in the buzzing, cavernous convention hall, relaxing and enjoying the people watching. There were thousands of name-tagged business professionals moving about, squeezing past one another, filling bags with freebies and checking out the loud displays that competed for attention.

When a visitor would wander close to the Your Resources booth, Anita would invite him or her to a five-minute demonstration of the latest and greatest in Human Resources administration software. She was always sweet and inviting, not pushy, and more often than not they accepted.

This was Anita's seventh trade show this year, and it was only June. Sometimes it would take a moment to recall where she was; the convention halls, bland and windowless, all looked the same.

Today and tomorrow was the Business Solutions Expo in Chicago. Late next week, it would be the HR Technology Forum in Seattle.

She had joked with her coworkers back in Sacramento that she should have tour T-shirts made with the Your Resources company logo on the front and her travel dates on the back, like a rock band.

ANITA SHERWOOD

NORTH AMERICAN TRADE SHOW TOUR

DENVER

L.A.

MIAMI

NEW YORK

NEW JERSEY

ATLANTA

CHICAGO

SEATTLE

The new job required a lot of travel, and she welcomed it. She didn't want to sit still. Movement was good. It was healthy to see the world outside the walls of her home and cubicle. In her marketing role, she interacted with a constant barrage of fresh faces, coming and going, no one connecting for too long. Once an account was landed, it became someone else's long-term project.

More than two years had passed since Tim's death, followed by her permanent departure from

Digital Learnings and her divorce from Dennis. She didn't miss either one.

The divorce was handled quickly, mostly between attorneys. Dennis came back a few times for some of his things—his Giants golf bag, some clothes, the stereo and CDs. Not much. The rest, including the aquarium, he told her to sell. He took the Jeep, she kept the Jetta. He had little to say. His emotions had been hollowed out. He was no longer there.

The tragedy had ruined Dennis beyond repair. She wouldn't let it ruin her, too. She sold the house in Rockridge and moved to a condominium in Sacramento. The new environment cleansed her mind. There were no memories here. Only new memories to be built from a new life.

She joined Your Resources, a company that specialized in software products for HR professionals. She started as a product designer but quickly sought out a new role. She simply could not tolerate long hours in a confined space at a PC anymore. When the marketing position opened up, she jumped for it. Her bosses were happy to oblige. Her strong grasp of software technology made her a smart and savvy sales rep.

Anita liked her new boss, Clifford, and her coworkers. They knew about her background, but didn't treat her differently, because there was no previous relationship for comparison. In her first week, Anita brought up the topic of Tim first, before they asked, and then let it drop. No one else retrieved it.

Not directly, anyway. In a strange manner, she became a magnet for others to share their own tragedies over lunch. A mother with cancer. A cousin in a fatal car crash. Anita listened and nodded with concern. Maybe she made them feel better because her tragedy dwarfed their own. As long as they didn't probe about Tim, it was fine.

Anita made new friends at Your Resources. She was starting over from scratch. Most of the Bay Area friendships had dissolved, unable to withstand the test of trauma. Granted, she wasn't the most enjoyable person to be around in the months after Tim's murder, but true friends should have stuck with her. A few did, like Maggie. Many did not, like Gilda, quietly slipping out of contact with her.

For a while, Anita felt tainted. She was certain that people perceived her as a downer, a frightening reminder of the fragility and cruelties of life. Who wants somebody like that around? Ignorance is bliss.

The absence of Dennis created a second hole in her life. Sometimes she missed Dennis terribly and regretted the divorce. Other times, she couldn't imagine staying with him. Either way, it still hurt.

In recent months, Anita had started dating. No one special emerged, but there were occasional glimmers of hope that romance could blossom again. And if that was the case, could intimacy be far behind?

She told her dates up front about her background. The men all offered sympathy and didn't openly appear bothered, but she could see the interest draining from their faces. A murdered child presented too much baggage for them.

Fine, she told herself. I don't want a man who can't handle it anyway.

They had to cope with a woman with severe psyche trauma and all of its side effects, which included a total lack of desire to rush into the sack.

Most recently, there was Will, a friend of a co-worker. Will had a nice build, but a goofy face that could not be masked by nice clothes and free weights. At the conclusion of their third date, parked outside her condominium, he was anxious to be invited up, and the invitation was not forthcoming.

He kissed her a little, and she gently drew back and reached for the door handle.

"The closer I move, the more tense you become," he said.

"I'm not tense," she lied.

"Do I make you uncomfortable?"

"No, but this conversation does."

Date four ended with Will calling her frigid.

"Am I supposed to be insulted?" she asked him, as they sat again in the front seat of his car outside the condominium. She didn't know if the frigid crack was teasing or if he was genuinely irritated. He was always grinning like an idiot.

"Hey, it's OK," insisted Will. "It turns me on. I like a woman who plays hard to get."

"You do?" she replied. "Then this ought to really get you off: I don't want to see you again."

She opened the car door, exited, and slammed it shut on him.

Dating sucks, she concluded. It was certainly not as fun or exhilarating as it was in high school or college. Now it was predictable, tedious, and consistently disappointing. But she was in no rush.

As she watched the trade show activity, a handsome young man with wavy blond hair and an expensive suit walked up to her table, smiling. "Hope I win," he said, flashing his business card.

There was a large jar on the table, collecting business cards for a raffle. Three winners would receive free software packages. All contestants became leads for the direct marketing folks back in Sacramento.

The handsome man didn't drop his card into the jar. Instead, he handed it to Anita, probably to show off the fact that he was the CEO of some no-name dot.com out of Indianapolis.

"If you get mine, do I get yours?" he asked, and the tone was not business.

"You get our brochure," she smiled sweetly in return.

He pressed on a little bit more, steering the conversation away from the software, asking questions about her, trying to reel her in.

Five years ago, maybe, I would play this game, she told herself. But not today.

He finally gave up. He wasn't the first one. There had been a few other men who flirted with her today, lured by the absence of a wedding ring. One had written his room number on the back of his business card. She wondered how many one-night stands occurred at these things. Many of them were probably married, inhibitions conveniently left at home.

When they toyed with her, she was flattered, happy and not interested. I guess I still look good, she thought to herself, and that was satisfaction enough.

She knew she had aged more than two years in two years. She had lines in her face. She had a few gray hairs, not many, but set against her jet black hair they definitely stood out. She had traded her longer hairstyle for a shorter, sophisticated look, and most of her outfits were conservative, not youthful but not bland. For summertime, she was pale, while everybody else seemed to sport tans, authentic or not. But she was still in good shape for a woman in her mid-thirties. Still able to turn heads at a business technology trade show, anyway.

For the first time since her jogging days in college, she regularly worked out. Instead of running, she exercised at the gym. When she traveled, she sought out the hotel's workout facility or pool. The benefits were twofold: It not only brought new energy to her body but also helped her emotional state. Shortly after she started working out, she found herself laughing in a conversation with a coworker. It was the first time she had laughed after Tim's death, and it immediately sounded strange and foreign in her ears. For a while, she felt guilty about laughing. But she accepted that it was all part of the recovery. Soon she might even feel genuine happiness again.

The simple truth was that she *was* feeling better and stronger every day. She had a new life. It wasn't disrespectful to Tim to enjoy life again, Dr. Andrew had told her during one of their last sessions together. Instead, it was honoring Tim's spirit to embrace life and not withdraw.

She could believe that, if she tried.

Day one of the trade show passed by pleasantly if uneventfully. Anita previewed the software dozens of times, distributed about half of her brochures and most of the free mouse pads. She had collected maybe a hundred business cards. The crowd swelled at the end of the afternoon when the final workshops and seminars let out, and then drained when cocktail time arrived.

The vendors hall shut down for the day at five o'clock.

"Not a bad turnout," said the rotund woman with chipmunk teeth at a neighboring booth. She sold WebSpy, a service that tracked (and busted) inappropriate employee use of the Internet. Anita had seen her before at other trade shows. "Better than Houston, not as good as Hartford," said the woman.

On the other side of Anita, a wiry, raspy man with a chiseled face shut off his kiosk with a loud sigh of relief. It had been playing a looped video clip all day, praising the virtues of benefits-enrollment software with relentless, chirpy theme music. "I don't want to ever hear that God-damned song again," he groused. "Christ, I need a smoke."

A pretty, twentysomething Asian woman in a black dress and black stockings walked over from her booth across the aisle to join the conversation.

"I've got a guy from a food company who wants me to come out and pitch to his vice president. In *Pittsburgh!* Gag."

"Are you guys going to the cocktail reception?" asked the WebSpy woman.

"Hell, yes!" scowled the wiry man.

"A group of us are going to Navy Pier for dinner," offered the Asian woman. "Anybody interested?"

"Sure," said WebSpy woman.

The wiry man grumbled something about getting drunk and watching a pay-per-view movie in his room.

Anita politely declined Navy Pier. "I appreciate the offer, but I'm going to do some shopping. I need to spoil myself."

"Right on," grinned WebSpy woman, adding, "My husband put an end to my out-of-town shopping after New York. I maxed out the credit cards."

As more booths shut down, the gathering of idle vendors grew. Anita finally packed up the laptop, took the jar of business cards, excused herself, and returned to her room.

In the elevator, she reflected on the day's interactions. Most of the people she encountered had no idea who she was. Usually, even if they didn't say anything, she could tell if they recognized her face or name from the news. The expressions softened, the conversation became tinged with awkwardness and delicacy.

It took a long time for her fifteen minutes of fame to end. The media wouldn't let go for months. But finally, other headlines and horrors filled its place. Thank God for other horrors.

As Anita walked down the corridor to her room, she passed a mother sweetly interacting with her toddler. A nonevent for anyone else, a momentary ache for Anita. There was a growing list of things she could now absorb without pain, but not moments like this. Not now. Maybe not ever.

In her hotel room, Anita ditched the name tag, put on comfortable shoes, and tossed aside the suit jacket to go sleeveless. She left a voice-mail message with Clifford that said all went well and promised him good leads.

The hotel was perched on the south bank of the Chicago River and a short walk from the Magnificent Mile, a stretch of North Michigan Avenue that boasted world-class, upscale shopping.

Hundreds of retail stores and boutiques lined the corridor and adjacent street. Anita looked forward to submerging herself in the latest fashions and accessories, even if her purchases would be slim to none. She was making good money, but not Michigan Avenue money.

She worked her way north on the east side of the street. It was a perfect summer day, bright sun extending through the late afternoon and into the early evening. The streets hummed with rush-hour traffic and the sidewalks were alive with people: the fast pace of workers heading home mixed with the slow amble of tourists gaping at skyscrapers.

Dipping in and out of stores, she advanced to the Water Tower Place Mall, a high-rise of shops directly across from the fabled historic Water Tower that survived the Great Chicago Fire in the 1800s.

Inside the mall, Anita wound her way up and down the levels, finding a lot of expensive nonessentials, the things you would buy if you had an unlimited supply of money, but otherwise simply provided great browsing and window-shopping. Too many of the stores were starting to look familiar—chains that weaved a web through every big city she visited.

After Water Tower Place, Anita decided to cross Michigan Avenue to hit the stores on the west side of the street and then head south back to the hotel. Along the way, she hoped to find a small, unromantic restaurant for dinner for one.

As Anita stood on the corner among a growing throng of stopped pedestrians, waiting for the light to change, a city bus pulled into view. The doors hissed open, a line of people climbed out, and then a line of people climbed aboard. The doors slapped shut, and the bus loudly lurched forward.

Anita saw the succession of faces in the bus windows roll past her. For a moment, her eyes locked with the sad eyes of a young passenger staring out. A frozen image, like a snapshot, then he was gone.

A little boy, maybe four years old.

A little boy with an uncanny resemblance to Tim.

Chapter Ten

For a moment, the city of Chicago disappeared. All sights, all sounds left her senses, leaving only the lasting image of the little boy with Tim's face staring out the bus window.

It grabbed her breath away.

Gradually, traffic noise returned, pedestrians swirled around her, the high-rises and blue sky reappeared. She saw the rear of the bus as it hurtled north on Michigan Avenue. The boy was inside.

Could it be Tim?

All logic said no. But the boy's sad eyes burned into her mind. She *knew* those eyes.

Not just the eyes—but the squat little nose, the thin lips, the chin, the straight-as-can-be mop of blond hair . . .

Anita knew she had to act fast if she was going

to get another look. The bus moved deeper into the congested rush-hour traffic. What should I do? she asked herself, followed by the answer.

Go.

Anita started running. She headed north after the bus, advancing to the next block. People were in her way everywhere, and she had to find openings, snake her way through them. "Excuse me, excuse me, *excuse me!*" she shouted. Some of them pulled away, widening a path for her. Others didn't. She knocked into elbows, shopping bags. More people began to take notice, turning and stopping and staring. They became an irrelevant blur.

Up ahead, she saw the bus brake for a red light. Anita weaved her way toward it, eyes glued on the traffic signal.

Don't change, don't change.

As she reached the rear of the bus, the light changed.

In a roar, the bus heaved forward, and Anita felt a blast of hot exhaust. She stepped into the street. She continued her chase, running alongside the curb.

"Lady, *move!*" hollered a bike messenger, draped in padding and reflectors. He zipped around her.

A car horn blasted so close that she nearly jumped out of her skin.

The bus was more than a block away now, and her chances of catching up were remote. She was panting, choking on the traffic fumes.

She saw a taxi slide past her. Immediately she waved and started to chase . . . but then caught a glimpse of a head in the backseat.

Anita whirled. She saw another cab approaching, three cars back. She began running south, against the traffic, toward it.

She caught the cab and grabbed the backdoor handle, but stopped short of scrambling inside when she realized there was a hunched old man with a cane in the back.

"Damn!" she cursed. She immediately reexamined the Michigan Avenue traffic.

Why are all the cabs going in the other direction?

But then a yellow taxi turned onto Michigan Avenue heading her way. And it appeared empty. About ten yards away she saw a businessman in a silver suit swiftly approach it.

Anita screamed and waved for the taxi with such hysteria that the businessman, frightened, stopped in his tracks.

"I'm sorry, it's an emergency," she said as she snatched it away from him. She yanked open the door and threw herself into the backseat.

"Follow that bus!"

"Bus?"

Anita tried to catch her breath, coughing between words. "Up ahead . . . two blocks ahead . . . you gotta follow that bus, wherever it goes. Please!"

She looked at the driver: Middle Eastern, perfectly relaxed, sunk in his seat, in no mood to raise his blood pressure. The drone of National Public Radio played at a near-subliminal volume. His name, Raoul, and ID were plastered on the back of his seat.

He didn't seem to understand the urgency, so she went into hyperdrive.

"Raoul—please, please, please—*my little boy is in that bus!*"

Without changing his placid demeanor, Raoul pressed hard on the accelerator and the cab shot forward, forcing a walkway of pedestrians to scatter.

"Thank you!" said Anita. The taxi sharply zig-zagged around a pokey Suburu, causing a chain-reaction screech of tires, followed by a symphony of horns.

He was her hero now. They were gaining ground.

The taxi was six or seven cars behind the bus. Anita's eyes remained fixed on it. She could read the route number off the back: 145. Memorize that, she told herself. 145. 145. 145 . . .

The bus barreled through an intersection as the traffic light turned yellow.

"Keep going!" shouted Anita.

Raoul swerved violently to gain a car length, tossing Anita against a side of the cab.

The light turned red.

Ignoring the light, the cab sped toward the in-tersection—then abruptly stopped, tossing Anita into the back of the front seat.

Red light or not, there was no place to go. Traffic was already streaming across the intersection and a throng of unleashed pedestrians filled the crosswalk.

"*Shit!*" said Anita

Raoul said nothing.

"If you catch up with the bus," said Anita, "there's a lot of money in it for you." She could see his eyes in the rearview mirror. He wasn't reacting.

Am I crazy? she asked herself, watching the faces of normal people with normal lives pass by in front of her, all shapes and sizes and races. *Have I lost my mind?*

It had been a long time since her last episode, where she thought she saw Tim in a crowd. There had been several wild goose chases during those first few months after Tim vanished. But those sightings usually ended with quick confirmation that it was not Tim. And they were children caught out of the corner of her eye, an incomplete glimpse. Not a dead-on look at a face like this. Nothing ever this vivid, this real—

Green.

A few people remained in the crosswalk, but an extended horn solo chased them away. The cab accelerated forward. "Keep playing that horn," Anita told Raoul. "I'll tip you five dollars every time you hit the horn."

The next obstacle was a stopped FedEx truck, lights blinking. The cab raced forward as if it was going to slam into the rear of the truck and then darted around it at the last possible second.

Watching through the windshield, Anita felt as though she was inside some kind of kinetic video game.

Way up ahead, the bus was veering right, heading toward an underpass. "Where's it going?" asked Anita.

"Lake Shore Drive," responded Raoul.

The taxi followed into the underpass and when it emerged, Anita got a comprehensive view of Chicago at rush hour.

Lake Shore Drive was a mess of merging traffic, a schizophrenic flow of vehicles moving at different speeds. The lanes were bordered by the party atmosphere of Oak Street Beach on the right and a handsome lineup of upscale residential highrises on the left. Directly in front of the cab, a sea of nervous brake lights popped on and off. The bus wasn't going very fast, but it wasn't getting any closer, either.

Raoul was stuck behind a woman with Tennessee plates. She was leaned into her windshield, very focused and very slow. Anita wanted to scream "Go around her!" but traffic was so tight, it really wasn't possible.

Or was it?

Raoul jerked the cab right and forced an opening between two cars. Angry horns followed and Raoul clearly didn't give a damn.

The cab moved from one bumper-to-bumper lane to another, to another, ultimately achieving very little.

Anita saw the bus ahead, accelerating.

"We can't lose sight of the bus," said Anita.

The traffic started to pick up a little. Raoul darted into the next lane and rushed to the bumper of a Mercedes convertible. Anita studied the traffic pattern like a constantly shifting puzzle to be solved. "Go to the left, go around the minivan, then you can get into the center lane, I think it's the fastest."

Raoul didn't pay her any attention and followed his own game plan. When he changed lanes, he didn't use his signal, so she helped by waving frantically at cars to let them in. Some did; some gave her the finger.

The traffic continued to increase speed. Anita saw that the cab was hovering near twenty miles per hour, which was progress.

The bus moved one lane to the right, shoving its way into traffic and succeeding. No one wanted to crash test their vehicle against the behemoth.

"The bus—" started Anita.

"I see it," answered Raoul.

Raoul swerved right into an open lane. His timing coincided with a Ford Explorer entering the lane from the other side. The two vehicles came within inches of colliding. Horns blasted, neither vehicle would surrender the lane, and for a moment Anita was certain there would be an accident, and the bus would be lost forever. . . .

But then the Explorer retreated, giving the lane to Raoul.

Raoul accelerated forward and the Explorer disappeared behind them.

The bus moved into the farthest lane on the right.

"He's—" said Anita.

"I know," said Raoul.

A sign ahead announced the exit: Belmont Avenue.

The traffic slowed down again. A growing number of brake lights spread across the lanes.

"Go right, go right," said Anita.

Raoul and Anita studied the lane for the precise moment to make a move.

"Now!" screamed Anita.

The cab shot right and tires screeched all over the place. They were in the same lane as the bus now, heading toward the off-ramp to Belmont Avenue.

The traffic slowed, slowed, stopped. Apparently, half of Lake Shore Drive wanted to exit here.

Anita could deal with the cab not moving, as long as the bus wasn't moving either. Waves of summer heat rolled in through the windows. Anita could hear car radios blending in the air, hip-hop layered with rock layered with . . . was that the Little River Band?

After five minutes of excruciating crawling and braking, Anita saw the traffic light that controlled the spill of vehicles onto Belmont. She watched intensely as it turned yellow-red-green, yellow-red-green, admitting about ten cars at a time.

The bus advanced to the front of the line. There was no doubt that it would make the next light.

But would the cab?

For a moment, stopped and going nowhere, Anita considered jumping out of the cab, running up the ramp of traffic, and catching the bus, hammering her fists on its doors.

The light turned green. The bus made an arching turn left onto Belmont, and she got a good look at its absurd long length, like two normal buses merged into one.

The cab advanced with the traffic flow toward Belmont.

Stay green, stay green, stay green, she prayed.

The cab got close, very close, and when the light turned yellow, it really didn't matter because they were so close . . .

But then the red BMW in front of them dutifully stopped. At a fucking yellow light!

Red now.

Anita screamed in aggravation.

The bus disappeared under Lake Shore Drive, heading west. Going, going, gone.

And, of course, the light took *forever* to change.

When the taxi finally headed west on Belmont, the bus was nowhere to be seen.

"No, no, no," moaned Anita.

Traffic slowed again. Pedestrians stepped between cars.

"We lost it," said Anita, sinking back in her seat.

Raoul looked nonplussed. "I know the bus route."

She perked up. "You do?"

When they reached Lake Shore Drive West—a road that ran parallel with its namesake—Raoul turned right. They were now in an area of residential high-rises.

The cab moved steadily, and then Anita caught a glimpse of bus number 145. "I see it up ahead!" she cried.

The rear bus lights flickered, then the vehicle stopped. As they got closer, Anita could see the bus doors split open. Passengers climbed off, while a few waited to climb on.

Nobody resembled Tim—he must still be on board.

The cab braked, four cars separating it from the bus. Anita opened her door. "I'm getting out here," she said. "Thank you, Raoul. You are the best. I gotta go." She left four twenties on the seat.

Anita ran up the street alongside the curb. She saw the last passenger get onto the bus. She heard the hiss of the bus doors shutting, the growing hum of the engine.

"STOP!" she screamed.

Anita threw herself against the bus doors with such force that it created a loud, violent thud.

She saw the startled face of the driver, a round Grandpa-type with a salt-and-pepper mustache. He hesitated, then switched gears and paused the bus from pulling away. He was not happy, but he did open the doors. "Don't ever do that again," he muttered.

"Thanks . . . Thank you," said Anita, digging money out of her purse. She didn't know how much to feed the box, so she gave it all her coins and two crumpled singles. There was no time to waste.

"Tim?"

Anita advanced down the long aisle, heart pounding. A sea of faces stared back at her. No one said a word. She examined them carefully.

Where was the boy who looked like Tim?

There were a few children, but no one resembling the person she saw in the window. When she reached the back of the bus, she turned around and headed back to the front for one more look.

This time, she received cold stares. She knew she looked crazy, sweaty hair in her face, still breathing hard.

"Ma'am, find a seat and sit down!" said the bus driver.

Anita ignored him. When she was certain she had scrutinized every row, she found an empty seat and sat down.

She wanted to cry.

I have lost my sanity, she realized. *I am hallucinating. I'm not recovering. I will never recover.*

Maybe it was her own wishful thinking playing tricks on her mind. A relapse into the desperate state she was in shortly after Tim was taken away. Maybe there was no face in that window at all.

Next to her, a middle-aged woman with a 1960s hairstyle and fake lashes adjusted in her seat to leave more distance between them. The woman focused somewhere out the window.

A yuppie across the aisle peered at Anita from behind *The Wall Street Journal* and then quickly buried his eyes back in the paper.

In the seat in front of Anita, a young black girl in braids had turned to face her. Her large dark eyes watched in rapt attention, as if something was going to happen.

The little girl's mother tapped the child's shoulder. "Amanda, honey, don't stare. It's not polite."

The girl turned around.

Don't stare at the crazy lady.

Anita leaned her head back and shut her eyes.

Back at the hotel, she continued to obsess over the feeling that Tim had been on the bus. She couldn't focus on anything else. The sterile, bland hotel room offered no distractions and only intensified her thoughts.

She showered. She ordered a room service hamburger and two beers. She flipped through the channels on her TV a few dozen times, watching nothing. Finally, she snapped it off.

This is madness, she told herself. But identifying it as madness didn't make it go away.

The numbers continued to stick in her mind: 145.

Where had the bus been? Where was it going?

Anita looked at her laptop, sitting on a desk

next to the TV. *Well, let's take a look.*

She plugged in and went online. She ran a search, found the Web site for the Chicago Transit Authority, and navigated her way to the bus schedules.

She found 145 and scanned its route. There was a map, and then she found an abbreviated list of stops.

"Holy shit," she said out loud.

According to the Web site, the bus stopped at the corner of Belmont and West Lake Shore Drive, the "inner drive." She had caught up with the bus at Melrose and the inner drive.

That meant that the bus made a stop during the time that Anita lost sight of it.

What if the boy got off at the stop?

Of course, that had to be it! She wasn't imagining the boy. He did exist. But he was gone by the time she climbed on the bus.

Anita felt renewed energy.

Followed by the crushing realization: *How am I going to find him now?*

She had two beers in her, she was feeling confident, and it suddenly all made sense: This was a job for the police. It was a child abduction, and the police would help find Tim.

She tracked down the general number for the Chicago Police Department and quickly made the call.

"Chicago Police Department," a male voice answered in a plain, undramatic tone, as if he was saying "Chicago Pizza Kitchen."

"Listen, I know this is going to sound crazy," she told the voice on the other end. "My son . . . My son Timothy Sherwood . . . was kidnapped two years ago in California . . . you may have heard about it, it was all over the news . . . his nanny took him . . . and she killed herself . . . and they thought she killed him . . . but today . . . in a bus on Michigan Avenue, number 145 . . . I saw him in the window."

Despite the numerous opportunities offered in her pauses, the voice on the other end wasn't reacting. This spurred her to continue, which was not a good thing because her story came out in an increasingly fragmented babble. She sounded ridiculous even to her own ears.

"I need help . . ." said Anita. "I think I know the stop where he got off . . . it's Belmont and West Lake Shore Drive . . . because I got on the bus after . . . and he wasn't there . . . you see, I was in a taxi . . . Raoul . . . the driver . . . he . . . we caught up with it."

Finally, she stopped. She wished she had thought out her words and described the situation better. Or was it just inherently ridiculous?

"What's your name and number," the voice said. "I'm going to have somebody from our detective unit call you back."

Anita thanked him profusely, provided the number, then hung up and waited for the return call. Maybe a few minutes?

It was two hours.

That was when a nasal, indifferent voice called

to tell her that he had spoken with someone at the Oakland Police Department and, with all due respect, ma'am, there was no longer a missing persons report and the case was closed. The boy had been declared dead.

She argued that the body was never recovered. She insisted that she had found him now. But when they pressed for a location, she could only offer a bus stop. When they asked for evidence, she could only state, "Because I know what my son looks like."

She tried to press on, but could tell the officer had reached a point where he was no longer listening. She could hear a lot of voices and activity in the background. She knew the Chicago Police were undoubtedly busy with other matters, rapes and robberies and murders every day, all over the city.

She hung up.

She sat on the bed. She didn't know anyone in Chicago who could help. Who could she call? Who would take her seriously?

She considered calling her parents, or Dennis, or Calcina, or one of her new friends back in Sacramento, and finally came to the conclusion that she needed more proof before she could start alarming other people.

There had been false alarms before. And what did she have to go on now, really? Three seconds of a face in a darkened bus window. A face that would have changed a great deal in the two years since she last saw it.

True, the whole thing sounded crazy and desperate.

But there was no body.

There was no body.

She was not about to give up the search. If she ignored this and went home, it would wind up haunting her forever.

It's probably not Tim.

But . . . what if it is?

Anita went downstairs to the concierge and obtained maps of Chicago. She brought them to her room and found the location of the bus stop where the boy may have gotten off.

She took a pen and circled a wide area around it.

This is where I'll begin my search, she told herself. I'll get up early and comb the neighborhood. I'll watch the bus stop. I'll search the parks, playgrounds, any place that a four-year-old child might go on a nice summer day.

Lying in bed, she felt everything spinning out of control again. The old wounds, fear, and confusion were back.

She tried to wrap herself up in the cocoon of the small room and sleep. The air conditioner hummed, drowning out all other noise, and the thick curtains were drawn, killing the outside light.

But she couldn't let go and drift off. She remained haunted by the sad little boy's face that stared out at her, pleading, before the bus took him away.

Chapter Eleven

Seven-thirty A.M. in Chicago meant 5:30 A.M. in Sacramento. Good. Her boss, Clifford, would not be in the office yet, so she could deliver scripted lies into his voice mail and avoid conversation. She was a bad liar.

"Clifford, hey," she said, pushing the words out painfully. "I think I have food poisoning. I really feel like crap. I'm not going to be able to man the booth today. But I've got a lot of leads from yesterday, so it hasn't been a total waste. It's been productive. I'll call you later. Bye."

She hung up and then called the convention's vendor manager to give her the same story. I hope I don't run into her on my way out, Anita thought.

The booth would be safe. There was nothing worth stealing; she had the laptop and business cards in her room. If someone wanted to run off with the rest of the brochures, or the banner with the company logo, well, then they could go right ahead.

Anita had room service deliver coffee, melon slices, and a bagel. She wolfed it down, then got dressed in gym shoes, jeans, and an orange cotton shirt. She gathered her maps and put them in her purse. Then she got brave and took something out of her purse that she rarely looked at but always kept with her. She forced herself to stare at it.

A small snapshot of Tim. Standing in the back-yard in Rockridge, holding his favorite truck, beaming back at her. Happy, safe, alive.

Anita took a cab to Lakeview, the residential neighborhood where she had caught up with the bus. She started at the bus stop at Belmont and West Lake Shore Drive. If he got off here, he can't live far from here, she reasoned. She picked a direction and started to go.

The area was very pleasant and eclectic, with a mix of small brownstones, vintage courtyard buildings renovated into condominiums, and some Victorian homes. The atmosphere was busy and youthful and trendy. Heading west, she reached the shopping scene, full of clubs, designer boutiques, thrift shops, and ethnic restaurants.

Anita turned north on a busy street and walked in the direction of Wrigley Field's light towers, which peeked from between buildings in the distance. Her eyes roamed the people on both sides of the street, stopping when she saw a child, examining faces, looking not only for Tim but any boy that may have been mistaken for Tim.

If she could find someone who even resembled him, that would do it. She could go home with a clear conscience.

Anita walked through a few diners and fast-food restaurants. She dipped into toy stores, children's clothing stores, bookstores. She even showed Tim's photo to a few clerks who responded with great sensitivity, but could offer no clues.

True, the photo probably did not reflect Tim accurately anymore. She tried to create a firm picture in her mind of Tim's height and build at four years old. *What am I looking for?*

She had to stop jumping when she saw two-year-olds. It wasn't him. It couldn't be him. Tim was four now. Taller, older, not the person she pictured anymore.

He had been gone now for the same length of time that he had been a presence in her life: two years.

Anita strolled the Lakeview neighborhood for hours. There were a few heart-stopping false alarms: children seen from behind, or obscured by others, who had Tim-like characteristics, but then unmistakably were *not* Tim.

When she found a park or playground, she stopped, found a place to sit, and stayed for anywhere between twenty minutes and an hour.

There was almost always children coming and going, and these locations provided the most opportunity.

Late in the afternoon, she returned to the bus stop at Belmont and West Lake Short Drive. She wandered the immediate block a few times but did not let the corner leave her site. Soon, it would be 6:25. The precise time that yesterday's Bus 145 stopped here, when Tim was believed to be on board.

Soon, she was checking her watch constantly. Thirty minutes to go, then twenty, then twelve, then seven . . .

Her heart beat faster.

At 6:25, right on cue, Bus 145 roared into view. Anita stood about twenty yards away as the bus pulled up to the curb and started letting people out.

A couple of young professionals . . . a Hispanic boy and his mother . . . a teenage girl all dressed up in gothic black lace and heavy mascara . . . and finally a tubby fiftysomething man with a crew cut, carrying a Radio Shack bag.

The bus roared off.

Anita stayed for three more buses and the results were equally benign.

Finally, she started walking again, west, until she reached Broadway. She ate dinner at the Melrose Restaurant, a twenty-four-hour sandwich joint, and watched the families, following every child's voice to a face, and came up Timless.

When the day succumbed to dusk, she took a cab back to the hotel. Anita stumbled into her room, depressed and tired from studying crowds, people, and faces for hours. She estimated she must have looked at hundreds of children.

Am I going to scour all of Chicago? she asked herself. This is ridiculous, Anita.

She sat on the bed and drew in her knees. What was the game plan? The trade show was now over. Her flight to leave Chicago was scheduled for 9 A.M. the next morning.

Maybe it would be best to go home and clear her mind of this entire mess.

She didn't move, thinking about it for a long time. The sun sank, and the room went from golden to shadows.

Finally, Anita got off the bed. She went to the phone. She canceled her flight.

"One more day," she said out loud to herself in the mirror. She looked awful: raccoon eyes, hair gone to hell. "One more day, and that's it."

The following morning, Anita dismantled and packed the Your Resources booth for shipping back to Sacramento. She endured a number of "Where were you yesterday?" inquiries from the other vendors, sticking to her food poisoning story, and even made up the name of a restaurant, Charlie's. Since she looked like crap anyway, they easily believed her.

By 9 A.M., she was back in Lakeview. She started again at the bus stop, watching a few loads of passengers climb off and on, before heading south. She would cover the same eight-block radius, but this time in a different order.

Soon, she felt dragged down by déjà vu. It was the same streets, the same buildings, the same school yards, the same storefronts, alleys, and restaurants. She even recognized some of the same faces. She did her best to examine people without staring. She didn't want to appear like a crazy lady stalking the streets, creeping everybody out.

By late morning, she was feeling more tired than ever. She had seen so many parents with happy young children that she was starting to fill with envy and depression. Her whole world was sliding back to a place she really didn't want to go.

This is pitiful, she told herself. Why would he be alive? Why here? Why now? What sense did it make?

At noon, she bought a sack lunch and took it to Belmont Harbor. It was a beautiful day to watch the yachts and sailboats, although she didn't see too many children. The water was turquoise and calm. She could watch it forever. The atmosphere relaxed her and gave her what she needed to regroup and begin her next walk.

She returned to the other side of Lake Shore Drive. After another uneventful hour of wandering, her feet began to scream pain. She had been ignoring the blisters up to a point, but now they really did hurt like hell. Fortunately, she knew the location of the nearest pharmacy. She had only walked past it four times since yesterday.

Anita bought a tin of Band-Aids and brought them with her to a small, crowded play area named Little People Playground. It was located between two large apartment complexes. She had been here twice already today. She found a bench, took off her shoes and socks, and began to cover the areas of her toes and heel where the skin had been rubbed away.

Anita scanned the crowd. Kids were climbing, running, chasing in and out of the playground equipment. Happy children's chatter filled the air, punctuated by shrieks and laughter.

Anita examined every young face. Her eyes made the rounds twice. No Tim.

She stuck the Band-Aid tin in her purse and slipped on her socks and gym shoes. There was still a lot more ground to cover. She stood up. Her feet felt better. She would be able to make it for a few more hours, at least.

Anita started on the path to the sidewalk and gave one last glance back at the playground. She caught something out of the corner of her eye.

A familiar little boy emerged from a covered fort at the top of a slide. Skinny, with blond bangs, a squat little nose, and dirt smudged on one cheek.

Anita gasped.

Dear God, it's Tim.

Her eyes locked on the boy as he stood. There was no mistake about it. He was taller, thinner, stretched out. A little boy instead of a baby. Moving with fluid grace and confidence, no longer a staggering toddler.

It was as if someone had taken her memories and old photos, added two years, and turned them into flesh and blood.

The boy looked around at no one in particular and then dropped to a sitting position. He slid to the ground, landing in the bark chips.

Anita felt tears rolling down her cheeks.

"Tim . . ." she said. She started to walk toward him.

The boy brushed off his pants and circled to the ladder on the back of the slide.

Anita broke out into a run. "Tim!"

The boy did not respond. He did not even turn his head.

"Tim!" she screamed. Why couldn't he hear her? "Tim! Tim!"

An explosion of adrenaline shot through her, sending a cacophony of emotions into her brain. She dashed across the playground, past the other children.

Anita caught up with him at the ladder. "Tim, Tim, it's Mommy!" She grabbed him from behind. His hands slipped off the rungs and he became wrapped in her arms.

The boy turned to look at her.

He screamed.

The piercing, high-pitched scream seized the attention of everyone on the playground.

"Honey, don't scream, it's *Mommy*—"

The boy squirmed violently, pushing her away.

Out of nowhere, a tall, angular blond woman ran at them. She was moving with lightning speed; her face was harsh, fierce. She had dark eyebrows. "Stay away from my child!"

The boy pulled away from Anita and grabbed the ladder for dear life. He was bawling, mouth opened wide, tears streaming. "*MOMMY*!"

The blond woman swept him up in strong, bony arms. "Jeffrey, it's OK," she said. "Mommy's here."

The boy clung to the woman, still crying. His face was red and wet.

"No!" shouted Anita, on fire. Her hands shot out for the boy, but the blond woman swung him away with daggers in her eyes. "Get away from him!" she shrieked so loudly that it echoed off the buildings.

"That's my Tim!" screamed back Anita, her hands clawing for him, getting a hold of his ankle before the woman screamed louder: *"Get away you crazy psycho!"*

Anita lunged again for the boy and the blond woman stuck out a hand, shoving hard.

The boy continued to cry with blood-curdling intensity. Then the blond woman began shouting: "Help! Help! Help!"

The world scrambled into chaos and disorder.

Strangers came running. Anita felt hands grabbing her. Words spilled into the air from all directions.

". . . crazy woman tried to steal that child . . ."

". . . don't let her go . . ."

"She's insane . . ."

"I've seen her casing the place . . ."

"Someone call the police . . ."

"Who has a cell phone?"

Anita struggled fiercely, but her arms were taken away as a growing number of angry faces surrounded her, pulled at her. She kicked at them wildly. Everything became a blur of faces, bodies, arms and legs filling her view, hiding Tim from sight.

Suddenly there was a hairy forearm across her neck and she felt the air pinched from her throat. She threw a fist behind her and connected with teeth. A man grunted, the grip loosened, and she squirmed free. She fell to the ground, scrambled beneath the slide, and turned around.

It was a man in a brown UPS uniform. He had a bloody lip now. There were seven or eight other adults circling her, along with some teenagers in sports jerseys. Behind them, a layer of wide-eyed children watched the commotion.

"It's my son!" screamed Anita from the ground. In the distance, through their legs, she caught a glimpse of the bony blond woman hurrying Tim out of the playground. They made it to the street and started to cross.

A new surge of strength pumped through her body.

On her hands and knees, Anita scrambled to the other side of the slide. The opening to her escape quickly filled with more people.

Anita managed to squeeze past and get to her feet.

The bony blonde and the boy were disappearing from sight.

Anita ran after them. But more people were entering the park in a hurry, all running in the same direction to head her off. The air was filled with shouts to stop her, stop her, *stop her* . . .

Anita tripped and fell hard to the ground. Pain exploded in her knee.

The crowd caught up. A swarm of hands grabbed for her and she felt her shirt rip. She screamed at them to let her go. She screamed and screamed until her throat went raw and she sounded like some kind of horrible wounded animal.

They didn't understand. *It was her child.*

The mob blocked out the sunlight. Someone very close to her ear shouted, "Crazy bitch!" And then in an instant, Anita went limp, sobbing.

In the distance, a police siren tore into the neighborhood.

Chapter Twelve

Anita sat in a hard wooden chair inside the Chicago Police station of the 23rd District on Halsted Street. She was filthy, covered in bruises and cuts, and felt like a dirty criminal. So far, they hadn't locked her up. Yet.

Everything was so surreal and bizarre, that she had gone numb. It was the day Tim had been stolen all over again, except this time she was the villain. Back then, everybody was supporting her. Now the world had turned against her.

The nameplate on the desk said LT. JONATHAN FORD. The desktop was orderly with small stacks of closed files. His chair had remained empty ever since an officer brought her here, fifteen minutes ago, and removed the handcuffs.

The wall was covered in black-and-white stills of Chicago architecture, giving her something to look at. Some of the perspectives were enigmatic, a collage of rigid lines and shadows.

When Ford showed up, his expression was not encouraging. He looked annoyed. And he let out the first of many big sighs. He was in his late thirties or early forties, red haired with green eyes. And tired.

"OK," he said, dumping his butt into a chair. "No charges will be pressed."

She felt no emotion about this one way or the other.

"The child you assaulted . . ." started Ford.

Assaulted?

". . . and the mother . . ."

Mother?

". . . were gone when the police arrived. We interviewed witnesses at the playground. We have good physical descriptions, but no one was able to identify the woman or the boy. Several people recognized them as regulars at the park, and we had two people who independently recalled that the boy's name is Jeffrey."

"Timothy," said Anita quietly.

Ford ignored her and kept going. "No one knows where they live. The playground is a popular one, it's in a dense residential area, a lot of apartment complexes, condominiums. People come and go. That's what we know about them. Here's what we know about you."

Ford opened a folder and began reciting surprisingly accurate information about Anita's past. He had all the details about the kidnapping in California and about Pam.

"So you know . . . I'm not some kind of insane child snatcher," responded Anita.

Ford didn't respond affirmatively. He sighed. "I've been on the phone with Mike Calcina of the Oakland detective unit. I have an understanding of where you're coming from. However, I am not on board with where you are taking this."

"There was no *body*," said Anita, forceful.

"This isn't the first time you have done this."

Anita looked at him, puzzled.

"Sears," said Ford finally.

"Screw Sears!" snapped Anita. "That was different. That was nothing."

"Many times, you have reported sightings of your son to the Oakland Police, and caused false alarm. It reached the point where they no longer followed up on your reports."

She was shocked by this. Was it true?

"Those times were different," she said. "It was right after Tim disappeared, I wasn't thinking straight."

"The case has been closed for more than two years," said Ford. "There is a very strong set of circumstances to support that your son is deceased."

He said deceased simply, without emotion, like a line on a police report.

"But they never found a body," said Anita. How many times did she have to repeat that?

"In drownings off the coast in that region, they

don't find the body a high percentage of the time. It's just not possible. The current's too strong, you have cliffs instead of beaches. I know that makes it difficult, but . . ."

"So you don't believe me?" Anita asked Ford, point-blank.

"The Oakland Police Department closed the case, and I don't have any evidence to support reopening it."

Anita looked down at the floor. She was too exhausted to become enraged. Tim was alive, that was fact, and they could all go to hell.

"So . . ." said Anita, slowly, looking back up at him. She looked him squarely in the face. Into his weary eyes. "What you're saying is that you refuse to help me."

Ford sighed. "Not entirely. I can do two things. Technically, if someone is kidnapped and taken across state lines, it's a case for the FBI. I will contact the field office and see if they want to become involved. There's no guarantee."

Anita nodded. "OK. Thanks."

"Second, I will take the descriptions of the boy and the woman, and I will talk to our beat officers in that area," he said. "This is off the books. But I will ask my men to keep an eye out. We're not going to give it priority over the rest of our work. But we'll see what we can do to at least ID these people."

"I have a photo," said Anita. She reached into her purse and pulled out the snapshot of Tim.

"Of course, he's older now, but you can make copies for the officers."

Ford stared at it for a moment, and then called over a woman named Lucy to make fifteen copies.

Anita felt better. Some help was better than no help. Sooner or later, something had to turn up.

"I'm going to keep looking, too," she said. "Can I have your direct number, so I can reach you if I find anything?"

Ford sighed. He opened a drawer in his desk and handed her a card. "Here's my direct number. But be responsible with it."

What am I, twelve years old, thought Anita.

"I know that you suffered a great loss," said Ford in a low tone. "I realize that they never recovered your boy's body, so you want to keep this hope alive, but . . . don't let your emotions overcome you. Stay level-headed and realistic."

Anita resented the condescending tone. All she could say in response was, "That boy was my son."

Lucy returned with the photo. Anita took it back and placed it in her purse.

Ford stood up. "Let me walk you out." Anita rose from the chair slowly, painfully, feeling soreness in her ribs. Her eyes again roamed the large assortment of photographs on the wall behind Ford.

He noticed her looking at them.

"I do some photography on the side," he said, offering his first smile. "Buildings and bridges, mostly for fun."

"They're really good," said Anita.

"Thanks," he said, almost in a tone of surprise.

On her way to exit the building, Anita noticed a bulletin board loaded with various wanted criminal posters . . . and then noticed missing children bulletins in the mix. She stopped.

"Lieutenant Ford," she said, stopping him. "Wait a second. We need a poster."

Ford struggled with a response. It was obvious that the answer was no, but at the same time he was softening since they had first met.

"Since your case is technically closed, *we* can't do one," he told her. "But . . . there's nothing stopping you." He took a pen out of his breast pocket. "Take out the card I gave you."

She handed it over. He wrote a name and phone number on the back.

"We have a woman, Donna Petersen," he said. "She's freelance. She does a lot of the missing kids stuff. She has this software where she can take a photo and give it what we call 'age progression.' She works out of her apartment, does Web consulting. She's not too far from here." He handed the card to her.

"Thanks," said Anita, adding, "You know what . . . you actually have been a help to me."

Ford sighed, shrugged. "It happens."

When Anita returned to her hotel room, she had a very important phone call to make. She had to call Dennis.

She was frightened that he would not be receptive, having been burned so many times before by false sightings and wild goose chases. She was uncomfortable that she had barely talked to him since the divorce. But now their world had changed again, and she needed him bad.

She tried the only number she had for him, a number in Los Angeles. It was old and, she quickly discovered, disconnected.

"Damn!" She slammed down the receiver.

What now? She thought hard and came up with a blue-haired solution: Myrtle Sherwood. Dennis's mother would have the new number. Myrtle lived in Kansas City. Anita called information and quickly became connected with one of her least favorite people in the world.

It had always been a chilly relationship, and the divorce had only made it worse. Myrtle resented Anita for everything: the crazy nanny, the crumbled marriage. And when Anita asked her for Dennis's phone number, the response was not accommodating.

"My son doesn't want to talk to you," she stated flatly.

"It's very important," stressed Anita.

"Why should I give you his number, after everything you put him through? You left him when he needed you most."

Anita let the old woman vent and kept her temper in check. She wanted to shout: *Put aside your prejudices for one damn minute!*

Instead, Anita said gently, "I know we had

185

problems. But this is very urgent. He needs to talk with me."

"He doesn't want to talk to you."

"You don't know that."

"Oh yes I do, honey."

"Please . . . let him decide for himself. If I give you my number, will you at least tell him I called?"

"You can give me your number, but he's not going to call."

"OK, good, here's the number—"

"Wait, wait, wait," groused Myrtle. "Let me get a dag-blasted pencil."

The old woman dropped the receiver with a loud, dramatic thud. Anita could hear the *Wheel of Fortune* spinning in the background.

When Myrtle returned, she said, "Yessss?"

Anita gave her the number, speaking very slowly, but Myrtle still griped that she couldn't keep up.

Finally, Anita made Myrtle read the number back. She did and added, "He's not going to want to talk with you."

Anita could take no more. She exclaimed, "*Tell him I found Tim and he's alive.*" She hung up.

After the upsetting call with Dennis's mother, Anita needed the reassurance of her own parents. They would provide sympathy and encouragement. Most important, they would wholeheartedly *believe* her, and she needed that to strengthen her for the search.

But she got the answering machine. And then

she recalled a recent phone call with her dad, and he had said something about an Alaskan cruise. Was it this week? Oh shit, it probably was.

Anita started to pace the small hotel room. Who could help? She couldn't do this alone and she certainly couldn't depend on the police. True, they were going to keep an eye out. But Ford had said it would be low priority.

There was no one in Sacramento to call. Co-workers, yes. Friends, yes. Close friends who would drop everything and fly out to indulge in this insanity with her, no.

Maggie was a possibility. But Anita hadn't spoken to Maggie in more than a year and couldn't imagine her leaving Digital Learnings at a moment's notice. Not when the evidence was so intangible. No one would really believe her, that was the problem. *No one knows the truth that I have seen.*

Why would anyone climb aboard this crazy train unless, like her and Dennis, they had a personal and emotional attachment to the tragedy?

Anita was staring out the window at the traffic below, brain working overtime, when the sight of a 7-Up truck brought a name to the forefront of her thoughts:

Roy.

Roy had a vested interest in the outcome of this search. His sister was a despised, notorious child murderer. If Tim was discovered alive, Pam's name would be cleared. The whole Beckert family would be relieved of a horrible burden that would stigmatize generations.

"Roy Beckert, B-E-C-K-E-R-T in Oakland," she told the woman on the information line for the Bay Area. A moment later, she had the number. It was late afternoon, his shift should be over—

Roy answered with a gruff "Hello!"

"Roy, this is Anita Sherwood."

Silence on the other end.

"I know it's strange that I am calling you," she continued. "But I have something very important to tell you."

Roy said, pensively, "Yeah?"

"I don't think your sister killed Tim."

A long pause. "What do you mean?"

"Tim is alive. I'm in Chicago. I came here on business. I saw him on a bus. I followed the bus to a neighborhood called Lakeview, and then, today, I saw him at a playground with a strange, tall woman who took him away. They got away from me, the police thought I was a kidnapper. I have to find them, and I need your help."

She knew that her story sounded off the wall. There was another long pause from Roy. In a very skeptical voice, he asked, "Are you sure about this?"

"I'm totally positive!" she said, flattening his cynicism with the most definitive, confident tone she had in her.

"What's your proof?"

"My eyes. I saw him. I know him. A mother doesn't forget. A mother *knows* her son. It's been only two years. Wouldn't your mother recognize you after two years?"

"This sounds a little crazy, if you want to know the truth."

"Together, we can search the neighborhood. We'll find him. I'll pay for your plane ticket and hotel room."

"Yeah?"

"You get to come to Chicago," she offered, which was lame, but whatever works . . .

"I don't know."

"Think about it, Roy. This is big."

"Who else you got out there helping?"

"No one."

"No one? What about your husband?"

"Not yet. We're divorced. I have to . . . He's not available at the moment."

"You guys got divorced?" said Roy, finding this interesting.

"Roy, listen to me. You can be a hero. If you help find him, you will be on the front page of every newspaper in the country."

Roy chewed on this. "Yeah, *if* we find him."

"We will."

"So he's in *Chicago*?" Again, the skeptical edge, the audible smirk.

"Roy, we can clear your sister. We clear her, we clear your family's name. I just need *help*, Roy." Her tone had turned to begging, pleading. She felt like she was going to cry at any minute.

"OK," said Roy suddenly.

"What?"

"OK, sure."

"You'll come out?"

"Yeah. I'll come out. I'll help."

"Thank you. Oh God, thank you. How soon can you get out here?"

"I don't know. When's the next flight?"

Anita felt a huge relief after her phone call with Roy. Brains or not, he would be a big assistance. She wouldn't be alone.

It was getting dark outside. She called room service and ordered a chicken sandwich and two beers.

Seconds after she hung up with room service, the phone rang.

Dennis!

He sounded aggravated. "I've been trying to get through for twenty minutes. What's going on? My mother said you called and were acting crazy."

"Dennis, thank God you called back," said Anita. "Tim is alive."

Dennis groaned, angry. "Oh Christ, Anita, we're back to this again."

"No-no-no, let me explain," she said quickly. She told him the full story, slowly and measured, rational and detailed, from the sighting on Michigan Avenue to the encounter at Little People Playground to the meeting with the Chicago Police.

Dennis seemed at odds with how to respond. "You've done this to me before. I can't take another one of your false alarms."

"This is different," she insisted. "I stared into his eyes. I grabbed him, Dennis, and I was three inches from his face. This is nothing like those other sightings. I know that it's him."

"But how is it possible? Did you ever stop to think about that?"

"I don't know. I don't know any more than you do. I admit that it makes absolutely no sense. But this whole thing has been nuts from the beginning."

"And the police are going to help?"

"Sure, but it's off the books. To be honest, I think they're just humoring me. I don't think they believe me."

"Anita, I swear, if you—" he started.

"I'm not crazy!" she countered. "Dennis, I need you here to help me. We can cover more ground."

"You want me to just drop everything for you?"

"It's not for me, it's for Tim."

"Anita, I'm in Orlando. I'm trying to rebuild a career. I can't just take off on a whim to search the city of Chicago because you saw a little boy who looks like Tim."

"What if I'm right, Dennis?" she asked. "Just stop and consider that for a moment. *What if I'm right?*"

Her words hung in the silence that followed.

Dennis finally relented. "I . . . can come out in a few days."

"A few days?"

"I have a job, Anita. It's delicate . . ."

"This is your son, Dennis!"

Dennis simply replied, "Yeah. Or somebody else's."

"It's pretty sad that I can get Roy out here faster than I can get you."

"Roy?"

"He'll be here tomorrow. We're going to start dividing up the neighborhood. We'll have posters."

"Roy Beckert? Have you lost your mind? Why would you get that creep involved?"

"I was *desperate*, Dennis." She was shouting now. "I didn't know if I would ever hear from you. I didn't even know if your mother would give you the message. The police don't take me seriously. I can't do this alone. I had to call *someone*. I need help."

Dennis muttered, "I don't trust that guy any-more than his psycho sister."

Anita reassured him, "I'll be fine. Don't worry about me."

"Why don't you just wait until I get there?"

"I'm not going to wait," said Anita. Her voice wavered. "I have already waited . . . for two years . . . for Tim to come home."

Dennis softened his tone. "OK. I hope you're right, baby."

"Me too."

"Otherwise, you're just reopening a big wound all over again. For both of us."

"I understand," said Anita. "It took me a long time to come to terms that Tim was gone. I would not be doing this unless I was absolutely certain."

For a brief moment, the old Dennis started to reappear. "I'm sorry. I didn't mean to get so mad," he said. He quickly followed with "I have to go. But give me a few days. I'll be there on Wednesday. And we'll see where it takes us."

Chapter Thirteen

Donna Petersen's apartment overlooked the right field wall of Wrigley Field, high enough to get a partial glimpse of the games. Even though the evening's contest was hours away, Anita could see a small gathering of street vendors and fans, dressed in Cub blue, scattered outside the park. She couldn't help looking for Tim, rotating her attention between the activity on Sheffield Avenue and the eerie image on Donna's iMac.

Donna was manipulating Tim's face with a software program. She was pinching, stretching, and deepening Tim's characteristics, starting from a scanned photo of Tim at two and altering him to create a boy of four. Anita provided guidance, based on the little boy she had seen at the playground.

Jonathan Ford was right, the woman could do

magic. With a series of mouse strokes and clicks, she adjusted Tim's cheekbones, eyebrows, nose, neck, and hair to create someone new yet familiar.

"You're like a plastic surgeon," she told Donna. The brown-haired woman in her fifties just chuckled and responded, "Yeah. I wish I made the same kind of money."

Illustrating the bony blonde who took Tim away was more challenging. There was no photograph to serve as a starting point. And Anita had not studied her appearance. The woman was seen in glimpses during the chaos and turmoil after the boy screamed.

Donna placed a large drawing pad in her lap and sketched with a charcoal pencil as Anita tried to remember details: the woman's severe expression; long and narrow nose; the full lips; the blond, shaggy hair; the dark eyebrows; the taut lines in the neck; the hard jawline. She was both attractive and a bit frightening, birdlike.

"I wish I could describe her better," said Anita.

"You're doing fine," assured Donna.

When the drawing was done, Donna scanned it. On the PC, she took both portraits and dropped them into a poster template. Beneath each picture, there was space for descriptive text.

Donna asked Anita to estimate the woman's height, age, and weight.

"She was tall, I remember that. Probably six feet . . . in flats." And gaunt, but muscular. "Maybe 150 pounds? And I'd guess somewhere in her early thirties or late twenties."

"Eye color?" asked Donna.

Anita thought hard. "I don't know."

Tim was easier. He was about four feet and forty-five pounds now. Blue eyes. She provided his birth date. Under it, they added the date he had first gone missing in California and the location where he had last been seen in Lakeview.

Then, painfully, the sentence: *Goes by "Jeffrey" (real name is Timothy Sherwood)*.

On the bottom, they added Anita's cell phone number and *Reward for Information*.

Donna printed out the poster and gave it to Anita to review. It felt potent in her hands, a huge step toward finding Tim.

"I can't thank you enough," said Anita. "How much do I owe you?"

Donna held up her hand. "Don't worry about it."

"No, really—"

"Just find your son," said Donna. "I like happy endings."

Anita couldn't stop staring at Tim's new face on the poster. Would this unlock the door to his whereabouts?

"Donna," she asked cautiously. "How often . . . do they turn up?"

Donna hesitated, searching for a soft answer. "I don't have a percentage. But I do know a lot of success stories." She opened a file that was buried under other papers on her desk.

Donna handed her a missing children poster

for Warren Weickert, aged seven, abducted at three. Warren had dirty blond hair, gentle eyes, and a sweet smile, not unlike Tim's picture. It hurt to look at.

"Disappeared on the West Coast, they found him on the East Coast last month," said Donna.

"What happened?" asked Anita.

"Black market adoption."

Anita had never heard of such a thing. "Black market? What . . . for children?"

"You'd be amazed," said Donna. "There aren't enough kids for adoptions, and there are people who are desperate enough that money is no object and, well, common sense goes out the window. The regular channels don't work, or take too long, or maybe they can't get approval from the state, so they find an alternative. They're told the kids are legit, that the real parents gave up the child and concealed their identities, when in reality, the child was stolen. The new parents don't check into the facts. It's 'Don't ask, don't tell.' "

"This really happens?" asked Anita, astonished.

"It was happening in a hospital in a poor part of the south where mothers were told that their newborns had died, when in actuality a doctor was involved with funneling the babies to an illegal adoption outfit."

"That's sick."

"They issued a new birth certificate, like there was no adoption at all, sold for cash, and there was no paper trail. The children grew up and, in some cases, never even realized that they were adopted. A couple years ago, they busted a baby ring where Mexican infants were smuggled across the border and sold in New York to wealthy couples."

"How much do people pay?" shuddered Anita.

"Anywhere between twenty thousand and a hundred grand," said Donna. "It's like robbing a bank, except easier."

Anita looked back at the poster. "But . . . this boy, Warren . . . he was found?"

Donna smiled. "He's back with his parents. He was not harmed. But you can imagine the psychological repercussions."

Anita said, "I guess you can't erase everything that's happened."

"He's alive and with his real parents today," said Donna. "That's the important thing."

"I don't think Lieutenant Ford believes me that Tim is alive," said Anita.

"If he was certain that Tim was dead, he would not have given you my number," replied Donna.

"I suppose." Anita handed Warren's poster back and asked for directions to the nearest copy shop. Donna wrote them down.

"Don't give up hope," Donna told Anita as she walked her to the door.

"I'm not leaving Chicago until I find him," said Anita. "I'll go door-to-door if I have to. I will find whoever has him and I will take back my son."

"That's the spirit." But Donna's parting words were "Be safe."

Anita hadn't thought about her safety before. Whoever had Tim would not give him up easily.

Anita made seven hundred copies of the poster on bright yellow paper at the copy shop. Then she headed east, passing under a thundering train on the El tracks, continuing until she reached the Halsted police station. It was time for a surprise visit to Lieutenant Ford.

He didn't exactly greet her warmly. He sighed.

Anita tossed thirty posters on his desk. "These are for your officers."

Ford just nodded. He looked very tired.

"What did the FBI say?" asked Anita.

"They asked me to keep them abreast of any developments, but they do not see enough evidence to support getting involved at this time," replied Ford matter-of-factly.

"What did you tell them?" Anita started to bristle. "It's your job to convince them—"

"Don't tell me my job," said Ford tersely, and it was obvious he was in no mood for her today.

"Have you even talked to your beat officers?" asked Anita.

"I am not ignoring you," said Ford. "But it's not the only thing on my plate. Frankly, it is not the most important thing, either. I've got a homicide three blocks from here, where a convenience store clerk was shot for fifty-five dollars and a six-pack of beer. I also have an elderly—"

"I don't want to hear your police log," said Anita. "I just want you to take me seriously. You have the posters now. All you have to do is give them to your men."

Ford nodded, but the nonverbal response didn't seem very committal.

"Fine," muttered Anita, and she left.

Anita hailed a cab outside the station house. It was almost four o'clock, and Roy would be arriving at the hotel soon. There was a lot of work for both of them.

She asked the cab driver to stop for a moment in front of Little People Playground. She examined the children, the adults, and did not see Tim or the tall blond woman. If the woman was truly guilty, she would not reappear, so there was something actually reaffirming about not seeing them.

"OK, keep going," Anita told the driver.

Anita was seated in an oversized chair in the hotel lobby when Roy entered. His eyes immediately took in the grandiose sight: spiraling balconies, glass elevators, water fountains, a flower garden, uniformed staff, and marble floors. She watched him for a few minutes before approaching. He did not appear as she remembered him. His rather grubby appearance from years ago had been replaced by better grooming and a slight fashion sense. For a split second, she even considered him attractive.

There were still traces of truck driver. He wore cowboy boots. His face had a weathered look that could not be wiped clean. The bent nose, never properly fixed from whatever broke it, still dominated his features. His sideburns were long.

He carried a single suitcase—the luxuries of being male—and wandered toward the front desk.

"Roy." Anita stood and walked over.

He turned and saw her. "Hey," he said simply.

"Thank you for coming," she said, resisting the sudden urge to hug him. She realized how alone she had been in her search until now. "I really, really appreciate this. I am not crazy. I saw my son."

"That's what you said," he replied. What kind of a response was that?

Anita started digging in her purse for a credit card. "I want to pay for your room. And I'm going to reimburse you for the plane ticket."

"No," he said.

"Come on, I mean it. I dragged you out here—"

"I said no."

He looked annoyed, and she didn't want to start things off on the wrong foot. "Are you sure?"

"I'm not broke, okay? I can pay my way."

"All right," replied Anita. "Listen, I'll let you check in, get settled. Are you hungry? We can grab a bite to eat."

"The airline food was crap," he said.

"OK, good, I'll find us a place to eat. When you're ready, give me a call. Room 708."

"Seven-oh-eight," he repeated, nodding.

"You got it?" she asked, and then realized her

tone was condescending, as if dealing with a child.

"I can remember seven-oh-eight," he said.

"Great," she smiled at him. "I really am happy you're here."

Then he smiled, almost shyly, self-consciously, a glimpse of Pam deep inside of him. "Yeah . . . I guess I can't resist a damsel in distress."

Back at her room, Anita cleaned up. She changed into a violet silk blouse and a skirt, something nice for a change. She was tired of looking like a shambles. And she wanted a decent meal.

She called the concierge and asked for a good steak-and-seafood joint, figuring it would appeal to both of them. After unsuccessfully trying to sell her on a place inside the hotel, the concierge gave her a nearby name and address. It was Karl's Ale House, but he promised it was more of a restaurant than a tavern.

While waiting for Roy to call, Anita plugged in her laptop and composed an e-mail for Clifford at Your Resources. She hadn't spoken to him live in days, leaning on voice mail and the Internet to communicate without conversation.

She wrote that she was delaying her return to California. The trade show booth and leads were on their way back to the office, but she needed to take a week off for an urgent family matter. She didn't fell obligated to embellish beyond that. She had been a good employee for a long time now, and there was enough goodwill in her bank to get away with this. If not, if Clifford didn't like it, well, too bad.

Nothing was going to get in the way of rescuing Tim.

Anita and Roy sat in a leather booth, not far from where a series of televisions broadcast the Cubs on monitors mounted above a long, rectangular bar. Occasionally, she caught glimpses of Donna's building over the right field wall.

The restaurant had a wood cabin feel to it, with hefty pillars and low lighting. Roy wolfed down a huge helping of beef ribs, getting barbecue sauce all over his face and the table. Anita cut into a lean, but tasty mustard-crusted pork chop. They both devoured mountains of the house specialty, redskin mashed potatoes. They also shared a bottle of red wine. Anita sipped. Roy gulped.

Anita indulged. It was the best meal she had tasted in a long time. Typically, she ate alone, and kept it quick and simple. But there was something about sharing a meal that made her upgrade her usual dining experience.

Throughout the meal, Anita told Roy the details of her discovery and pursuit of Tim. He nodded a lot, and she couldn't tell if he was buying it.

Finally she asked him point-blank, "Do I sound like I'm making sense or do I sound crazy?"

"You're not crazy," he offered. "But it is kind of a crazy story."

"What do you mean?" she shot back, a little defensive.

"Well, think about it. Why here? Why now? Who took him? Where did they get him?"

"I've been thinking about that. And I don't have a clear answer, just some speculation. Maybe someone stole Tim from Pam. She ran off with Tim, and then they met up with some crazy third party. Like a second kidnapper."

"A second-kidnapper theory," Roy said, sarcastically, but she let it go.

"Or did Pam hand off Tim to someone else?" continued Anita. "Maybe it was part of the plan all along. And maybe that someone killed her, or else she killed herself out of guilt."

Roy shrugged.

"I know, I know," said Anita. "It doesn't quite add up."

A copy of the poster was on the table between them. She had given it to him when they first sat down. Now it had splotches of barbecue sauce on it.

"This picture could be a hundred women," said Roy, looking at the drawing.

"It's better than nothing."

"So we're just going to walk around and look for them?"

"You and I, we'll split up the neighborhood," said Anita. "We'll put these posters up, we'll stop and talk to people, we'll look at people. They live somewhere in that area. They can't just hide in-

side, they have to come out for food and whatever."

"What if I find him?" said Roy.

The statement struck her for a moment. It filled
her with a rush of excitement.

"Do you have a cell phone?" she asked.

"No."

"Well, I do. You'll find a pay phone and call me.
We can't just take him. We'll need to get the police involved. That's the lesson I learned from the
playground. We can't just grab him back. If we
see him, we stay in the shadows, we stay in control, we call the cops."

She caught him staring at her. Not an "I am
listening to you" kind of stare, but something
more discomforting. She couldn't put her finger
on it. Maybe Dennis was right, Roy was creepy.

Anita finished her glass of wine.

"Let's get another bottle," said Roy.

She shook her head. "No. I'm a lightweight
these days. I think I've had my max."

The wine did feel good in her system, like a tiny
massage right down to her fingertips and toes.
She finally asked a question that had been in the
back of her mind all night.

"Roy, tell me about Pam."

"Pam?"

"Just, you know, growing up with her. Being
her brother. How close were you?"

"I don't know. We got along. We weren't really
. . . friends. I didn't call her all the time, if that's
what you mean."

"Did she have, like, a dark side?"

Roy's eyes narrowed, the question had an impact. "No," he finally said.

"To this day, I still find it hard to believe that she would hurt Tim."

"Pam didn't hurt people," said Roy, and he looked into his empty wineglass. Anita reconsidered getting another bottle to really open him up, but not tonight. She was losing energy fast.

"Then why do you think . . . it all happened?" asked Anita.

"I have no idea," Roy said.

"But as her brother, you must have some insight—"

"She never told me she was a kid snatcher."

"That's not what I mean."

"Then what do you mean?"

"There must be something in her past . . ."

". . . that I'm not telling you? Like she used to kidnap other girls' dolls when she was little? Well, I'm sorry to disappoint you, but there's nothing. Nothing."

"Did Pam talk much to you about Tim?"

"No."

"Not at all?"

Roy slapped his hand on the table, silverware rattled. "Listen, I didn't come here to get the third degree. I came here because you said you found Tim, and that we could clear Pam's name. Where are you going with this?"

"Right," said Anita softly. "I'm sorry. And I want

you to know that I really appreciate you coming out so quickly."

When the check came, Anita reached for her purse, but Roy was all over it.

"I got it," he said.

"Oh come on . . ."

"I drank most of the wine. I had the apple pie."

"I made you come out—"

But he had already thrown cash on the table. "That should cover the tip, too."

As they stepped outside the restaurant and onto the sidewalk, Roy suddenly had a gleam in his eye.

"Let's go for a walk," he said. The city lights were in full bloom, reflecting into the Chicago River.

"I'm so tired . . ." said Anita.

"C'mon, it's Chicago. Where's Rush Street?"

Anita laughed to herself. Maybe it was his first trip to Chicago?

"I'm serious," he continued. "The night is young."

"But I am old. Roy, we need to get some rest. Tomorrow is going to be a big day."

Roy was disappointed, like a teenager told he had a curfew. He accompanied Anita back to the hotel.

They split up in the lobby. "I'll call you in the morning," said Anita. "Around seven?"

"I get up early," responded Roy.

She thanked him again for coming out. She stopped short of telling him how badly she needed him. Above all, his presence made Tim's rediscovery feel less dreamlike and more real. She wasn't on her own anymore.

Back at the room, Anita stripped and sank into a hot bath. She placed a wet washrag over her eyes and tried to release the tension that still clung to her body. She imagined all the grime and anxiety falling off her skin and into the tub, to be released down the drain.

She tried to think of nothing.

She had almost dozed off when a sound startled her awake.

A small *click.*

Followed by slow, heavy footsteps scraping the carpet.

Anita sat up, pierced by abrupt terror.

"Who is it?" she said, trying to sound firm and not scared out of her wits.

No response. The footsteps stopped. Was somebody entering her room? Who?

Not housekeeping, not at this hour. And there had been no call for room service.

Anita remained very still, listening. Then she heard another footstep and a faint scrape.

Donna Petersen's parting words returned to her: "Be safe."

The bathroom door was shut but not locked. Somebody could burst in at any second.

And here she was ridiculously vulnerable—naked, confined, thousands of miles away from home in a city of strangers.

Her cell phone was in her purse on the bed, out of reach. Big mistake. Her eyes frantically searched the small bathroom for anything that could offer protection . . . serve as a makeshift weapon . . .

A hairbrush . . . toothpaste . . . water glass . . . soap . . . towels . . . snap at them with a wet towel? *Shit!*

Then she heard a voice murmur, softly. She couldn't make out the words.

Anita's heart pounded at her rib cage.

"*Who's out there?*" she demanded, rising from the tub now, water falling off her body. "I will scream," she said forcefully, hoping the words would buy her time because, at the very least, she needed to wrap herself in a towel. *I will not let them attack me nude.*

She knew that her escape route was not far. The hotel room door was in close proximity to the bathroom. If she moved fast, she could dive out of the bathroom, seize the door to the corridor and escape . . .

There was silence from the other side of the bathroom door. Covered in a towel, she silently stepped forward. She wrapped her hand around the handle.

One. Two. *Three.*

Anita threw open the door. She jumped toward the hotel room door. She had it open and was halfway out when she quickly turned to glance . . . and saw no one pursuing her. The room was empty.

Leaving the hotel room door open, she cautiously stepped back into the room. She checked the closet . . . under the bed . . . behind the curtains . . . and found no intruders.

Then she heard more footsteps and murmured voices. Coming from the other side of the wall, in the next room.

"Christ, I am an idiot!" she said out loud.

Anita shut the door and sat on the bed. It took a good fifteen minutes to stop shaking. Even though it was a false alarm, the fear remained.

Someone out there had Tim. Someone who might fight to keep him. Someone who might not hesitate to harm her—or kill her—to protect themselves.

I don't know what I'm up against.

She wanted Dennis here, now. He was still three days away from joining the search. Could she stay safe that long?

Anita got dressed back into her street clothes. Hair still wet, she went to see the concierge and asked him for a late-night pharmacy or convenience store that would sell her mace. The concierge directed her to a small food mart two blocks away.

Anita found it, following the green glow of the neon LOTTERY TICKETS sign in the window. The store manager listened to her request. He was a heavy man with a missing front tooth and no shortage of nose hair. He examined the crowded racks of items behind him, going past the stock of porno magazines, and found a black canister of pepper spray. It was small enough that she could conceal it in her hand. It was actually a key chain.

He explained how it worked, reading off the packaging. There was a trigger that locked. It contained five bursts of one-second each. It was effective up to eight feet. And it was very potent.

One spurt of the stuff would shut the eyes of an attacker and make breathing difficult. At twenty dollars, it was a wise investment.

The manager rang it up. "But don't forget," he told Anita, "the best defense against a rapist or mugger is a good, old-fashioned kick in the balls."

"What if it's a woman?" replied Anita.

The manager was surprised by the comment and paused for a moment. "A woman rapist?" He chuckled. "Hey, you find one, you let me know."

Ugh, thought Anita. She left the store with her purchase, and the manager cheerily called after her, "Have a good night!"

Chapter Fourteen

Young voices filled the air at Little People Playground. The children fed off the energy of the morning sun, darting and climbing in perpetual motion.

Anita and Roy sat together at a far corner on a bench, each wearing sunglasses. Roy had the big, mirrored kind that had gone out of fashion an era ago. Between them, two maps were spread out with blue ink outlining separate territories in the Lakeview neighborhood. They each had a bag containing about 350 posters, a roll of tape, and a staple gun. "We're going to divide and conquer," Anita said.

Lieutenant Ford had told Anita to stay away from the playground after the confrontation, and Anita initially agreed. But Ford wasn't holding up to his end of the bargain: helping. Anita could sense she was slipping down his top 10 list of priorities, and possibly off the charts entirely.

"This will be our meeting place," she told Roy. It was 8 A.M. "Every two hours, back here, to touch base." Then she conceded, "They probably won't reappear here. But we can circulate the posters. Someone is bound to know something."

Roy nodded, studying his map for a moment.

"Remember," Anita told him, "if you think you've found them or you have a good lead, don't intervene. Stay invisible. Get to a public phone as fast as you can and call me on my cell phone."

She waited for a response.

"Pretty straightforward," he finally said. "I'm ready."

Anita folded up her map. "Me too. Let's go find Tim."

They headed off in different directions. After about a block, Anita looked over her shoulder and could see Roy in the distance attaching a poster to a telephone pole. Good boy.

The posters had to produce some results.

Anita unloaded about a hundred of them in the first hour. She passed them out to pedestrians, posted them on poles, and asked to place them in storefront windows.

She received a lot of cooperation. After all, who could turn her down? They couldn't. At least to her face. As the morning progressed, she realized that some of the small shop owners agreed to display the poster, but subsequently did not. It was probably too much of a downer to put alongside their cheery DISCOUNT SUPERSALE! signs.

At 10 A.M., she returned to Little People Playground, where Roy was already sprawled comfortably on a bench.

"You been here long?" She eyed him suspiciously.

"Just got here," he stated.

"How'd it go?"

"I put up a lot of posters."

"Did you give them to people? Did you ask questions?"

"Nobody's seen him. But they look at it pretty fast. They're on their way to places, you know."

She sat down next to him. "OK." She reviewed the kids and parents at the playground. There was no one she recognized from the other day, so it was time to circulate. "I'm going to hit the crowd here," she said. "You wanna help?"

Roy grumbled. "Sure."

Most of the parents reacted with apprehension. "We've got a child abductor in our neighborhood?" asked a freckled woman with a paperback. Her freckled daughter threw bark chips at a boy nearby.

"Well, he was taken in California, but he's been seen in this neighborhood," replied Anita.

The woman's face lit up with concern. "How terrible, how terrible," she said.

Another mom reviewed the poster carefully, nodding, and said, "I heard there was a crazy lady loose in the neighborhood. She tried to steal a little boy from this playground a couple days ago."

Anita couldn't quite tell her, "Actually, that was me." Instead she asked, "Do you know anything about the boy that she . . . tried to take?"

"No," the mom responded. "Just some four-year-old who lives around here."

After every parent at the playground had a poster, Anita returned to Roy. "Well, let's go pound the pavement. See you back here at noon."

She covered another series of blocks, this time residential. She put posters under the windshield wipers of parked cars. She gave one to every person who crossed her path.

All she needed was one person who could make the identification or provide a location. One lousy person.

Anita was taping a poster on the side of a mailbox, when her cell phone rang. She snatched it and almost answered, but stopped.

She recognized the number on the display. It was Sacramento. It was Clifford. It was work.

She chose not to answer it. It was the last thing she needed right now. It would mess with her focus. Clifford had her e-mail, that would have to do for now.

After she found Tim, Clifford would understand.

Another phone call came fifteen minutes later, as she was sharing a poster with a twelve-year-old girl with a ponytail who looked ready to cry. "This is so, so terrible," the girl said.

Anita didn't recognize the phone number. She answered. It was Roy.

"I think I found him," he said quickly.

Anita's heart nearly jumped out of her chest. "Oh my God. Roy, where are you?"

"At McDonald's."

"The one on Broadway?"

"I think so. Yeah."

"Check your map."

A rustling noise on the other end. "OK . . . Broadway. Yeah."

"What's he doing?"

"Eating."

"Don't draw attention to yourself. I'll be right there."

She hung up, feeling shivers climb up her body. The ponytail girl was staring at her.

"Did you find him?" she asked.

"Maybe." Anita turned and headed up the sidewalk.

"Can I come with?"

"Whatever you want." Anita was in a daze. She started to run, tugging the bag of posters with her. The twelve-year-old followed.

Four blocks later, badly winded, Anita entered McDonald's and immediately started looking at faces. She tried not to look obvious.

A lot of kids to examine. One by one, she checked them off.

Not Tim, not Tim, not Tim, not Tim . . .

Roy. He was seated alone at a small table, sipping on orange soda.

Anita slid into the plastic chair across from him. "OK. Where?"

Roy unwrapped a finger from his drink and pointed over her shoulder.

Anita turned.

"Where?"

"The booth. Under the clown picture."

Anita saw a boy and a woman.

Not even close.

"That boy is probably seven years old!" Anita lost her temper. All of the tension inside of her erupted. Another hope dashed; she couldn't take this. "He looks nothing like Tim. Nothing! Did you even look at the poster?"

Roy shrunk back. "OK, OK. I'm sorry. So it's not him."

The ponytailed girl entered, also out of breath, face eager to see a reunion. She spotted Anita and headed over.

"It's not him!" growled Anita, and the ponytailed girl backed off. She looked like she was going to cry again.

Roy nervously sipped his drink until it was just ice, and the cup gurgled.

"I'm sorry," Anita told Roy. "I'm on edge. You can understand?"

"I'm just trying to help you," he said.

"I know, and I appreciate it."

They stayed for hamburgers, and then returned to their respective searches.

For Anita, it was a lousy afternoon. Her cell phone number on the poster merely provoked crank calls, cruel ones, including a demented voice that exclaimed, "I cooked him and ate him!" There was also a shrill woman who was pissed off at Anita for posting posters on a tree on private property. Anita didn't remember doing that, so it was probably Roy.

Outside an elementary school, a teacher reprimanded Anita for passing out posters in close proximity to the students. "Several of the younger children have seen the poster, and they are asking questions, and it is making them quite upset."

"Talk to them about it. Make it part of their education," Anita answered. "Ever heard of 'stranger danger'?"

Then, during the final meeting with Roy at Little People Playground, a short balding man in jean shorts and a Chicago Bulls T-shirt approached her and started yelling: "Get away from here!"

Anita looked up at him.

"I know who you are. I saw you here Saturday trying to take that kid. You better leave before I call 911."

Roy stood up. "Listen bud, you don't know the real story."

The short man shouted, "Who the hell are you, her accomplice?" Other parents and kids were staring now. "I mean it, I will call the police unless you get off this playground."

Roy took steps toward him. "You can't make me do shit, asshole."

Anita grabbed Roy's arm. "Don't, don't. This won't help. Let's leave."

Roy and the man continued glowering at one another, but when Anita tugged again, Roy relented and left the playground with her.

"I could have kicked his ass," said Roy

"Then I would have kicked your ass," responded Anita.

Evening put the cap on a crummy day. They returned to the hotel in a cab, tired, without leads, but several hundred posters lighter.

"How about if I pick a place for dinner?" asked Roy as they stepped back into the hotel lobby.

Anita looked at him, shrugged. "OK. I don't know how hungry I am . . ."

"How about Mexican and margaritas?"

"Sure." At the very least, chips and salsa sounded good.

They split up, cleaned up, and Roy tracked down a Mexican restaurant. It wasn't too far, but they cabbed it.

The restaurant, Siesta, was located in a dark, glamorless strip somewhere between Michigan Avenue and Navy Pier. There wasn't much nightlife nearby: a couple of big, mostly empty parking lots for daytime commuters, a closed currency exchange, a scary-looking liquor store, and a shuttered automotive parts shop.

"The food here is supposed to be great," said Roy as they stepped out of the cab.

"I hope it makes up for the ambience," Anita replied.

Inside, the crowd lacked tourists and had a gritty feel that seemed to reenergize Roy. He finished his margarita before she had taken two sips from hers.

Anita had brought the Lakeview maps and started to open one. "OK. Here's the plan. Tomorrow we'll widen our search."

"Can it wait until morning?" asked Roy. "Please?"

She refolded the map. "Sure, I guess."

Anita tried Ford on her cell phone. She had tried several times before without an answer. This time, he answered.

"Have you received any leads?" she asked.

"If I had heard anything, I would have called," Ford said with a sigh.

She told him about the posters, and he was nonresponsive. He eventually cut the call short. She could hear a lot of activity in the background.

"I have to be a pest," she explained to Roy after putting away the phone. "I won't let them forget about me."

Roy grumbled, "The police are worthless. You shouldn't even bother with them."

"Really," agreed Anita.

"I would give up on the cops helping you," he

said again, pouring more margarita down his throat.

"Well, in two days, Dennis will be here, so that will give me a boost."

Roy appeared startled. "What, your ex?"

She nodded.

He became curious. "What's he coming out here for? You guys still have a thing?"

"No," replied Anita. Now she needed to pour down some margarita. "We're over. It all fell apart when this stuff happened, you know. It was a horrible time. I don't know how any couple could survive it."

"So if you find Tim, are you guys getting back together?"

She chuckled. "I'm not thinking about that."

"So he's here in two days?"

"That's the plan."

Roy seemed to focus on this for a moment. Anita dipped a chip. The liquor was making her drowsy.

When their combo platters came, she could barely eat half of her meal. Roy finished most of his and consumed a steady succession of drinks. He became quiet.

In many ways, he is similar to Pam, thought Anita. Not the conversational type. But not shy like Pam. Just private.

As the waitress cleared away their plates, the cell phone rang. Anita inspected it before answering to make sure it wasn't a Sacramento area code. Then she clicked on.

"I saw your poster," said the boyish voice on the other end.

"Do you know something?" asked Anita.

"How much is the reward?"

She had never really established a number. How much did she have in savings? "Twenty thousand," she replied. Was this for real?

"I'll tell you where they are for twenty thousand. In cash."

"Why cash?"

"You know, uh, taxes."

"I'll cover the taxes." Anita's initial surge of hope was giving way to skepticism. "I can't pay in cash."

"You can get it."

"Who is this?"

"Uh, Robert."

"Robert, where's the little boy?"

"No, no, no. I want the money first."

"I see."

"Meet me at ten o'clock at the corner of 43rd and Western."

"Where's that? In Lakeview?"

"Hell no."

"I'll tell you what, Robert. You'll get your reward, but I'll have a policeman deliver it. Just to make sure you're not some liar who thinks they can take advantage of a woman who might be a little desperate and vulnerable."

"A policeman?" The tone was disappointment.

"I have your number." She read it back to him from the display. "I can use it to get your address.

"Wait, no, no. Don't do that."

"What's wrong?"

The voice struggled for a response.

Then Anita heard another person on the line, snickering.

It sounded like a couple of teenage boys.

"How old are you?" asked Anita.

"Ah, go to hell, lady," said the caller. The other voice on the line exploded into laughter.

"You little shits—" started Anita, but before she could get any further, Roy had snatched the cell phone out of her hands. He was on fire.

"Listen you cocksuckers I am going to personally come over to your house and pull your fucking brains out of your eyesockets and wipe the streets with you."

Roy pressed to end the call and handed the phone back to Anita.

She was speechless. She had never seen Roy like this before. It scared her.

He grabbed his latest margarita and finished it in a gulp.

When the bill came, they both reached for it.

"Come on, Roy, my turn," she said.

"What, you think I'm poor white trash?" he snapped, and she immediately let it go.

Roy pulled out his wallet. He had a thick wad of bills stuffed inside. *Where does a truck driver get all that money?*

As they stepped outside the restaurant, Anita immediately started looking for a cab. But no cab. Hardly any cars. A cool breeze swept the air from the direction of Lake Michigan.

"Let's walk it," said Roy.

"You haven't seen my blisters—" started Anita.

"Do you want to go somewhere for drinks?"

"No. I've had one, that's enough."

"How come you don't like to drink?"

She considered telling him about Dennis and his alcohol problems, the whole history, but decided not to go there. "I'm tired," she said simply.

They began walking back toward the direction of Michigan Avenue. They would have to cross the bridge over the Chicago River to get back to the hotel. Anita kept her eyes peeled for a cab.

Roy hovered close. He was silent. He was starting to creep her out again. There was no one else around, no pedestrians, not enough streetlights. More than anything, Anita wished that Dennis was here, now, at her side.

Anita started to think about the pepper spray in her purse. She tried to pick up the pace, but Roy was walking slowly.

"What's your hurry?" he asked.

"It's late. It's dark. I don't really know where I am."

"It's a nice night. Enjoy it." His tone was weird. Was it the alcohol? She looked at him. He had an eerie, blurred look in his eyes.

A lone car drove past and disappeared. No other cars were forthcoming.

Anita suddenly felt very, very frightened.

What was Roy's story anyway?

Fragments of information began moving in her mind, combining like some kind of equation.

He immediately flies to Chicago when she tells him she saw Tim . . .

He's got wads of cash . . .

He's acting weird, he discourages contact with the police, he's apprehensive about Dennis . . .

He takes her to a restaurant in the middle of nowhere and tries to feed her drinks . . .

What if Roy is somehow involved in all this?

Then the thundering thought: *black market adoption.*

She picked up her pace.

"Slow down!" said Roy.

"No," she responded. She stepped off the side-walk and into the street, into the light.

He quickened his pace to keep up with her.

What if Roy killed Pam . . . staged Tim's death . . . and sold him to someone in Chicago?

"Anita . . ." said Roy.

"I see a cab!" she shouted. In the distance. Heading her way. She waved frantically.

It started to turn in the wrong direction.

"Taxi!" she shrieked.

It stopped. Reversed. Came at them.

"Jesus Christ," muttered Roy.

"I told you, I have blisters," said Anita.

Roy said nothing during the cab drive back to the hotel. She tried to calm down. *If I panic, I*

*won't handle this correctly. I need to think, I need
to regroup . . .*

Inside the hotel lobby, she told Roy, "I'll call
you in the morning."

"I'll walk you to your room," he said.

"No, thanks, I'm fine." She headed for the elevators.

"There are crazies in this city. They've got your
phone number now."

"They don't have my room number." She
jabbed the elevator button.

"C'mon . . ."

"No," she said firmly. The doors slid open and
she entered. She pressed seven.

Just before the elevator closed, Roy stepped inside. The doors shut behind him.

He said nothing on the ride up, standing near
her. She could hear his breathing. She saw sweat
on his sideburns.

When the elevator doors opened, she stepped
out and simultaneously reached into her purse
for her card key. He followed.

The corridor was quiet, empty.

Heart pounding, she stood at her room door.
"Thanks for walking me up. I'll be fine now."

He didn't budge. "Can I come in for a sec?"

"No," she said. "Why?"

"I need to talk with you."

"Then talk."

"Not out here," he said.

"Can it wait until morning?"

He looked at the carpet and shrugged. "I suppose."

"Thanks," she said. Time to move quick. "Good night, Roy." Anita unlocked the door and slipped inside. Immediately she turned to close it.

Roy jammed his foot in the way. The door wouldn't close.

"Stop it!" exclaimed Anita, in full panic.

Roy shoved hard and the door opened wide. He pushed his way inside.

Everything happened in fast motion, a flurry of movements.

Roy came toward her as she frantically stuffed her hand into her purse. She felt the pepper spray canister graze her fingertips. She clutched at it. Was it upside-down? Was the trigger unlocked?

He had her cornered against the wall. As she brought the pepper spray out of her purse, the canister fumbled from her grasp. It landed on the floor. Roy's shoe knocked it, sending it spinning across the carpet. He moved in on her.

Anita opened her mouth to scream.

Roy kissed her.

A drunk, margarita-and-quesadilla-tasting kiss, not rough, but not gentle, either. She had no reaction for the first few seconds, stunned into compliance. Then she grabbed his arms and pushed him away. He stumbled backward.

She stared at him.

He looked dopey now, drunk and pathetic. She

did not see a killer in his eyes. Just a sad sack, a buffoon.

"Shit, I didn't . . . I'm sorry," he said. He appeared genuinely startled. By her mortified expression or his own behavior?

"What the hell is wrong with you?" she asked, breathing hard, eyes locked on him.

"I lost my head," he mumbled.

"I thought you were going to kill me," she said, heart still pounding.

He looked perplexed. "Kill you?"

She nodded.

"Why would I want to kill you?"

Anita didn't reply.

Roy continued looking at her. He stumbled on the words, but they still came out coherent enough to sting. "Anita, I think I love you."

She was speechless for a moment, and finally said, "You're drunk."

"No. I've felt this way since I got here."

"It can't work," she said.

"Why not?" he asked. "We've got some chemistry."

"We do?"

"Come on, haven't you noticed?"

"My mind . . . has been on other things, Roy."

"Then let those things go for a minute," he said softly. He moved forward and kissed her again. This time, she accepted it for a long moment. She shut her eyes and took in the adrenaline rush. It felt good, reviving a faraway sensuality . . . but finally she jerked away again.

"No," said Anita. "This won't work."

"Because why?" he said. "Because you think I'm out to kill you? I don't understand."

"Neither do I. Why are you here, Roy? Really?"

"I came here to clear my sister, just like you want to find your boy."

She fixed him with a skeptical stare.

He stepped back for a moment and gave her space. He started to unbutton the top of his shirt.

"What are you doing?" she asked instantly.

"Hold your horses, it's not what you think." Roy opened part of his shirt, reached in, and took out a thin gold necklace. He showed her the small cross attached to it.

"I wear this everyday," he said. "It used to belong to Pam. I know I'm not real good about showing my feelings, but Pam was my sister and she's dead. She wasn't a bad person like everybody says. She was the nicest person you'd ever know. She's no murderer."

Anita watched Roy's face soften. His eyes looked sad.

"I want to get to the bottom of this just as bad as you," he said.

"Good," said Anita. "Then, please, let's just stick to that mission. I can't get involved with you, Roy."

"Yeah," he said, returning the crucifix inside his shirt, buttoning up.

"Are we still on for tomorrow?"

"Of course."

"Thank you. From the bottom of my heart,

thank you for helping me and thank you for believing."

She moved toward the door, and he understood the signal. He joined her and opened it.

"G'night, Anita," he said. He stepped into the hall. He gently shut the door behind him and was gone.

She locked it.

"Holy shit," she muttered to herself.

She wanted to go to bed, but her drowsiness was all shot to hell now. She returned the pepper spray to her purse and turned on the TV. She tried to concentrate on Jay Leno. She was not successful. She paced the room.

She couldn't get the kiss out of her mind. *He's infatuated with me.*

Anita kept replaying the encounter in her head. Did she have feelings for him or was it just the blast of relief that he wasn't a killer, the excitement of the moment that created electricity, which she had not felt in a kiss for . . . years.

Sure, he was handsome in a rough kind of way, but it would never work. Never work. Not the brother of the woman who . . .

. . . who what?

She sank into a chair, overwhelmed by confusion, realizing she didn't know what to think or who to believe anymore.

Part Three

Chapter Fifteen

Thunk!

Roy stapled another poster to another telephone pole, wincing as the sound pierced his head. He felt like shit. The sun was too bright. The air was too hot. He was hungover. And he was a goddamned idiot.

Last night's embarrassment clung to him like a leech. Too many drinks, a sloppy, impulsive kiss, and a most definite rejection. He couldn't help it. He had always been struck by Anita Sherwood's looks and drawn to her intensity, ever since that day she came home in the hot red dress, all tits and ass and mascara, to find him in the living room. The day his ding-a-ling sister lost her ring down the kitchen sink.

Anita gave off the vibe of a sexually repressed mommy who needed someone to pop her cork.

But the next time he saw her, the whole Pam-Tim thing had erupted, effectively wiping out any romantic fantasies. He had never given it another thought until she pulled him out here, out of all the possible people in the world. She pleaded with him. She *needed* him.

Joining her in Chicago, he had cleaned up, dressed up, treated her to meals, paid his way, tried to impress her as being something better than what he was . . . a bread truck driver. The drama of their search together only stirred him up more. They had laughs, they made a connection. On their first dinner out, she dressed in a tight skirt and heels, all done up like a date. Her husband was out of the picture.

True, she was a sophisticated college grad and businesswoman, and he was a blue-collar knucklehead who didn't even own a computer. They were the odd couple for sure. Yet through the death of Pam, they were bonded forever.

He was drawn to her. So he drank too many margaritas and gracelessly made a move. And she freaked. She said she thought he was going to kill her.

What the hell was that all about?

Then, to confuse things further, she accepted a second kiss with just enough return change to tantalize him. Then he was shown the door.

Roy had a theory for all this. Anita Sherwood was not sane. The missing kid thing had messed up her mind real bad. Evidence? There was the psycho fit when she saw Roy at the pharmacy, looking at a magazine. There was the well-publicized incident where she closed down Sears. There was the buzz in the community that, well, the woman had lost it, ditched her job and husband, fled the area and gone into seclusion.

People whispered about her. They gossiped. And he felt a kinship, because he knew that the same thing happened to him. People gave him funny looks. Anger, sympathy, freak-show curiosity, all of the above. After all, he was the brother of Pam Beckert, the infamous baby killer—

Whap whap whap.

Teenagers were playing basketball in a small court outside a youth center. The pounding of the ball on the pavement prodded his already sensitive skull. Roy swiftly moved out of the area.

Coffee. I need more coffee, he told himself. Any kind would do, nothing fancy, none of that Starbucks crap. Gas station sludge would be welcome.

Roy headed up Belmont Avenue, away from the apartment buildings and town houses and into a busy business strip. His bag of posters didn't feel much lighter, but he knew he had posted dozens in the past hour.

Was it worth it? He had been helping Anita for three days now. He was having serious doubts that she really saw her son. It simply didn't make sense. Anita's mission was desperate, fueled more by hope than logic.

During the mostly silent breakfast they shared together in the hotel café, he had asked her, "How many days are you going to do this?"

"As many as it takes," she stated plainly.

He didn't tell her then, but he was already determined to leave soon. In all honesty, he couldn't afford a bunch of nights in a fancy Chicago hotel. He wished he had accepted her offer to pay, but no, he had to act cool, be a hotshot, like money was no big deal.

Money mattered. And this was costing a lot. But there was another factor telling him to go home. Anita's ex-husband would be arriving tomorrow. And two's company, three's a crowd.

Roy bought a large cup of coffee, no cream, no sugar, at a convenience mart that already had one of the missing Tim posters in the window.

He brought the coffee with him to a small adjacent parking lot and found a spot to sit on a concrete block. Not too comfortable, but he had to rest for a few minutes. The hammers in his head said so.

As Roy sipped his coffee, he took out one of the posters and stared at it to refamiliarize himself with the faces he was looking for.

The illustration of the woman didn't have much distinction and looked like a lot of people. It was everybody and nobody. But the photo of the boy definitely made an impact. The eyes seemed to stare right out at you. He looked like a good kid.

And he was probably dead.

My sister murdered this little boy?

The police and FBI said so. But they didn't know Pam. They didn't know how crazy and implausible it was.

Pam Beckert? The frail, passive little thing that got beat up so many times in grade school that he finally took it upon himself to pound her attackers for her?

True, she was something of a nut job, but a nice one. That's what everybody used to call her: "Nice." How could she go from nice to evil overnight? Does it happen to people?

People just snap, one cop had said. Even good people.

Maybe the whole Tim thing was a release of thirty-eight years of pent-up aggression. Maybe Pam was unhinged from the start. He just didn't know.

Roy and Pam were never particularly close, but they always got along. He wished he had talked more with her. Unfortunately, the lasting image Roy had of his sister was the broken, drowned, pale corpse that he had to identify for the police. It was gruesome, something out of a horror movie, and stocked him up with nightmares for months to come.

A few days before her burial, he retrieved her necklace, the one with the small gold cross. It was the only thing he owned that had belonged to her, and he wore it around his neck as a lasting statement.

You're my sister, maybe you did this horrible,

awful thing and maybe you didn't, but I will not abandon you.

Most everyone else did. Pam's funeral hardly attracted a handful—even close relatives stayed away. Meanwhile Tim's funeral drew an overflow crowd and all the public sympathy.

Pam was the monster, as he was reminded countless times through the vicious crank calls and anonymous, scribbly letters shoved in his mail. "Your whole family will rot in hell" was one of the classics. Many contained religious rants or death threats.

At least he was strong enough to handle it. They could all kiss his ass. But his mother—

Roy swallowed. It hurt to think about this, but he couldn't stop.

Their mother took all the impact and then some. Without a doubt, it caused the stroke. It destroyed her health. Dad was useless to help, as always, a pitiful fool who simply increased his hours at the hardware store, hanging out there with his cronies, even when he wasn't being paid.

At least Dad had cronies. Roy's own friends faded away overnight, as if they feared getting arrested for talking to the brother of a killer. It didn't help him find a steady woman in his life, either. But he could usually snag a one- or two-night stand before the realization hit and his phone calls went unreturned.

Screw it. Most of them were bimbos anyway.

Roy shook the moping out of his head. This was not helping his hangover. He finished his coffee in a long gulp and crumpled the cup. It was time to circulate more posters. If Anita saw him taking a long break like this, she'd probably lose it. She wasn't exactly keeping her cool lately.

Roy walked the sidewalk, looking at kids and moms. He smiled politely when they caught his stares. Nobody matched the poster people.

He stopped various folks to show them the poster, and received the usual shrugs, nonreactions, and funny looks. Some of them were already familiar with it. Hell, it was everywhere now.

As Roy returned to the residential area he had been assigned, he noticed a bunch of poles he had missed during his first go-around. Then it seemed like he had overlooked entire blocks—but he knew he hadn't. This was territory he had covered just hours ago.

Then he noticed the remains of one of his posters clinging to a post. It had been torn down.

At first, Roy didn't think too much about it. Somebody had torn down a poster because it was considered litter, creepy, unauthorized, whatever.

But then Roy noticed that his posters were removed throughout the area, and they had been singled out. Other posters—for bands playing at clubs, dieting schemes, dog-walking services, you name it—remained.

Someone was deliberately removing Tim's posters.

After another block of this, Roy came across a

garbage can containing a dozen or more crumpled yellow posters. From their position amid the other contents, they must have been placed there a while ago. He took one out, flattened it, and stared at it.

Who is doing this?

And why?

For a second time, Roy stapled posters on the poles. He kept his eye out for anyone who might remove them.

It filled him with anger.

Roy felt motivated to stop more people and show them the poster. He received more responses of "I'm sorry," head shaking, and shrugs.

And then a breakthrough. He handed off a poster to a teenage girl with a pierced belly button as she Rollerbladed past him. She continued another twenty feet, then stopped.

"Hey mister, I know a Jeffrey."

Roy caught up with her in an instant.

"You do?"

She handed back the poster. "I mean, I don't know if it's the same kid, but there's a little boy Jeffrey that lives across the street in that building. I don't know the last name. His mom kind of looks like that. Are they in trouble?"

"No. Not at all." Roy wanted to kiss her on the braces. He couldn't believe how excited he suddenly felt. "Thank you!"

The Rollerblade girl said "Good luck" and continued on her way.

Roy crossed the street. It was a residential complex that spread halfway down the block, dozens of units compiled in identical, U-shaped sections with courtyards.

He approached the entrance to the nearest section. This was the building the Rollerblade girl had pointed to.

Roy stood outside the front door. Now what?

After a few minutes, a lean black man with round glasses stepped out of the building.

"Excuse me," said Roy. He showed the poster to him.

"I don't know," the man responded. He appeared to be in a hurry and walked away.

Roy waited patiently at the entrance and gently interrogated people as they were coming or going.

Some ignored him, and a few reacted with suspicion or disdain. "Who are you? Are you with the police?" asked one woman, heavyset, triple chin, in overstuffed polyester.

"No," said Roy.

"Then why should I tell you anything?"

But it didn't take long for the next jolt of progress.

A little old lady on her way inside stopped, put down her grocery bags, and studied the poster for a long moment.

"Oh yes," said the old woman. "The Riskins. They're on six."

Dazed, Roy mumbled words of thanks, and she entered the building, unaware of the enormous value of the information she had provided.

Roy felt hornets in his stomach. Should he find a phone and call Anita? Maybe not until he got a look at the Riskins. The last thing he wanted was another Anita outburst over a false alarm, like the day before at McDonald's. She was a hot head.

Inside the vestibule, the entrance to the building was locked, but Roy was patient. After ten minutes, an acne-ridden teenager exited and Roy strolled inside, holding out his keys, acting like a resident.

The mailboxes for the units lined one side of the lobby. Roy examined them until he found what he wanted.

RISKIN 612.

He felt his heartbeat accelerate. He had a name, he had an apartment number.

Roy took note of the name on the adjoining mailbox.

WILHOIT 614.

He tucked the bag with the posters and staple gun under his arm and went to the elevator. As he entered and pressed six, Roy mentally rehearsed his routine:

Knock on 612, and then when someone answers, apologize and explain that he's got the wrong apartment—he's looking for *Wilhoit*.

That would enable him to get a good look at whoever lived inside before they closed the door, enabling him to determine whether or not the Riskins resembled the woman and the boy on the poster. And if they did—find a phone and call Anita pronto.

The elevator doors opened on the sixth floor. Roy stepped out and began examining apartment numbers. 616 . . . 614 . . .

612.

Roy studied the door for a moment. He couldn't hear any activity inside.

He recited his lines again in his head. I'm looking for Wilhoit, Wilhoit.

Roy knocked.

There was a long silence.

Then the sound of some shuffling on the other side.

Another long silence.

Then the loud thunk of a bolt being unlatched. A doorknob rattling.

The door swung open, and Roy found himself staring into the face of Dennis Sherwood.

Chapter Sixteen

Dennis was puffier, bearded, and without his glasses, but it was definitely him. Roy recognized him in an instant. And the intense gaze and wry smile from Dennis indicated that he recognized Roy as well.

"Hello, Roy," said Dennis. "I saw you through the peephole. Sorry for the delay answering the door, but I had to get something."

Dennis raised his arm to reveal a sleek, black semiautomatic pistol. He aimed it at Roy.

"Please come in," said Dennis.

Roy remained where he was. He felt a trembling ripple through his body.

"Don't be afraid. I just want to talk with you," assured Dennis. Then his tone curled with menace. "You *will* speak with me, Roy."

Roy knew he had a choice: run and maybe get shot; or stay and maybe get shot.

"I'm not going to hurt you," continued Dennis. "Unless you choose to act stupid."

"What do you want to know?" asked Roy, trying to keep his voice even, unafraid.

"Not here. Inside."

When Roy lacked a response, Dennis brought the end of the handgun forward until it nearly touched his navel.

"Your stomach would make a nice silencer," said Dennis.

They locked stares. Dennis had bloodshot, unblinking eyes.

"OK," said Roy. "We'll talk."

Dennis backed up to let him in, continuing to hold the gun steady.

Roy entered the apartment and Dennis shut the door. He locked it. Bolted it.

"Put your bag on the floor," instructed Dennis. Roy set the bag down.

The living room was partly furnished and partly in boxes. The boxes were neatly stacked against a wall. Against another wall, a stereo system with huge speakers was set up, bookended by CD towers. Beyond the living room, there was a small dining room area that connected with a kitchen on one side and a corridor on the other side. The corridor probably led to bedrooms.

It all looked perfectly comfortable, domestic and nonthreatening . . . including one heart-stopping element.

Trucks. A half dozen toy trucks, some small and metal, some big and plastic, scattered near a low coffee table. On the table, a book of puzzles and games with a cartoon rabbit on the front, "for ages 3–6."

Tim is here.

Dennis gestured to a large chair next to the sofa. "Have a seat, Roy. Your feet must be tired from handing out posters all day. Take a load off."

Roy didn't react quickly, standing in the middle of the room.

Dennis repeated, more firmly, "Sit down."

Roy slowly stepped back and sat in the chair. He kept his eyes on Dennis.

"Thank you," said Dennis.

Behind Dennis, Roy caught a glimpse of something yellow on a table. He realized it was a stack of the yellow posters, torn and bent.

Dennis followed Roy's stare to the posters. "Yeah, those," said Dennis. "I've been tearing them down for two days. They're very bothersome."

Dennis sat down on the sofa alongside Roy, keeping the gun on him. "My poor wife and kid, they can't go outside ever since the crazy woman came after them. The neighborhood's just not safe anymore."

Dennis intensified his glare. He hardened his voice. "Where is she, Roy?"

"Who?"

"Who else? Anita."

"Right now?"

"Right now, pal."

"I don't know," replied Roy, and that was pretty much the truth. "She's covering a different area." After a discomforting silence, he added, "All she wants is her son."

Dennis erupted. "*Her* son is dead. Now there is only *my* son."

Then he grumbled, "You would be a lot better off if you had stayed home and stuck to your bread truck."

Roy's eyes kept returning to the gun. He was familiar with semiautomatics; he knew a driver who carried one and showed it off. The guy drove a cigarette truck, made a lot of night stops in bad Oakland neighborhoods, and had been beaten up a couple of times by winos and crazies for cartons of Marlboros. Finally, enough was enough and he bought a gun.

It was a single-action, requiring manually cocking the hammer for the first shot. To do that, you pulled back the slide. All subsequent shots simply required pulling the trigger.

Roy thought, *If I could get it away from him . . .*

Dennis promptly stood up. "You want a drink?"

Roy shook his head no.

Dennis walked over to an elaborate, oak-wood liquor cabinet. Behind little glass doors, various brown, green, and clear bottles were lined up, labels facing out, orderly and dignified. A shrine to booze.

Roy watched Dennis carefully, but Dennis did

not turn his back to him. Dennis did not put the gun down.

Roy calculated that he and Dennis were roughly the same size, although Dennis had some belly, and Roy was probably in better shape.

I could probably take him, Roy figured, *if he puts the gun down . . . or if I can catch him off guard.*

Dennis filled a glass with vodka for himself without taking the gun off Roy.

"So what else do you want to know?" asked Roy. *How long would this last?* The living room curtains were drawn. He could hear birds chirping outside, but they felt a million miles away.

"Tell me about the investigation," said Dennis. "Are the police involved?"

"Not really."

"Not really," echoed Dennis. "That's not much of an answer, Roy."

Roy said nothing. The condescending tone angered him.

"She hired a private detective yet?"

Roy remained silent. Maybe it was better to let him fear the worst. Let him think the jig is up.

Dennis took a long swallow of vodka and put the glass down. "I don't think you appreciate the disruption you've created in my life. Do you know what a hassle it is going to be, changing my name again. My son's name. My wife's name. I kind of liked Riskin, too."

Dennis picked up Roy's bag of posters from the

floor. He placed it on the table with the other posters, pulling one out to examine.

Dennis frowned. "I don't like how you made her nose look, it looks like a beak. That's rude. She's a beautiful woman, Roy. She made the last twelve months of my marriage with Anita bearable." He crumpled the poster and tossed it at Roy's feet. Then he returned to his vodka and took another drink.

Keep drinking, thought Roy. *It'll just slow your reflexes.*

"Anita and I, we grew apart," said Dennis. "Our marriage had cancer, Roy. It was inoperable. She figured it was her career causing it, and that when she quit her job, everything would be cured. Well, Roy, as you know, that didn't work out so well."

Roy remained silent, eyes glued on Dennis.

"If I didn't care so much for my son, it wouldn't have come to this," said Dennis. "It would have been a simple divorce. But I didn't want to lose my son. If you had a son, you would understand. There's a bond that you have with your child, it's deeper than anything else in life. This is all about . . . love."

Dennis sat back down on the sofa, gun in one hand, vodka in the other. He looked at Roy. The alcohol had not taken the edge off his intensity. "In a divorce with Anita, I never would have gotten custody of my son. Not with my history. The drinking. The domestic battery charge. No, not when she's the one who gives up her career to take care of him, even though I'm the one supporting them both."

Dennis sighed. "Roy, she would have gained custody of him in a snap. It's not right, but that's the way the system works. Us guys get screwed, Roy. Being a father puts you at an immediate disadvantage. Check the case histories. It's not fair. Fine, then I don't *play* fair."

Dennis took another swallow of his drink, anger growing. "I have been really happy for two years, Roy. I completely disconnected from my old life, started a new one and kept my son. Then one day, it all comes crashing down. And do you know why? The Shedd Aquarium. We took my son to see the whales. And we took the bus. All of this because of some beluga whales."

Dennis gestured to the boxes on the other side of the room. "You saw the boxes? Yes? It's time to move on. I had hoped we'd be gone by the time you found us. One more day, and this would have been an empty apartment. Anita expects me to arrive in Chicago tomorrow. But it's backward. That's when I'm *leaving* Chicago."

Dennis finished the vodka and his face hardened. "I have a beautiful new wife. I have a beautiful son. That's all I want. Nothing will fuck that up, Roy. Do you understand me? You and Anita will not fuck this up. I worked way too hard to get here."

Dennis let his words hang in the air.

Roy had kept quiet for most of the tirade, but now it was his turn. One simple question.

"What did you do to my sister?"

"Oh, Roy, you really don't want to know."

"You killed her."

"No, no. She killed herself, remember?"

"That's bullshit."

"She killed herself and killed Tim, case closed. Read the papers and learn a thing or two. Or don't truck drivers read?"

Roy felt rage. His words turned to steel. "You are going to burn in hell for this."

Dennis' expression didn't change. He leaned forward on the sofa and brought his face close to Roy's face. Roy could smell the stink of his breath. He could see the tiny dots of perspiration on Dennis' nose, the gray in his beard, the broken veins in his eyes. Dennis locked a stare on Roy for at least half a minute.

Then he asked, "Do you like The Who?"

"What?"

"Not The What. The Who. Rock and roll, Roy. Heard of them?"

"Of course."

Dennis leaned back now, strangely jovial in a jarring shift of moods. "I like The Who a lot. Always have. I like The Stones, too, but The Who more. Better dynamics, they rock harder. Roy, do you have a favorite Who album?"

Roy was speechless. Dear Christ, this man was totally insane.

Dennis continued, "I have most of them. The good ones, anyway. Especially the Keith Moon period. Boy, could that guy bash the drums." He gestured to the wire towers of compact discs alongside the stereo. "Go pick a Who CD."

Roy didn't move. *I'm not going to engage in this conversation. It's ridiculous.*

Dennis jumped to his feet. "Then I will." He put the vodka glass aside and leaned over one of the CD towers. He ran his finger down the CD spines until he found what he was looking for. He moved quickly, and Roy studied him, adrenaline racing, wondering if this would be his best shot at tackling the bastard . . . or should he wait until Dennis consumed more alcohol . . . *Shit, what should I do?*

Dennis turned from the CDs, pistol aimed at Roy in one hand, a copy of *Who's Next* in the other hand. "Got it."

Dennis punched a few buttons on the stereo. Various lights popped on, the CD tray slid out.

"This is their magnum opus," said Dennis, inserting the disc, never fully turning away from Roy, never lowering the gun to the floor. "More than thirty years old, but it's got the energy of *right now*. Listen to this track. It's called 'Bargain.' "

Dennis entered the track number and turned away from the stereo, beaming.

The song started softly, Dennis nodding along inanely, watching Roy's reaction. "Ohm Walsh speakers," Dennis said, and it meant nothing to Roy, but at least Dennis was impressing himself. "Wait until you hear the bass on these things."

The music suddenly shifted tempos. A burst of

drums, followed by thundering guitars and the familiar, soaring voice of the lead singer. Roy couldn't remember his name, although he had heard this voice on the radio a million times since childhood. Peter . . . Daltrey?

"To really appreciate The Who, they have to be played loud," said Dennis. He gradually turned up the volume, grinning as the rock and roll thrashed with monster intensity, filling the room.

The guitars stung, the drums exploded, the bass throbbed. Dennis was singing along now, his voice straining above the booming stereo. He placed dramatic emphasis on the lyrics. *"I'd pay any price just to win you, surrender my good life for bad."*

Then he stopped to shout at Roy, "HOW ABOUT THOSE SPEAKERS? AREN'T THEY GREAT? I CAN'T EVEN HEAR MYSELF!"

Dennis turned around, facing the stereo receiver. *Is he going to turn it up louder?* thought Roy. *Does it even go louder? Will he shut the fucking thing off?*

Suddenly, Dennis spun around, and Roy realized in an instant that he had not been fiddling with the stereo.

Dennis had cocked the hammer on the pistol. He aimed the gun at Roy. There was no time to react. Dennis fired two shots, sudden cracks, buried under the noise of the music.

Roy slammed into the back of the chair. He felt a searing burn in his chest. He felt his hands and feet twitch and prickle. He choked for breath, shuddering. His lungs were filling with blood.

Dennis gradually reduced the volume on the stereo. The music shrank. "Better turn it down," Dennis said. "Don't want to upset the neighbors."

Roy slid to one side of the chair, still choking, feeling a cold wave of nausea rise over him like a blanket. His shirt was soaked with blood. He felt it rolling in little streams to his waist. He wanted to stand, but could not. The pain spread like wildfire.

Roy's mind raced even as his body shut down. He knew. He knew he was dying. How many minutes left? Who will find me?

Slumped over the chair arm, immobile, Roy's eyes stared forward, his focus trapped on a portrait hanging on the wall.

A family portrait of the Riskins. Proud father. Beaming mother. Smiling son. Looking all the world like the perfect all-American family.

Roy's vision turned cloudy, giving way to a swarm of fireflies. The pounding in his ears became a faraway ebb. Then Roy Beckert's final thoughts fragmented and dissolved away.

Chapter Seventeen

Dennis watched the life drain out of Roy as if he was observing a science experiment. The skin color shifted from pink to white to grayish. The body, slumped over the chair arm, shifted ever so slightly, then moved a few more inches as muscles relaxed.

Suddenly, the body pitched forward. It landed on the rug with a loud thump.

Dennis placed the handgun in the liquor cabinet, behind several bottles, high enough to be out of Tim's reach. Safety first.

Cary entered the living room. She wore a white T-shirt and red shorts, skinny and long, all arms and legs.

"Is Tim all right?" asked Dennis.

"Jeffrey," she corrected him.

Dennis shut his eyes. "I know. Right. Jeffrey."

"He's watching TV in our bedroom," said Cary. "The loud music scared him for a minute, but he's fine." Her eyes rested on the dead body of Roy leaking blood onto the carpet.

"That's just great," she said in a monotone.

"It doesn't change anything," said Dennis. "Keep packing. Just pack what's essential. We're still getting out of here."

Cary cautiously stepped over the body, keeping her tennis shoes out of the blood.

"We'll roll up the carpet and bring it with us," said Dennis. "The chair, too. I'll take care of this."

"Are you sure he wasn't being followed?"

"He and Anita split up the neighborhood. He has a map. They aren't covering the same ground."

Cary couldn't take her eyes off Roy's body. "Everything was going so well . . ."

Dennis remained cool. "We'll just start over someplace new. We've done it before and we can do it again. We're pros now, honey."

He walked over and kissed her cheek. He took her hands and she turned her attention to him. He looked into her blue-gray eyes. "Go pack. We're fine."

She made a thin smile. "I hope so."

He touched her short, shaggy blond hair. She smelled good. She always smelled good. He rubbed against her. Her skimpy summer outfit unveiled long stretches of skin, turning him on. It didn't take much. He felt the hunger for her.

He wanted to push her on the couch right then and there.

"Mommm. . . ." cried a young voice, followed by footsteps.

Cary pulled away and turned, alarmed. "Jeffrey."

"Keep him out of here," said Dennis sharply.

Cary moved quickly to intersect him and guide him back into the bedroom.

Dennis watched Cary disappear, following the lines and curves of her body, down to the tattoo of a thorny vine that wrapped above her left ankle.

No one will get in the way of my new family. That was everything in a nutshell. It was very simple, really. Anita out, Cary in. Anita no, Cary yes. The bitchy, boring worker bee replaced by vibrancy and fresh sex appeal. Cary was his beautiful, wounded kitten, who needed him and appreciated him. She was full of life, while Anita had become dead tired.

Long ago, Anita had been something of a prize, brimming with fire and spice. But she rapidly lost her sense of fun after college, a rude case of bait and switch. She called it maturation, he called it dull. She called it responsible, he called it nagging. They disconnected, unplugged, had nothing more to say. It was sad. He was still young. He didn't need to surrender the rest of his life to a bad choice.

Anita out, Cary in, Tim stays. So simple.

Dennis looked at Roy. A dead man on the floor.

Also remarkably simple. Dennis examined the body with a determined detachedness, as if he were staring at a piece of furniture.

He was pleased with his lack of fear or guilt. No remorse, no revulsion, no feeling of any kind, really. Just another necessity to achieve the goal.

Frankly, he felt proud of himself for handling this whole thing in such a controlled manner. No panic, no sweat.

This was even easier than the first time.

He was cool and collected then, too. There wasn't a choice. Anything less would unravel every plan he had for the future. It was a carefully plotted sequence of events, hinged on the credibility of his performance. There was no margin for sloppiness . . .

"Shit!"

Dennis slammed the brakes, stopping the Jeep Liberty as it backed out of the driveway.

"What is it?" asked Anita.

"My wallet," grumbled Dennis. "I left it in the house."

"Well, good thing you remembered it now," said Anita.

"Wait here," said Dennis. He stepped out of the Jeep. "I'll be right back." He slammed the car door.

Anita remained in the passenger seat, all dressed up for the good-bye dinner that awaited in San Francisco with her work colleagues. The engine was running. Dennis gave her a quick glance before he entered the house, shutting the front door behind him.

Gotta act fast.

"Pam!" he called.

"Mr. Sherwood?"

Pam approached from the family room, where she had been picking up Tim's toys. Such a good nanny.

"I forgot to tell you about Horsey," said Dennis.

Pam smiled but wrinkled her forehead. "Horsey?"

Dennis chuckled. "Come on, I'll show you."

He took her to the fish tank in the living room. It was a large, rectangular saltwater tank, sixty gallons, propped on a heavy stand. The contents, collected over time included anemones, clown fish, puffer fish, a blue tang, a yellow tang, angelfish, starfish, coral, and seahorses. Dennis removed the hood of fluorescent lights and delicately placed it against the wall.

"One of the seahorses is sick," he said. "It's the little one. Tim calls him 'Horsey.' We need you to give Horsey his special medicine about ten o'clock."

"No problem, Mr. Sherwood." Pam examined the fish tank. "Which one is Horsey?"

Dennis stepped back so she could get a better look. "The little one. Do you see him?"

Of course, Pam would have to study the tank. The two seahorses were the same size. There was no smallest one.

"I'm not sure." Pam moved closer to the tank. "Is it the one on the right?"

"No, keep looking. You'll see him." Dennis quietly stepped back to the closed drapes that covered the living room window. He reached behind the drapes and grasped the handle of a Barry Bonds Louisville Slugger baseball bat.

Dennis told himself: *grand slam.*

"They're so cute," said Pam. "But I don't see a small one."

Dennis stepped forward with the bat. "Keep looking. He's probably in the coral." Dennis brought the barrel of the bat back, prepared for a level swing, and aimed for the back of Pam's head.

"Horsey, where are you," sang Pam lightly, tapping the glass of the aquarium.

Dennis wanted to crush a 450-foot home run into the bay beyond the walls of Pac Bell Park. But he knew he would have to check his swing. A love tap. Nothing messy; just enough to make her sleepy . . .

Dennis drove the bat forward and wood met bone, filling the living room with a sickening *crack.*

The momentum of the swing knocked Pam away from the tank to dive onto the rug. She rolled, then remained there, limp, her butt in the air, her limbs pointing in all directions. Her thick, nerdy glasses rested nearby.

Out cold.

Gotta act fast.

Dennis dropped the bat. He took off his jacket. He rolled up his shirtsleeves to the elbow. He took ahold of Pam by the hair and collar. He yanked her up. She jerked passively like a rag doll. Her face was turning fat and swollen. A huge purple welt bulged out of one side of her head.

Dennis sunk Pam's face into the fish tank, making sure the mouth and nose dipped beneath the surface. The fish scattered, while bubbles rolled out of Pam's nostrils and lips.

Drown you pathetic troll.

Dennis counted to himself. "One one-thousand, two one-thousand, three one-thousand . . ." His heart pounded madly, his pits and groin dampened with sweat, but he wouldn't let emotion interfere with this very critical task.

Pam stirred, barely conscious. But her tiny struggles were no match . . .

Dennis held firm. He continued to hold her face in the water, even when resistance persisted. Sure, it was horrific; she would soon be dead; but he couldn't think about that. He continued to keep emotions in check, telling himself, this is just a job I gotta do. Like changing the oil, or digging out a dead bush from the backyard, or . . .

Don't think of the action, Dennis told himself. *Think about the results.*

A new family of Cary and Tim.

He imagined the three of them on a picnic on a picture-perfect summer morning. Tim full of love and happiness for his parents. Cary wearing her sweet pink halter top, long legs folded beneath her, fantastic smile and those lips . . .

The pictures in his mind provided a beautiful substitute for the grotesque agony of Pam's final minutes.

When Pam's struggles ended, her body went slack and she emitted a horrible gurgly gasp. Her mouth opened wide in the water and the stream of bubbles became a trickle.

Gotta act fast.

Dennis removed Pam's face from the fishtank. Being careful not to let water drip on his clothes, he picked her up and kept her face held out over the floor. She was small, but not necessarily light. Dead weight.

Dennis swiftly carried Pam's body to the family room, and over to the door that connected with the garage. He reached out, pushed the door open, and then dumped Pam into the dark, onto the pavement.

He shut the door and hurried back to the living room.

Gotta act fast.

He returned to the fish tank for a quick look. The fish appeared to be returning to their routines, after the rude interruption of Pam's big, ugly face.

Everybody fine? You won't tell, will you, little fishies?

Dennis reached in and delicately returned the little toy scuba man to a standing position.

Then he returned the aquarium hood above the tank and secured it.

Everything normal? He did a quick count of the fish, missed one, and counted again . . . then again . . . *Shit!*

One of the clown fish was missing.

How could that be?

He searched frantically around the tank. *I don't have time for this.* He couldn't find it anywhere. Then he remembered Pam's gaping mouth as she drowned in the saltwater, and it dawned on him—

She inhaled one of the fish?

Dennis started giggling nervously. He couldn't help it.

He hurried into the kitchen, dried off his arms with paper towels, rolled his sleeves back down and buttoned them. He put his jacket back on.

Gotta act fast.

Dennis ran up the stairs. He hurried into the bedroom and grabbed his wallet from the dresser. Then he opened the top drawer to rummaged through it for a moment and create a scene. He had already removed the cash earlier in the week.

Next, Dennis went into Tim's room. Tim slept in his crib, undisturbed, clutching his bear.

Dennis looked at him softly. Such a fantastic, lovely boy. He kissed a finger and brought it to Tim's lips.

"Sweet dreams," said Dennis. "Don't be scared. Daddy will see you again in a few months."

Gotta act fast.

Dennis returned downstairs, where he unlocked the back door that led from the family room into the backyard. He snapped the back porch light off—then on—then off again.

Another minute later, Dennis was back behind the wheel of the Jeep. Sweating a little bit, panting slightly, but under total control. Anita barely looked at him; her focus was on the farewell dinner ahead.

Think: Academy Award, he told himself before he delivered his lines.

"Something's not right," said Dennis. He backed out of the driveway and into the street. "I think I caught Pam off guard. She was crying."

"Crying?" said Anita.

"She was picking up some of Tim's toys in the kitchen. She was staring at them. She seems distraught." He told Anita: "I feel like crap, but why should I?"

"You shouldn't," Anita said.

They discussed Pam's sorry state some more, and then Dennis popped on the stereo. The Who blasted out of the speakers. Dennis let out a heavy sigh, drowned out under the music.

The Jeep swung around a curve, making its way out of Rockridge and heading for the lights of San Francisco.

Chapter Eighteen

In the backyard of the home of Dennis and Anita Sherwood, Cary blended in with the night. Tucked in the brush, out of the sightline of neighbors, she waited with supreme patience. She was as still as a statue, every joint and muscle locked. Only her eyes moved.

Then: the signal. The back porch light flicked off-on-off.

Cary felt a mad surge of excitement.

Shit, he really did it, she told herself. Right on schedule.

The rush of emotions provoked panic, glee, arousal, all of the above. This was more intense than any other high. She worked to regain focus, clear her head, stay calm.

Now it's my turn.

The next steps had been planned very carefully

and she had them memorized. She would not fuck up.

"Do it right, and we will have our dream family," Dennis had told her. "Forget a step, do it sloppy, and we all go to jail. There is no in-between."

Cary moved quickly to the back door. Wearing gloves, she turned the door handle. It opened.

Cary entered the house and locked the door behind her.

She froze for a moment and listened.

Silence. Absolute silence.

She took a moment to take in the family room. Just like the exterior, the inside of the house sparkled perfect, like it belonged to one of the ideal TV sitcom families from her youth. The brightness, the cleanliness, the soft furniture, happy portraits, all the toys—it was laid out in front of her like a big cozy hug.

Growing up, living in Hell House, Cary's escapism was the Bradys, the Huxtables, the Cleavers—all cheerful, warm, and loving, wrapped in appreciative laugh tracks. There were never any serious threats, and the occasional conflicts were resolved neat and tidy before the half-hour mark. It was both exhilarating and foreign. When she was little, the other kids were into *Star Wars* or *Batman,* but her fantasy life was *Family Ties.* She wanted to know: *How can I enter that world?*

Then, as she grew up, wised up, got knocked around one too many times, she realized the simple truth: You don't always get the life you want. Sometimes you just have to take what you need.

Right now, more than anything in the whole wide world, she needed Dennis and Tim and the cleansing future of a perfect family. They would buy a house together just like this one, but far-away, maybe in New York, or Chicago, or Dallas. She would decorate it with love.

And that would destroy the memories of Hell House. Tear it to the ground.

Cary opened the door that connected the family room to the garage. And there she was, just like Dennis had promised. The crumpled, dead nanny. Ugly and small, with clumps of wet hair wrapped like big spider claws across her face.

Dennis did his part. Now Cary had to finish up.

She started gathering items, using the checklist in her mind.

She retrieved the baseball bat and the nanny's glasses from the living room. She pulled the nanny's coat out of the closet. She found the nanny's purse, checked it for the cell phone, and took out the nanny's car keys.

Cary pocketed the car keys. Everything else went into the garage, on the floor in a small pile next to the nanny.

Next, some clean up. She took towels out of the kitchen cabinet where Dennis had planted them, neatly folded.

Cary wiped up the water on the sides of the fish tank and the legs of the stand. She soaked up wet spots in the carpet in front of the aquarium and then dried some smaller water spots along the path to the garage.

When she checked the aquarium one last time, she found two long strands of the nanny's hair in the tank. Cary took the hairs out, placed them in the towel, and checked carefully for more.

When she was satisfied that no clues remained, Cary brought the towels into the garage and placed them with everything else that was going to be removed from the property, including the body.

Dennis had left a waterproof bedsheet folded up, hidden behind the lawn mower. It was rubber and stain resistant, intended for toilet-training toddlers. She brought it to the nanny to cover her up.

Cary couldn't help glancing at the nanny's face before she dropped the sheet.

It wasn't the first dead body she had ever seen in her life, nor the most startling. That honor belonged to Meg, one of her old roommates in Berkeley, who overdosed on heroin on Halloween while dressed as Vampira. Cary was high on ecstasy when she found the body, which complicated things. She waited for the ecstasy to wear off before she called an ambulance to the apartment. She later felt occasional guilt about it. Maybe they could have saved Meg if the call came earlier, but she doubted it.

This wasn't even the first murder caused by someone she knew. Nick, the biker she hung out with for four months, claimed he killed another man in a bare-knuckle fight outside a bowling alley, but she always suspected he was just saying that to impress her.

As Cary stared at the dead nanny, she noticed something strange snarled in her hair. It looked like a little fish. She reached down and slid it out. It *was* a little fish, orange with white stripes, dead. She would have to tease Dennis about this later. She placed the fish in one of the towels.

Then Cary dropped the bedsheet on the nanny's face. Time to get the car.

Dennis had placed an extra garage door opener on a shelf with the garden tools. She took it, jabbed it. The garage door rolled up, offering a view of darkness on Vernon Road. She stepped outside the garage and scanned the surroundings.

Quiet. Still. No one's around.

Ex-cellent.

Cary walked to the curb and climbed into the nanny's Toyota. She started up the engine and backed the car into the garage, next to the Jetta, being careful to stop short of the body. She parked, climbed out, and closed the garage door.

It rolled shut with a definitive *slam*.

So far, so good.

Time to load the trunk. She opened the lid and placed the bedsheet on the floor, spreading it out. Then she placed the various items inside: the baseball bat, the towels with the hairs, the coat, the glasses, the purse.

And, finally, the nanny.

She was a little chick, but flopping all over the place. It took several shoves to move her up and over the lip of the trunk. She landed inside in a ridiculously awkward position, looking like a circus contortionist.

Cary slammed the lid shut.

One more item left on the checklist.

Cary went upstairs into the little boy's bedroom. He was asleep. Looking at him, she felt her heart fill with good, happy feelings. Jesus Christ, he was a beautiful boy.

And she would be a good mom. Better than this Anita woman that Dennis described. Anita had no time for this precious child. She neglected her son and her husband. What kind of a mother was that? Cary needed to set things right. She was simply taking what Anita didn't want.

Cary would be perfect in the perfect family. A good wife, a good mother. Great husband, great kid. She would not abandon them, ever, not like her own mother had done. And she would not become an evil, stifling bitch like Aunt Margo, turning childhood into Hell House. No, Cary would be the best mom ever.

All the pieces were sliding into place now. She reached into the crib and gently picked up Tim. He maintained his grip on a stuffed brown bear.

For a moment, he seemed to stir and squeak, and Cary freaked. She had not prepared for this. What if he started to scream and cry?

She held him close to her chest, stroked his hair. He smelled so clean. His little arms and legs moved, then relaxed. He sighed. A beautiful sigh. Then he drifted back to sleep . . .

Cary brought Tim into the garage. She placed

him in his car seat in the back of the nanny's Toyota. The straps took some time to figure out, but she managed to secure him safely and calmly. He stirred some more, but did not make noise.

Cary checked her watch: 9 P.M. Everything had gone like clockwork. Time to leave and head north.

She pressed the garage door opener and brought it into the car with her. Without turning on the headlights, she backed the car out of the garage, shutting the garage door when she reached the end of the driveway.

Mission accomplished. *Ex*-cellent.

The Toyota entered Vernon Road. Cary departed from the neighborhood and blended into growing streams of evening traffic, without making a ripple.

Mile after mile of Highway 101 disappeared behind her into the night as the hours rolled by.

We did it, Cary told herself over and over. Dennis is mine.

Dennis had said he would never leave Anita unless he could bring Tim. At first it seemed impossible. But, really, nothing is impossible if you set your mind to it.

If you are determined enough, if you have the balls to do whatever it takes, you can spin miracles.

Cary checked her watch frequently, timing her

progress with the sequence of events developing back at the Sherwood house.

Anita and Dennis wouldn't arrive back home for at least two hours . . . then allow another hour to ninety minutes until the police are fully engaged . . . that should give her plenty of time to reach her destination.

Her new life was waiting. She couldn't get there fast enough. The old life would be dead and buried, RIP, good-bye to twenty-two years of shit with a capital S.

For the first time, she would have a real family, not the sack of garbage that stole her childhood. She hated them all. The seriously messed-up father, currently back in jail for another bungled string of armed robberies. The schizo mother who barely made appearances or any sense. The evil stepparents of Hell House: grabby-hands Uncle Jack, the fat sicko pervert, and sadistic Aunt Margo, aka scowlface, old yeller, the wicked witch of the world. All gone, all erased. Not her family anymore.

This felt so good. This felt even better than when she torched Hell House on her way out of San Diego two years ago. The fire didn't kill Uncle Jack or Aunt Margo or even do much damage to the house, but it did send an effective statement about her feelings at the time. With two suitcases of possessions, she took a bus to Berkeley, found the seediest part of town and moved into a two-bedroom apartment filled with a rotating occupancy of six to eight dropouts, drifters and burnouts. To get by, she dealt a little dope, mooched, and shoplifted. She got wasted for days on end and spread her legs for any semiconscious stoner with a sufficient hard-on. This was her "fuck you" period, Total Rebellion, but it never felt all that good and eventually became a depressing extension of everything that had come before.

It still wasn't the life she wanted.

So she did a 180, cleaned up, found a real job, and left the apartment of losers for her own tiny place three blocks away, a basement unit on the other side of a boiler room.

The real job was bartending. Her willowy looks and long brown hair drew business, even if she was clumsy and slow. She worked for four months at Sanford's, a small corner tavern and then, for much better money, accepted a similar gig at the Green Hills Country Club near Rockridge.

Talk about culture shock.

Green Hills was a different class of people than she had ever been exposed to before. Instead of the skanky late-night crowd at Sanford's, this was afternoon groups of golfing buddies, rich and immaculately groomed. They were almost entirely male, wearing expensive watches, nice sweaters, neatly ironed slacks, smoking fat cigars, and tossing her horny stares. It was fun to flirt with them, serving up beer and chatter. She even bedded a couple of the guys, catching on when they slipped off their wedding rings, usually after the third or fourth beer.

They meant nothing to her. Just recreation.

Then she met Dennis.

There was something different about him. For one, he was not stuffy or condescending like the others. He had a boyish charisma. The age difference didn't matter. She looked older than her twenty-two years, he looked younger than his thirty-two years, so they met somewhere in the middle.

Unlike the others, she felt like she could connect with him. He reached in and touched her soul. He made her feel special, not cheap. Sex meant something, it wasn't just a lay.

Dennis was smart, confident, classy, great to look at, a wealthy real-estate broker. He had it all.

Unfortunately, that included a wife.

From the beginning, he talked about how the passion had left his marriage. His wife had become a workaholic who cared more about her job than her family. She was never home. He wanted to leave her. But he couldn't bear to leave his son.

Dennis's deep devotion and love for his son was the most beautiful thing she had ever known. She wanted him so bad it was breaking her heart in a way she had never felt before. She couldn't sleep or eat.

When Dennis announced that Anita was leaving her job to spend more time with their son, Cary became alarmed that it might repair the marriage. But Dennis remained adamant about cutting loose from Anita. He continued to see

Cary as often as he could, often showing up at her apartment between real-estate showings.

She wanted to spend the rest of her life with him. He said he wanted to spend the rest of his life with her . . . but could never leave the boy, Tim.

In a divorce, Anita would gain custody, and that was unthinkable to him.

As the passion burned, Cary and Dennis dedicated themselves to finding a way to make it work. She suggested killing Anita, but he wouldn't go there.

Initially, he said it was because he still had feelings for her. Later, he admitted it was a flawed plan because it would be too logical to connect them to the crime.

After several Saturday afternoons of long talks in the clubhouse, scribbling half-baked ideas on napkins, they found a twist that was so unexpected, it was perfect:

Fake Tim's death in order to take him away.

Everything fell into place after that. The weirdo nanny was an ideal scapegoat. Dennis took glee in plotting out the scenario. He had an incredible mind. He was a college graduate, bursting with knowledge. He had all the confidence in the world.

And so did she.

On a Saturday afternoon so beautiful that it chased everyone else outdoors, Cary and Dennis sat at a table in the back of the clubhouse, sharing a bottle of white wine like some kind of storybook romance. Dennis proposed a toast.

"To our new family."

For the first time since she was a child, Cary cried.

Cary was making great time. Driving in the middle of the night will do that, she concluded.

She only made stops for gas and milk. The milk was for Tim, who murmured and acted fussy about fifty miles from their destination. She bought and filled a sippy cup for him. He gulped about half of it down and returned to sleep. Her presence did not seem to alarm him; although he never appeared fully awake.

Far up the northern California coast, she pulled off Highway 101, following the route so carefully researched and mapped out by Dennis. She took a small, unpaved road that hugged the coastline, coming across no other cars. It was incredibly dark. The redwoods shut out the moonlight, and she drove slowly. She realized she was returning to a bad habit—chewing her fingernails bloody.

"Stop it, Cary," she told herself.

Suddenly something reflected in the beams of her headlights. It was a parked car. It was the black Acura that she and Dennis had tucked there the prior day.

Destination reached.

Cary killed the engine. She looked back at Tim. He was in a deep sleep, his head to one side, the sippy cup tipped over in his lap, the stuffed bear tucked under an arm.

Cary stepped out of the car and opened the backdoor. The air was cold and the wind howled through the trees. Cary could hear the crashing waves of the ocean nearby.

The black Acura had been fitted with a brand-new baby car seat. Cary transferred Tim from one car to the other. Briefly, he opened his eyes. For a moment, Cary feared he would freak out, but instead he simply clung closer to her for warmth. He was asleep by the time she strapped him into his new car seat. Cary placed a blanket over him and shut the door.

She faced the nanny's car. "OK, Pam," said Cary. "Now it's your turn. Time to go for a swim."

Cary approached the trunk, holding the key. She took a deep breath and inserted the key into the lock. She twisted, it *clicked*. Cary lifted the trunk lid to peer inside.

Pam burst forward, mouth twisted open, screeching like a crazed animal. Her face was distorted into something monstrous. She swung the baseball bat wildly, connecting with Cary's hand. Cary felt the blow, yelled in alarm, and stumbled backward onto the grass.

Pam continued to scream, raw and horrible, like nothing Cary had ever heard before. The nanny scrambled out of the trunk, maintaining her grip on the bat, facial features purple and swollen, teeth bared. Cary returned to her feet just as the bat sliced the air near her chin.

She could see Pam's terrified eyes, magnified

huge in her glasses. She was panting in deep, hoarse gasps.

The two of them simply stared at one another for a moment, trying to identify positions in the dark. Then Pam took another swing with the bat. Cary dodged it. She would not get hit again. Her hand stung like hell.

Cary sized up Pam.

This was not part of the plan. But no matter. This puny mouse did not stand a chance against her. Hell, she had beaten up *guys* a lot bigger than this.

"Give me the bat," spat Cary.

"No!" Pam swung it wildly, which was exactly what Cary wanted, because after it swished past, while Pam was still off balance from the lunge, Cary moved in, and she grabbed the barrel with both hands.

They struggled, both of them grasping the bat, but Cary kicked the smaller woman squarely in the shin, and it loosened her fingers just enough to lose the bat.

Pam started crying.

Cary didn't waste any time. She struck the bat against Pam's cheekbone.

Pam crumbled, screamed, begged.

Cary felt no pity. This little mouse was not going to destroy her new family. No fucking way, no fucking how.

Pam managed to get on all fours, her hands clawing at patches of grass. She was frantically looking for her glasses.

"Please . . ." she said.

"No thank you," said Cary, and she struck again.

Pam was still partly conscious when Cary tossed aside the bat and began to move her. Cary was punching, kicking, and shoving. To avoid the blows, Pam kept scrambling away, crawling off balance and broken, like a dog with three legs.

She was going in the right direction. Cary directed Pam to where the trees vanished and the earth disappeared into an abyss.

The waves below roared and crashed. When Pam realized where she was, it was too late.

Cary gave one final, ferocious shove, sending the smaller woman over the edge. Pam's hands clutched desperately at the air, and she screamed into the stars. She plummeted.

Cary lost trace of Pam's descent, but then heard the smack when she hit the rocks, and caught a quick glimpse of her broken body before the black, violent waters sucked her up and took her away.

The threat was over.

Cary took off her gloves. She examined the fingers on her left hand. They hurt like hell, but she could bend them, so they probably weren't broken. Bitch.

She put the gloves back on. Now on with the show.

Cary returned to Pam's car. She removed Pam's purse and coat from the trunk, setting them aside. She gathered the towels, wrapped them in the bedsheet, and placed the bundle in the trunk of the Acura. She added the baseball bat. It was cracked. She closed the trunk gently, so not to wake Tim, who remained asleep in the backseat, blanket still tucked up to his chin. Positively adorable.

Cary went back to Pam's purse, picked it up by the straps, and plopped it on the front hood of the Toyota. She took out the cell phone and turned it on. She quickly entered the text message that she and Dennis had composed earlier in the week. Pam's tearful admission of guilt.

"I LOVE TIMMY. I AM MORE OF A MOTHER . . ."

When she was done, she entered Anita's cell phone number and pressed SEND. She shut off the phone. She tossed it in Pam's front seat. Next, she took the five hundred dollars of cash Dennis had given her and stuffed it in Pam's purse. She placed the purse next to the cell phone. She tossed Pam's coat on top.

Anything else?

She checked the inside of the car. She checked the trunk, closed it. All seemed good to go.

Then she realized: Jesus Christ, don't forget the mouse's glasses!

Pam's bent glasses were in the grass behind her car. Cary picked them up. She carried them to the cliff and flung them out to sea.

That was it, except for one last task. Cary returned to Tim and gently eased the stuffed toy bear out of his grasp.

"I'm sorry, honey," she whispered.

She took the bear to the cliff and tossed it, watching as it seemed to almost float, twisting in the wind, turning tiny and tinier, until it was gone.

Good-bye, Tim. Hello, Jeffrey.

As the first strains of daylight streaked across the sky, Cary drove Jeffrey to their new temporary home, a small, isolated ranch house outside of Sonoma Valley. The house was a rental, arranged by Dennis, who made good use of his real-estate resources to mask her identity under a bogus name.

Jeffrey's room in the house was already prepared. It had been a joyous experience: shopping for the crib and changing table, picking out the clothes and toys, buying his diapers and food. There were balloons and clowns on the wallpaper. She eagerly looked forward to future trips to buy his things.

She delicately put Jeffrey to bed, under clean new covers. He looked so totally at peace, untouched by the ordeal of the past twelve hours. He was young enough to adjust to the changes—and forget.

The hardest part was over, but there was still so much more to do. Tomorrow she would cut her long brown locks dramatically short and dye her hair blond. She would do it herself in the bathroom mirror.

Cary left Jeffrey's room and went to the phone in the kitchen. She dialed Dennis's voice mail at work. After it picked up, greeted her, and beeped, she waited exactly ten seconds before handing up. The silent message was her signal to him that all had gone according to plan. Well, more or less . . .

Now it was simply a countdown until Dennis joined them.

Six months, to be exact. That's what Dennis had promised.

"She will throw me out of the house the second week in August," Dennis had assured her. "I know exactly what buttons to push. Just you watch."

And he was right, as always. On August 10, Dennis slapped Anita hard across the face.

Following the loss of their child, the loss of his job, the loss of his affection, and his return to alcohol, the slap was truly the last straw in a marriage that had actually been dissolving for years.

Anita told Dennis to leave and never return.

And Dennis obliged.

On the single best day of Cary's life, Dennis returned to her arms. He returned to his son. The perfect family was now complete.

Immediately, they started plotting their next move. They would relocate far from California and become lost in a large city. They would have new names and new looks. In this new life, there would be no mention of Anita and no memories of Hell House.

It would be a fucking paradise.

Chapter Nineteen

Anita checked her watch again. Now Roy was thirty-five minutes late. What gives?

He had been good, if not totally prompt, about meeting every two hours. Now it was the end of the day, time to return to the hotel and regroup. The meeting place hadn't changed: the corner bench at Little People Playground.

But no Roy.

Anita didn't know what to do. Did he get lost? Possibly, but Roy had a map and her cell phone number. A more troubling thought emerged: Did he simply take off?

Roy did seem to be losing interest in the search. He was quiet throughout the day, probably feeling awkward and dejected about the kiss the prior night. Earlier, he had muttered that if they didn't make any progress, this would be his last day. He was edgy. He was probably low on money. He didn't look well, probably hungover. And he had been fairly cynical from the start.

Maybe he blew me off, she thought. Maybe he went to a bar. *Or maybe he ran into trouble.*

That last thought sent a chill through her. What could she do?

Nothing. Except wait.

After an hour had passed, she took a cab back to the hotel. At the hotel, she checked his room. No answer. Maybe he went back to California? Anita checked with the front desk, but they told her he had not checked out.

Unless he blew out of town without paying his bill, Anita thought.

Anita sat in the silence of her hotel room, watching night descend over the city. The phone did not ring. She ordered a room service salad, but couldn't finish it. There were new knots in her stomach. She tried his room several more times. She left messages.

"Roy, it's Anita, I'm worried, *call me.* I'm in my hotel room."

She returned to his door several times to knock on it, loud, in case he was asleep or passed out. When Dennis drank, it took an earthquake to wake him.

Dennis. His name brought relief to her thoughts. Dennis would be arriving tomorrow afternoon. Dennis would help sort through this mess. Dennis would know what to do.

She needed him now more than ever.

Anita awoke with a jolt the next morning. She immediately called Roy's room. No response. Again.

Great, she said to herself. Now I have two missing persons.

Anita's head swam. Two nights ago, she was afraid Roy was out to kill her. Now she was worried for him.

Anita debated whether or not to call the police. Wasn't there some kind of rule about waiting twenty-four hours before reporting a missing person? She decided to call Ford anyway, even though she could predict his weary, exasperated response: "Now you lost somebody else?"

But Ford wasn't there. She left a message, babbling a bit, and realized after she hung up that it would be a while before Ford called back. If he did call back.

There were probably more rapes and murders last night to keep him busy. She was just some kook from California who kept seeing her dead son in buses and on playgrounds.

Anita grew antsy. She could not sit in the hotel all day. She studied her map of the Lakeview neighborhood. She knew she could probably pinpoint within a few blocks where Roy was located late yesterday.

She decided to trace his footsteps.

* * *

The skies were gray, threatening but not delivering rain.

Anita walked the Lakeview streets, covering block after block, stopping now and then to dial Roy's hotel room on her cell phone.

This is madness, she told herself. Now what do I do, create a missing poster for Roy?

As the hours advanced toward noon, her legs ached from days of hitting the pavement. Anita chose to return to the hotel and wait for Dennis to arrive from Orlando.

She needed a fresh mind to tackle this. She was positively fatigued.

On her way to Belmont Avenue to grab a cab, Anita passed an alley between two apartment buildings. Tucked about one hundred feet in, she caught sight of a parked, open U-Haul van. Several items were placed in the gravel near the truck, including an ironing board, a couple of chairs, and a child's bicycle.

Anita paused. It was a boy's bike.

She stepped into the alley to get a better look. She hung to one side, near a series of winding back stairways that led up to apartments. The gravel crunched under her feet. Flies buzzed from nearby Dumpsters. She kept her eyes fixed on the back of the van.

Suddenly the tall blond woman entered Anita's sight. Anita froze. She felt shock waves. It was the woman from the playground. She was carrying a large cardboard box of clothes. She added the box to the rear of the truck, among other boxes and plastic bins. She did not see Anita.

Anita ducked into the shadows beneath a back stairwell. Her mind raced. *It's her. I found her. She's skipping town.*

Then Anita saw Tim. She thought her heart would explode. Walking evenly across the gravel like a young man, he joined the blond woman. He held a cookie. He exchanged words with the woman, but Anita couldn't hear them.

Anita felt her throat tighten. She wanted to sob. She had to clamp a hand over her mouth to stop from shouting out his name. More than anything in the entire world, she wanted to run at him, scoop him up . . .

But she was under better control this time. She would handle it right. She would not blow it again. She had waited too long for this . . .

Anita reached into her purse and took out her cell phone.

Don't panic, she told herself. *Don't scare them off. They won't even know I'm here. I'll call the police. Read them the license plate number off the truck. The police will be here in minutes. I will save my son.*

Hands trembling, Anita turned on the phone. She kept her eye on Tim and the woman. The woman was rearranging items in the back of the van while Tim stood at her side, watching.

Anita shook so much that her fingers could barely connect with the tiny buttons. With great focus, she dialed 9-1-1. She waited for the call to go through.

Abruptly, an arm shot out from behind her. It snatched the phone from her grasp.

Anita gasped and spun around. She opened her mouth to scream—

—and then didn't.

Instead, Anita broke out into a smile, her shock immediately replaced by relief.

"*Dennis!*"

"You don't have to call the police," he said. "I already did." He hung up the phone with a jab of his thumb.

Dennis had a beard, he was missing his glasses, but it was still him, the familiar face, the greatest thing she could have hoped for at this time.

Anita grabbed his arm. "Thank God you're here. Dennis . . . that woman has Tim—" She was trying to keep her voice low, but hysteria pushed it higher.

"I know, I know," said Dennis calmly. "Settle down. *Look at me.*"

She nodded, took a deep breath, heart still racing. She looked into his eyes.

"We have to be very quiet," said Dennis. "The police are on their way. I took care of that."

"How did you know?"

"I have a real-estate contact in Chicago who knows the landlord to this building, and he called me with this tip. I came out as fast as I could. I tried to reach you at the hotel."

"I've been out every day, looking for him. Dennis, I can't believe you're here. How did—"

He held a finger up to his lips to quiet her. "We'll talk about it later. We have a lot of catching up to do. But first . . ."

Dennis gestured to a narrow space nearby, an area behind the Dumpsters, against a wall of the brick building. It was dark and hidden. "We need to stay out of sight, until the police get here."

Anita nodded. "Right. OK."

"Don't make a sound." Dennis beckoned her to follow.

Anita looked at the U-Haul and the blond woman and Tim.

"Come on," said Dennis. "They're not going anywhere."

"I know," said Anita, and she started to turn, but then glanced back at the truck. Something had caught her eye.

There was a flash of something familiar inside the U-Haul. She strained to get a better look.

The blond woman was rearranging the contents. She moved a box and stepped to the side, giving Anita a complete view of the item she had glimpsed. Anita gasped. Terror seized her entire body.

The San Francisco Giants golf bag.

"Come on, come on," urged Dennis. "What are you waiting for?"

Anita felt paralyzed. She was in a state of shock.

Not Dennis. Oh my God, no, no, no . . .

"Anita . . ."

She turned to face him. "I . . . think . . . I'll go wait . . . at the curb . . . for the police to arrive . . ."

"No," said Dennis firmly. "She might see you."

Anita took a step backward. "I'd really . . . rather . . . do that . . . Dennis." Her voice shook. She couldn't keep it even.

Dennis knew something was wrong.

Anita saw Dennis remove his gaze from her. His eyes lifted, looking over her shoulder.

Dennis saw the golf bag. Then his stare returned to Anita.

In a horrific instant, his eyes changed to evil slits and his mouth twisted into a frown. He dashed the cell phone to the ground where it exploded into pieces of plastic. He took a big step toward her . . .

Anita turned to run.

Dennis caught her by the wrist. He yanked her back and spun her around.

"Dennis!" She pulled violently, but his grasp was iron.

She saw him reach into his waist. She saw the butt of a pistol. He pulled the gun out. He began to raise it.

Anita frantically dug her free hand into her purse.

Dennis aimed the gun between her eyes.

"It's over, Anita," he growled.

"*NO!*"

Anita shot Dennis full in the face with the pepper spray.

Dennis yelled and let go. He flung himself backward, out of the stream of the spray. He let loose with a string of profanity, waving the gun blindly.

Anita kicked him hard in the groin.

Dennis dropped to the ground.

Anita ran.

Chapter Twenty

The pain sucked him to the ground.

The burning clamped his eyes shut. His chest tightened, squeezing his breath, causing him to cough and drool. His balls screamed.

Helpless and on all fours, Dennis clutched the dirt, enraged. Anita had attacked and gotten away.

"Dennis?"

He couldn't see her, but knew the voice. Cary was standing over him.

Her hands took ahold under his arms. She helped him to his feet. He still couldn't open his eyes.

"What happened?"

"I got maced. It was Anita."

"Anita?" said Cary, under her breath.

"Did you see which way she went?"

"No. We were packing the van. I heard you shout, we came running."

"Is Tim OK?" he asked.

"*Jeffrey* is fine," she replied. "He's right here with me."

"I can't see a thing," Dennis growled, his face hot and tingling.

"Are you OK, Daddy?" asked Tim.

"I'm fine, Jeffrey, fine. A bad lady . . . sprayed something in my eyes . . . and ran away . . . but I'm—" He was out of breath. He couldn't continue the sentence.

"You dropped your G-U-N," said Cary. "I put it in my purse."

"Jesus Christ," muttered Dennis.

"She's probably getting the P-O-L-I-C-E," said Cary.

"Well, I can't fucking see!" snapped Dennis. He sucked in air. "You're going to have to drive. We've gotta get out of here *now*."

"The stuff in the apartment . . ." started Cary.

"We've got what's important, right?"

"I think so."

"Then let's hit the road."

Tim asked, "Are we going to our new house?"

"Yes, dear," said Cary.

"It's only our new house for a little while," said Dennis.

"It's not our new house?" said Tim, sounding disappointed.

"Not forever," replied Dennis. He stuck out his

hand. "Now get me to the van and let's get out of here."

Cary guided him to the front of the truck. He waited as she placed Tim in the center of the seat, securing him with a lap belt. Then she helped Dennis to sit alongside Tim, by the window. Once they were situated, she went to the back of the van.

Dennis heard Cary retract the loading ramp, roll the cargo door shut and lock it. Then he heard her climb behind the wheel.

As Cary started up the engine, Dennis managed to open his eyes a little bit to allow some light. His eyes and nose watered profusely. Air returned to his lungs. He felt dizzy. His balls ached. He loathed Anita . . . *loathed* her.

"If I ever see that bitch again—" he started.

"Jeffrey," reminded Cary, cutting Dennis off before he went into a profanity-filled, murderous rant.

The U-Haul van left the alley and turned onto the main road.

"Just get us to the highway," muttered Dennis. He knew that Anita was probably rallying the police at this very minute.

"Rest your eyes," said Cary. "We'll be across the state border before you know it. Nobody's gonna find us."

"We're going to need new names, new IDs, new looks," said Dennis, "all over again."

"That's cool with me," replied Cary. She

thought about it for a moment, then declared, "You know, I've always wanted to be a redhead."

Deep darkness.

Rumbling.

Occasional bumps and jolts.

Anita's hands roamed her surroundings. She could feel plastic bins to her left, rolled-up carpet behind her, a child's box spring and mattress to the right, and cardboard boxes directly in front. By the sound the boxes made when they jiggled, they probably contained dishes.

If she listened real hard, she could occasionally hear the muffled murmurs of Dennis and the woman he called "Cary."

Anita didn't know where they were going. But she was along for the ride.

After spraying Dennis, she had quickly circled to the other side of the U-Haul, out of the view of Cary and Tim. When Cary and Tim reached Dennis, she slipped into the back of the van. She hid deep in the back, behind the piles and stacks.

It was a mad impulse, but she had to do it. There was no way she was going to let them drive off and escape. No way she would allow them to begin new lives of anonymity somewhere else. Not with Tim.

There would be no more searches. She would not lose him again.

Now she understood why Dennis didn't want her to begin her search until he got there—because he was planning on never showing up. He was buying time to leave Chicago. He had been under her nose this whole time, while telling her he lived in Orlando.

Anita tried to piece it all together in her mind. How could Dennis be behind all this? Somehow he faked Tim's death so he could leave her . . . but not lose Tim.

The whole thing was so convoluted that no one would ever think to make the connection. Pam provided an easy, vulnerable scapegoat.

What did they do to her?

The truck hit a bump and Anita quickly stuck her hands out to prevent a stack of boxes from toppling on her. Dennis's golf bag leaned into her and she shoved it back.

The space was cramped, forcing her into uncomfortable positions, and she adjusted continually. Her muscles ached. The air was stale and hot, and her clothes stuck with perspiration. She moved about in the darkness. As she stretched, her hand landed on . . .

. . . another hand.

It was all she could do to stop herself from screaming.

She pulled back. The hand didn't move. Anita regained her composure, swallowed hard, and touched the hand again.

It was cold.

She placed her thumb on the wrist and pressed for a pulse . . . there was none.

Dead.

Holding her breath, she ran her fingers up the

arm . . . following it into what felt like a down comforter. Then she touched a zipper and realized it was a sleeping bag. A dead body in a sleeping bag.

Her fingers reached a shirt. It was crusted and damp with . . . blood?

She wanted to yank her hand back, but continued to trace the body in the darkness, searching for its throat.

When she reached the throat, she found the thin chain around the neck. She followed the chain with her fingertips until she felt the small gold cross.

"Oh my God," she said very quietly.

Roy.

She held back the crying, stifled it into small hiccups. Anita knew that the man and woman in the front seat would stop at nothing to keep their secret alive. Roy had been murdered. Dennis had been prepared to shoot her in the alley.

This was no longer the man she once married, the charming frat boy from Berkeley. Somewhere along the way, he had succumbed to insanity. The glimpses of the violent man she witnessed during drunken rages were not another person created by alcohol. The alcohol simply stripped away the mask and revealed the true man.

Anita's hands searched in the dark until she felt Dennis's golf bag. She felt the various clubs and picked one with a thick, heavy base. A driver. She slipped it out of the bag.

Anita held the golf club tightly. If she needed

to, she would crush it into his skull, into her skull. If it was kill or be killed, there would be no time to hesitate.

Anything goes in the fight for Tim, Anita realized. It was an all-out war. There were no rules. Only winners and losers.

Chapter Twenty-one

Anita's mind raced in the dark, running through countless scenarios, but the truth was, she didn't know what was going to happen. She didn't know where they were going. She didn't know how long it would take. She didn't know what would happen when they arrived. She just knew that she was along for the ride. She could not escape if she wanted to. The van was locked from the outside. She was like a caged animal, coiled for the moment of release.

The wait was agonizing. It continued for hours. The worst moments came when she heard Tim. His delicate, high-pitched voice, speaking in articulate sentences, unlike the Tim she had last known. He was growing up and she was missing it all. At one point, she heard him crying and it brought silent tears to her own face. He cried for a full five minutes about something. She could hear the blond women, Cary, yelling at him to shut up already.

The truck made three stops. Each time, Anita scurried to hide herself deeper behind the cargo, clutching the golf club. But the rear door did not open. For the first two stops, the sound effects of various clunks and hisses told her that the gas tank was being refilled.

On the third stop, she heard Dennis shout "Don't forget the beer," followed by a door slam and a lengthy stillness. She could hear the occasional rattle of shopping carts, which indicated Cary was stocking up on groceries. If that was the case, they must be close to their destination.

Anita was right. Before long, the van maintained a slower speed and made frequent stops at intersections, away from the steady flight of the highway. Soon, the sounds of other vehicles faded away. The smooth pavement gave way to miles of uneven terrain. She could feel the gravel and dirt roads rumbling under the wheels.

When the van made its next stop, the engine shut off. Anita knew this was the end of the line.

Doors opened and slammed. Everybody was climbing out. Anita tucked herself tightly behind Dennis's big stereo speakers. She held the golf club in one hand, the canister of pepper spray in the other. There was a long period of silence.

They must be taking care of Tim first, Anita thought. Putting him inside? How late is it? Day or night? Will they leave the rest of the van until morning?

Finally, she heard a metallic *clang*. Light spilled into the van. It shocked her eyes and took a moment for them to adjust.

The loading ramp rolled out. She could hear Dennis and Cary bickering.

"So that's the best you could do?" she said. "It's a dump."

"Can it, we're safe here."

"It smells."

"It's been vacant, we'll air it out."

"The water's brown. The phone's disconnected . . ."

"We have the cell phone. Just chill out."

"I'm still waiting for our dream house."

"Well, not today," he snapped.

"When do we pick up the new car?"

"Tuesday." Dennis moved something and grunted. "Why don't you grab that, I'll get this . . ."

Dennis and Cary removed items from the van. They did not touch the stereo speakers or sense her presence. Dennis and Cary left the van, and their voices trailed away. Anita heard the slap of the screen door shutting.

Now.

Anita scrambled forward, pushing items aside, careful not to create any obvious disturbances, but also moving as swiftly as she could.

At the edge of the truck, she peered out into an area of heavy woods. It was early evening and the sun, muted by dark clouds, was sinking behind the trees. Anita's eyes roamed the surroundings. She saw a small, tired-looking garage . . . a small, weathered cottage . . . and an unpaved road that wound back into the forest and disappeared. That was it. No other houses in sight. Just nature and isolation. Perfect seclusion for a pair of criminals.

Holding the golf club, Anita stepped out of the truck. Then she heard Cary's voice.

Anita scurried into the woods, going deeper and deeper, about thirty yards in. Then she quickly knelt, crouching behind a thick tree and heavy brush.

They couldn't see her. But she could see them.

Anita watched as Cary and Dennis unpacked the rest of the truck. Wordlessly, load after load. Cary was strong, handling large bins with ease. When Dennis grabbed his golf bag, she shuddered. But he didn't notice the missing driver.

Tim remained inside the house, probably propped in front of a TV. She kept waiting for a glimpse, but he did not come out.

After numerous trips, Dennis returned without Cary. Instead of going to the truck, he headed into the garage.

Moments later, he emerged dragging a shovel. It scraped against the dirt. He leaned the shovel on a tree near the U-Haul. He stepped into the back of the van.

When Dennis reappeared, he was pulling a

stuffed, blue sleeping bag. It was heavy. It was Roy.

Dennis pushed the sleeping bag down the ramp. It tumbled and hit the ground. An arm popped out.

Dennis hopped to the ground. He shoved the arm back in. He grabbed the shovel and slid it into the sleeping bag with the body.

Anita watched in horror as Dennis started to pull the sleeping bag along the ground . . . heading in her direction.

Anita didn't know what to do. If she got up and ran, he might see her. Her footsteps would make noise in the leaves and sticks. But if he continued in her direction, she would be discovered for sure.

Dennis continued in her direction.

Anita crouched lower, knuckles tightening around the handle of the golf club. Her heart pounded.

Dennis advanced into the woods. He stopped about thirty feet away from where Anita sat in the brush. He did not see her. She remained very still, breathing silently through her nostrils.

Dennis let go of the sleeping bag. He bent down and pulled out the shovel. Then he picked a spot and began to dig.

The shovel cut into the earth, tossing dirt, steady and repetitive. Dennis grunted, sweated and swore. Anita could see the butt of the handgun sticking out, tucked into his waist.

The forest darkened as night crept in. Anita

maintained a painful stillness. Mosquitoes buzzed by her ears and landed on her face. They stung her neck and cheeks. But she couldn't move her hands up to her face. She couldn't move at all for risk of making a noise. A snapped twig could end her life.

She wanted to scream.

Every so often, Dennis paused to survey the surroundings. He looked around her, past her, but never at her.

A sprinkling of raindrops began hitting the leaves above.

"Goddamn it," muttered Dennis. He dug faster. When the hole appeared wide enough and deep enough, he threw the shovel aside. He tackled the sleeping bag, rolling it several times until it tipped into the hole.

Not quite deep enough. Part of the bag extended out of the hole. Dennis swore loudly, sending birds fluttering from nearby trees.

The rain persisted. She felt a steady scattering of drops soak through her clothes to the skin. She could see wet trickles cling to Dennis's face. He stared at the sleeping bag for a long moment. Then he jumped on it.

Dennis stomped on the sleeping bag, violently, repeatedly. Anita could hear ribs breaking.

Dennis flattened the bulge to ground level. Then he snatched the shovel and started dropping dirt over the hole. Each scoop of dirt splattered with a pop when it hit the sleeping bag.

When the bag was completely covered, Dennis

hastily gathered some fallen branches and leaves. He scattered the debris over the grave. He stepped within twenty feet of Anita to grab a fistful of twigs. His next trip brought him within ten feet. Anita held her breath, watching his eyes. They missed her.

When the body appeared sufficiently hidden, Dennis picked up the shovel and examined his work for a moment. He glanced around the forest one last time. Then he headed back to the house.

Anita remained frozen. She waited until she heard the slam of the screen door.

The forest was gray now. The rain grew denser, louder.

Slowly, Anita stood up. Her legs ached. She vigorously scratched at her face, then forced herself to stop before she scratched herself raw. She moved toward the house, taking a zigzag path to stay behind trees and brush.

The interior of the house was lit up, illuminating each room. The home appeared cheaply furnished, very plain. Probably a rental, Anita figured. He probably paid cash, minimum paper trail. Someplace in the middle of nowhere to lay low . . . to start planning a new identity and new life.

Anita examined the layout. It wasn't a very big house. She could see the master bedroom . . . and a small bedroom for Tim.

The most encouraging sight was the open window to Tim's room. A direct route to his rescue. It beckoned to her from across the overgrown lawn. Other windows had been opened, too, in an effort to air out the house.

The sight filled her with new strength and resolve.

Anita moved to another part of the yard. She slipped behind a tree and got a good look into the kitchen.

She watched Dennis enter the room. He washed his hands in the sink, lips moving, but no words, like a silent movie. Tim was already seated at the kitchen table in a booster seat. He drank milk from a coffee mug. Cary was taking a pizza out of the oven. She placed it on the counter and cut it into slices. Then she brought the pizza to the table.

Dennis grabbed a beer out of the refrigerator. He sat down at the table next to Tim.

Watching Dennis wolf down a piece of pizza, Anita realized how hungry she was. How long had it been since she ate? She decided she didn't want to know.

Tim reached over and stuck his fingers in the pizza. He started to pull off a piece of pepperoni. Cary caught him and slapped his hand hard. Her face turned ugly as she scolded him.

Tim pulled his hand back, on the verge of tears.

Cary continued speaking sharply to him. She made a big production of presenting him with a napkin and then a small slice of pizza on a paper plate. Tim looked sad, withdrawn. He didn't touch his pizza.

Anita felt renewed rage surge throughout her

body. She tightened her grip on the golf club.

Dennis chugged his beer. Cary sat down and took a slice of pizza. Cary looked very tired.

Anita's eyes roamed the kitchen. She saw keys on the counter. Car keys.

The van keys.

The rain was coming down hard now. Anita heard distant thunder. It rumbled in the air and beneath her feet. She was soaked.

Anita's eyes surveyed the house from front to back one more time. She made a mental note of where everything was. *Remember this.* Then she crouched low and quickly headed for the garage.

Anita pushed open a small side door and slipped inside. It was dark, windowless and musty, buzzing with flies. She cautiously stepped forward.

Immediately, there was a rustling noise coming toward her. She gasped and didn't know which way to turn. She felt something brush past her legs. It was a raccoon, scampering off into the night.

Anita regained her composure. Another rumble of thunder rolled across the skies, trembling the garage walls. The rain pounded aggressively on the roof. The next sound of thunder brought a flash of lightning.

Anita leaned against a wall inside the garage. She shut her eyes tight. She had to plan her next move. Her whole world narrowed to a single goal. Nothing else mattered. Nothing would stop her.

I'm going to get my son.

Chapter Twenty-two

The storm gathered strength, raging louder as it bent trees and battered the earth. Rain and debris blew in through the sidedoor of the garage. The rickety structure shook until Anita feared it would collapse. Lightning stabbed at the sky, illuminating the forest in glimpses.

Anita remained hiding, watching the house with tremendous patience. She had waited years for Tim's return, what was a few more hours?

Finally, a window in the house went dark. Then, shortly after, another. And another. After twenty minutes, the light in the master bedroom went out. The entire house was in darkness.

Anita checked her watch. She decided to give them one hour to fall asleep . . . before she went inside.

During that hour, she ran the plan through her

mind over and over. It was not a complicated plan, but its success or failure meant life or death.

Slip inside the house. Get Tim. Get the van keys. Slip out.

She felt confident that she could drive the U-Haul van. And if the sound of the engine woke up Dennis and Cary and brought them outside, so be it. She would gladly run them over in her escape.

War. No rules.

She envied the sleep they were now getting. She was exhausted and dirty, drawing deep from a pool of remaining strength. Every bone and muscle ached in protest. But her work was not done.

At the one-hour mark, without any light or motion seen inside the house, Anita decided to make her move.

She gripped the golf club, waited for a flash of lightning to pass, and dashed into the pouring rain, covered by darkness.

When Anita reached Tim's window, she found her entry blocked. The window had been shut and locked, shade closed. *NO!* Her heart sank. *This can't be happening . . .*

As the rain continued to assault her, Anita conducted a quick survey of the other windows. They had all been closed and latched in the recent hours, probably when the storm turned ugly.

OK, OK, she told herself. Now what?

Anita spotted a window well that led to a small basement window. She stepped inside the well. Her gym shoes sunk into a large puddle.

The window was rectangular and wooden with three square panes. Anita held the neck of the driver. She placed it inches from the glass of one of the panes. She waited . . .

At the sound of the next crash of thunder, she smacked the pane, breaking it. The timing was perfect. The sound of the breaking glass was lost in the storm.

Anita reached inside and found the latch. She opened the basement window. It was a tiny opening.

Can I make it?

Taking the golf club with her, she squeezed through, feet first. She scraped her butt, cursed her figure, but did not get stuck.

Anita landed in pitch-black darkness. She didn't know which way to turn and didn't want to crash into anything to announce her arrival. She waited for the next flash of lightning to send some light.

After a minute, the storm obliged. A blink of illumination shot through the room, followed by thunder. Anita quickly got her bearings. It was a cramped, unfurnished cellar. All concrete and clutter. She glimpsed a furnace, a washer, a dryer, and several loads of their boxes and bins.

More importantly, she saw the stairway leading upstairs.

She made her way over in the dark. Spiderwebs

tickled her face. When her foot hit the bottom stair, she groped for the handrail and started to climb. Her gym shoes squished with each step. Her clothes were soaked, chilling her to the bone. She pushed wet strands of hair out of her eyes.

At the top of the stairs, she felt a door. She listened carefully and heard nothing. She took ahold of the handle, turned it, and opened the door a crack . . .

. . . it *creaked*.

Shit!

Anita froze. She listened again. She heard the sounds of the storm. And nothing else.

Anita opened the door wider, very slowly. When there was enough room to slip inside, she advanced into a small corridor.

From her earlier examination of the layout, she had a sense of her location. Everything was on ground level. The bedrooms would be to the right. The kitchen and family room area would be on her left. Straight ahead, there was a bathroom.

Anita knew that Tim's bedroom was nearby. Looking down the corridor, she could see his doorway opened halfway. A little further down, the door to the master bedroom was shut.

The corridor had wood floorboards. Anita stepped cautiously toward Tim's room. One hand gripped the golf club and the other reached out to avoid walking into the walls. Her wet shoes continued to squish. Worse, some of her footsteps caused the floor to creak. It was like maneuvering a minefield.

She could hear the rain pounding away at the roof. It provided a constant din that distracted from her sounds. The thunder continued to crash with irregular frequency. Every hit sent a jolt though her nerves.

Anita advanced in slow, measured steps to Tim's doorway. When she reached it, she peered inside.

The room was small and plain. Several boxes lined the wall. Tim slept in a toddler's bed. It was a startling sight. When he had been stolen, he was still in a crib.

Anita could see Tim's face, relaxed and beautiful, resting on a pillow. His tiny fingers peeked out from under the covers. He was still just a little boy, surrounded by adult horrors.

Anita felt a sudden lump in her throat. She removed her eyes from him. *Can't get emotional. I've got to stay in control.*

She gave Tim one more look. *I'll be right back. Don't worry. Mommy's going to take you home.*

Anita headed for the kitchen, making careful steps. She grimaced at every small creak. When she reached the kitchen, the floor was linoleum. Her footsteps were silenced.

The kitchen windows offered just enough light for Anita to find her way around. She recalled the layout from earlier, and found the van keys on the counter.

Anita pocketed the keys.

She also discovered a road map of Wisconsin. *So that's where we are,* she realized. *Hiding out in the Wisconsin woods. This map will come in handy on the drive out of here.*

She slid the map into her back pocket.

There was one more item grabbing her attention. Pizza. Anita was famished. Two pieces remained on a plate near the sink.

Anita walked over. She scooped up a piece of the pizza. It was cold and tasted fantastic. She finished it in several big bites. Food for strength.

Out of the corner of her eye, Anita noticed something glisten in the sink.

A knife. The knife Cary used to cut the pizza.

Anita reached into the sink, took the knife and held it to the window for a better look.

It was a good-sized knife. It could offer some added protection.

She took out the road map and unfolded part of it. She placed the knife inside. She refolded the map around it.

Anita carefully returned the map to her back pocket. She untucked her shirt over it.

Anita consumed the second slice of pizza. She felt revived.

She moved over to the backdoor that connected the kitchen with an outside path leading to the driveway. She studied the door. *Better unlock it now, so when I have Tim in my arms, I can move fast.*

She turned the knob on the latch.

It made a loud *snap.*

Damn it!

Anita froze. That was the loudest noise yet. *Please God, don't let them wake up.*

Fortunately, judging from the beer cans that littered the counter, Dennis was probably out like a light. And Cary had looked exhausted earlier, no doubt wiped out from the move. . . .

Anita waited several minutes. She heard nothing.

Time to get Tim.

Anita returned to the corridor, back to the floorboards. Again, they creaked in random intervals, sending shudders of fear up her spine. She stepped as softly as possible, focused on her plan:

She would very gently lift Tim out of bed. Best-case scenario, he would not wake up. But if Tim did awake and become alarmed, she would put a hand over his mouth to stifle any noise. She could not afford to let him scream. She would move him very fast through the house, out the door, and to the truck.

Tim's bedroom door loomed ahead, growing nearer and nearer. Her heart pounded faster. Her skin prickled. She reached the doorway.

Anita stepped inside.

Cary stared back at her.

Cary stood at the foot of the bed, gaunt and fierce, nostrils flared, eyes on fire. She was draped in a robe. She held Tim in her long, bony arms. Tim clung to her.

Anita gasped. She spun around . . .

. . . and faced Dennis. His face was tight with rage. He wore a pajama top, sweatpants, and slippers. He held a gun in his hand. Pointed at Anita.

Dennis snatched the golf club out of Anita's grasp. He threw it to the ground. His voice simmered with venom.

"What the fuck are you doing here?"

Anita could barely breathe. She wanted to cry. She wanted to scream.

Dennis kept the gun parallel with Anita's sternum.

"Take care of her," hissed Cary.

Dennis stared into Anita's eyes. She could see the cold hate inside him. There wasn't even a glimmer of the man he used to be. That man was long gone.

"Give me what's in your pocket," Dennis said. "Now."

Anita remained frozen. "What?"

"You don't have a chance in hell of protecting yourself," said Dennis. "So give up what's in your pocket."

The knife, she realized. *He knows I have the knife.*

He continued aiming the gun at her. "Give it to me now. *Now. NOW!*"

Anita started to reach in her back pocket, under her shirt.

Dennis boomed, "The mace! Give me the goddamned mace!"

Anita hesitated. She brought her hands forward. The pepper spray was in her front pocket. She slowly pulled out the small black cylinder. She handed it over.

Dennis snatched it. "Thank you. Now come with me."

"Where are we going?" asked Anita.

"I suggest you come with me, unless," said Dennis, "you would like Tim to see you die."

Anita turned and looked back at Cary. Tim was awake in her arms, eyes wide and frightened. His little arms and legs were wrapped around Cary's side.

Abruptly, Anita felt a hard blow to the back of her head. She reeled, seeing stars, but managed to keep on her feet. Dennis had hit her with the gun.

"I'm not going to ask again," said Dennis. "You're coming with me."

Anita felt tears well up in her eyes. She couldn't stop looking into Tim's scared face.

Was this the last time she would ever see him?

"You are *Tim*," she told him, putting every ounce of emphasis on his real name. "You are my son. *I am your mother.* I love you, Tim."

Cary turned away, shielding Tim from Anita. "Don't pay any attention to that crazy lady," she said, stroking his hair. "You're having a bad dream."

Cary took him away. She closed the bedroom door, shutting it on Anita's face.

"Ready?" said Dennis.

Silent tears rolled down her cheeks. Thunder rumbled, rattling the windows.

"Let's go, move," growled Dennis. He shoved Anita, pushing her several steps down the corridor. "We're going outside."

Dennis pulled back the slide on the gun, cocking the hammer.

"Hold tight," he called out to Cary. "I'll be back in two minutes."

Chapter Twenty-three

With Dennis shoving and prodding, Anita moved through the house, the walls winding past her. He directed her down the hall corridor, into the kitchen, and toward the back door. When she slowed, he struck her in the back to pick up the pace.

"Dennis, please . . ." she begged.

"Outside," he replied.

She advanced through the backdoor into the yard. The rain continued to pelt the earth in the dark, creating long puddles. The trees shook violently, dumping branches around them. The wind stung through her wet clothes.

"Keep going," said Dennis. Every time she slowed down, he shoved harder, nearly knocking her down. It was getting difficult to see where she was going. Her hands were outstretched into sheets of rain. She stepped between trees and pushed past wet brush. The mud gripped at her tennis shoes.

Dennis drove Anita deeper and deeper into the woods.

"You brought this on yourself," shouted Dennis above the storm. "I didn't want to have to do this. This is all your doing. You should have stayed home. You never should have left California."

She couldn't see the cottage, but could sense that it was shrinking behind them. They were soon in the vicinity of Roy's grave.

Dennis ordered her: "Stop!"

She stopped. The wind howled, the rain blew sideways.

"Look at me," said Dennis.

Anita turned to look at her ex-husband.

Dennis sprayed her in the face with the pepper spray.

Anita screamed. She dropped to her knees, in the mud.

Her eyes burned. She could not open them. Her chest tightened, reducing her breathing to coughs and gasps. Her entire face stung powerfully.

"How does it feel?" snarled Dennis. "Doesn't feel too good, does it? A dose of your own medicine."

She couldn't respond. She couldn't even cry. It was all she could do to get oxygen into her lungs. She felt the skin around her eyes swelling. She tried to force them open. She couldn't. They shut involuntarily.

She was blind.

She knew he was standing over her. Then she felt something cold and metallic touch her temple.

"You can't see, can you?" said Dennis. "Then let me tell you what's happening. I am aiming a gun at your head. I am going to put a bullet in your brain. You are going to join your buddy Roy in the ground. You are going to be worm food."

"Dennis, wait . . ." she pleaded.

"You're not going to get any sympathy, Anita."

Anita, choking, groped at her surroundings. Her knees slipped in the mud. Dennis laughed at her.

"You really look fucking pathetic right now," he told her.

The kitchen knife was still in her back pocket, under her shirt, inside the map. If only she could see . . .

She had to buy time. She had to make him talk, listen hard to pinpoint his location, and then strike with her instincts. She would only have one chance.

If I miss, I'm dead.

"Dennis . . ." said Anita, still coughing. "Why did you do this?"

"Some fathers will just go the extra mile for their children," he said. "Do you think I would leave you and let you keep Tim? He's my boy. He's *mine*. Let's face it, Anita, you were never really there for him anyway. You were a lousy mother. You couldn't care less about him."

"That's a lie!" she shouted.

"You saw him maybe two hours a week, you were so goddamned self-absorbed. Well, you know what, he doesn't know you. He never did. A few more years, and you will be a forgotten memory. You will not mean shit to him. He's got a new mother now. She will be his mother for the rest of his life. You will be . . . nothing."

Anita reached an arm behind her back . . . lifted the shirt . . . and touched the map in her back pocket.

"Well, I guess this is it, sweetie," announced Dennis. "I look forward to digging your grave."

Still reaching behind her, Anita fumbled with the map . . . extracted the knife . . . and got a solid grip on the handle . . .

"Good-bye, Anita," said Dennis. "Put a nice image in your head. Because it'll be the last—"

With every ounce of strength in her, Anita lunged. She drove the knife forward into the dark. The knife hit a solid target. The blade sank and kept going.

A loud *bang* shattered the forest.

Horrific pain pierced Anita between her shoulder and neck. A bullet had grazed her collarbone. Anita splashed backward into the mud. She could hear Dennis thrashing wildly above, screaming into the storm. He was still standing, capable of taking another shot.

Anita whirled her momentum forward. She

crashed into Dennis . . . felt his punches . . . seized at his body until she found what she was looking for . . .

Anita grabbed the knife handle with both hands and used all of her might to drag it wider and sink it deeper.

Dennis howled and both of them tumbled into the mud. The pain in Anita's shoulder was unbearable, but she seized on the agony to keep going, like a vicious, wounded animal.

Dennis continued to flop violently. Their arms and legs entangled into a single being, everything soaked in mud. She could hear his panting and wheezing near her ear. Gritting her teeth, she forced her eyes to open halfway.

The first thing she saw was the gun moving toward her face. She shoved it away and a bullet fired into the trees. A shot of thunder followed that lit up the sky. She could see Dennis jerking his body in a frenzy. His eyes bugged liked a psychotic. The arm with the gun swung wildly.

Anita rolled away from him and desperately searched the ground. Where was the knife?

Dennis struggled to return to his feet. The knife remained in his chest, protruding grotesquely from a bloody shirt.

Anita threw herself into him. She grabbed the knife handle. He shoved her away, which caused the knife to leave with her.

Dennis, face half-blackened with mud, looking like some kind of deranged creature, swung the gun back in her direction.

Anita aimed for the heart. She drove the knife back into his chest.

Dennis let out a piercing cry. He squirmed spasmodically, gurgling. He stared into her eyes, shocked, and in a chilling instant, became the old, lost Dennis from long ago. Then he went limp and rubbery. He sank into the mud. He dropped the gun. He crumpled.

Anita kneeled over him. Dennis did not move.

A flash of lightning lit him up. The rain continued to splash down on his face, into his open eyes. Dennis did not blink.

Anita turned away, grasping, and shuddering. Sharp pain burned in her shoulder, shooting down her left arm, up her neck . . .

I've been shot.

Her shirt was soaked and she couldn't tell what was blood, what was rain, what was mud. Her left arm felt useless and numb. She looked skyward and let the rain splash on her face and eyes, wiping away the pepper spray.

When her sight improved, she looked back at him.

Dennis was dead. One hand remained locked into a clawlike position. The gun remained at his side.

Anita reached to the ground and picked up the gun.

She looked back to the house, lit up, like a beacon that beckoned in the dark.

She rose to her feet. She locked her sights on the house.

OK, Cary. Now I'm coming for you.

Anita stepped into the house through the door to the kitchen.

Cary's voice sounded from another room. "So you shot her? The bitch is dead?"

Anita followed the sound of the voice. She left a trail of mud and blood on the linoleum. Her left arm remained limp at her side . . . but her right arm was good and strong and gripped the gun. The searing pain did not matter.

Anita entered the living room. Cary sat in the dark, dressed in shorts and T-shirt, smoking a cigarette. She looked up and saw a bloodied, soaked crazy woman with wild hair and a dangerous expression pointing a gun at her.

Cary jumped to her feet, tossing the cigarette. "Shit!"

Anita aimed for Cary's bosom. "*Give me my son.*"

Cary stared at Anita in horror. Then, in a flash, she dashed from the sofa to a nearby doorway.

Anita had the gun fixed on her. But she hesitated pulling the trigger for a split second. That split second was all Cary needed to flee the room.

DAMN! Anita quickly followed.

Anita entered the hallway and then heard noise in Tim's room. She heard Tim squeal and burst out crying. She dashed to the bedroom and stopped in the doorway.

Cary had pulled Tim out of bed. She held him tightly—roughly—in front of her. A human shield. Tim was startled, eyes wide with terror.

"You want to shoot me, you're going to shoot him first," said Cary.

Tim's legs kicked. Cary's fingernails dug into him. He howled.

"You think I care about him anymore?" said Cary. "You ruined everything. You destroyed this family. It's over. This child means nothing to me."

"*Put him down,*" demanded Anita.

"On the contrary," said Cary. "You put your gun down. Or I will break his neck." She grabbed Tim by the hair, pulled his head back. "Don't think that I can't do it. I will fucking kill him unless you hand over that gun. The gun and the keys to the van."

Anita trembled. She didn't know what to do. Cary looked deadly serious and desperate.

Tim cried, tears streaming down his face. His anguish was too much.

More than anything, Anita wanted to throw down the gun . . . retrieve Tim . . . hold him tight in her arms . . . reassure him that everything was going to be OK . . .

"*Give me the gun!*" screamed Cary, gripping Tim's scalp harder, pressuring his head to one side.

Tim squirmed fiercely. His little arms and legs kicked.

Cary started to lose her grip . . .

"That's right, Tim," cried Anita. "You can do it. Come to your mommy."

"*I'm* your mother," Cary snarled.

"No, Tim, it's me. You don't remember . . ." Anita felt a rush of crying bubbling up inside her. "I'm your real mother—"

"Tim, I'm your mommy," insisted Cary, trying to inject sweetness into her voice, but straining. "Don't listen to her, she's a crazy lady. She's a crazy monster lady from the woods who wants to hurt you."

Tim continued to struggle, panicked.

"Tim, please, that is not your real mommy," pleaded Anita. "She is not who you think she is."

"*I am your mommy, goddamn it!*" shouted Cary.

"*NO!*" cried out Tim. "*I don't like you!!*"

Tim flopped wildly. His weight became unbalanced in her arms. He started to pull free . . .

Cary regained her grasp. She clutched at him madly, harshly, hurting him. Tim cried. She squeezed him back into her arms with such pressure that he reddened.

Tim bit Cary's arm *hard.*

"Ow! You little bastard!" screamed Cary.

Tim tumbled to the ground.

Cary lunged for him.

Tim scrambled away.

Anita squeezed the trigger on the gun.

The force of the shot sent Cary crashing into the wall. Tim screamed, covering his ears. He ran from the room, past Anita.

Cary fell to a sitting position on the floor, a bullet hole in her stomach.

"Oh my God," Cary moaned, in shock. "You shot me."

Anita kept the gun aimed at her. Should she fire again?

"I'm going to die . . ." gasped Cary, wide-eyed, suddenly childlike, petrified. "You shot me, I'm going to die . . ." The blood seeped in a widening circle under her shirt.

"Where's your cell phone?" asked Anita.

"In . . . in our room," said Cary.

Anita went into the master bedroom. She found the cell phone on the dresser. She grabbed it and returned to Cary. She tossed the phone at her.

"I guess you better call 911," said Anita. "And tell the police how to get here."

Cary gave Anita a long look. Her body shuddered with every breath, her face had gone ghastly pale.

"I don't know you . . ." murmured Cary. "But all I wanted . . . was the same as you."

Anita stared at her. She had nothing left to say to this woman. Anita turned away. She left the room to go find Tim.

Anita discovered Tim hiding in a corner of the bathroom, crouched in the corner. He was covering his ears and crying.

She placed the gun in the sink. "Tim," said Anita gently. She bent down to one knee. "Tim, everything is OK. I know you're scared. But you're safe now. It's over. Mommy's here."

She pleaded softly with him for several minutes. Finally, Tim turned. He looked at her from under his blond bangs, uncertain, still crying.

"Tim," said Anita. "Everything is better now. I'm your mommy."

Tim looked at her for a long moment.

"You're safe, honey," she said, feeling the tears on her own face.

Tim took a hesitant step toward her. Then another. The third step brought him into her arms.

Anita hugged him tight with her right arm. Very tight. It felt so good. His little arms wrapped around her neck. They both cried.

She told Tim that she loved him. And she promised never, never to let him go.

Chapter Twenty-four

The first snapshot showed Anita bathing Tim, small and pink and three weeks old, in the kitchen sink. His hair was soaped together into a protruding point, unicorn style.

The second photo was outdoors, more than a year later. Tim was learning to walk. He wore blue overalls and tiny black sandals. One knee was dirty from a prior tumble. His face showed great concentration. Anita stood nearby with a big grin, clapping her hands.

The next picture was Tim on his very first day, bundled and secure in Anita's arms in the hospital. His face was flattened and ruddy, eyes shut, hair askew, a startled new entry into the world. Anita held him close, glowing. It was the happiest moment of her entire life.

Anita continued through the small stack of

photographs, narrating them as Tim watched in rapt attention. They sat on a blanket in a Sacramento park on a day where the blue sky stretched from end to end without interruption and the weather was so perfect it felt like no weather at all, except for the gentle rays of the sun.

Anita was reacquainting Tim with his past. Jeffrey was fading a little more every day, like a bad, distant dream. Tim asked a lot of questions, filling in the pieces where his memory couldn't. She was delighted with his curiosity.

The counselor had said it would be a gradual recovery. He said not to expect miracles. Tim had a lot to get over. But he was young. He could outgrow the scars. He was in good hands. The odds were in his favor.

When Tim grew older, Anita knew she would have to tell him the truth about what happened to his father. And she would have to tell him about the bad woman in prison who helped his father do very bad things. It wouldn't be easy. But every day was a little better, a little closer to some kind of normalcy. She would gladly accept the slow pace, the baby steps.

He would be five years old in a few months. His teachers at the daycare center said he was smart for his age, among the brightest in the class. And they were excellent teachers, surrounded by degrees and professional accreditation. It was a large facility, stimulating and creative, with a low child-adult ratio. Tim was comfortable there.

Putting Tim in daycare was the hardest thing imaginable, but as a single mom she had little choice. Fortunately, she found an arrangement that made it easier.

Shortly after returning to California, Anita left Your Resources, took some time off to be with Tim, and then began a new job hunt.

Her criteria had changed since she left college. The job she now sought had little to do with money or power. She focused on companies that were known for a family-friendly work environment.

She found what she was looking for at Huber, a large technology corporation twenty minutes away, near Sacramento. The company had flexible hours, family-oriented policies, and generous benefits. Best of all, they had a quality, on-site daycare center. Tim was never more than five minutes away.

She visited him at lunch. She snuck over on breaks. Then she initiated a project that would allow her to check up on him as often as she wanted.

Anita's new job put her in charge of the company's intranet. One of her first brainstorms was placing Webcams in the daycare center so that employees could check on their children online. The other parents who used the center rallied behind her, and soon Anita's proposal became a reality.

In the beginning, she surfed to the site constantly, or kept it minimized in a small box in the corner of her screen. She always found him busy, playing, interacting, well treated, happy. Her compulsive watching got in the way of her work, but over time she learned to trust the center and check up on him less frequently.

Sometimes she touched his image on the monitor, drawing strength from the connection. His smiles kept her going through the day.

Anita's boss had two daughters and a thorough understanding of the demands of family. She gave Anita total trust and flexibility to adjust her work schedule for Tim's needs, whether it was colds or counseling appointments. In fact, she grew angry when employees with families worked long hours. It was the first truly nine-to-five job Anita had ever experienced.

She had plenty of time to share with Tim. He was the center of her life. She would wrap him up in love and truth and protection. She would never take him for granted.

When she had finished flipping through the photographs, Anita could sense Tim was growing restless. He was watching some of the other kids at the park. They were running, chasing, and tumbling. In particular, he was focused on a sturdy tree with low branches that had become something of a jungle gym for several of the children.

"Hey," he said. "Can I go climb the tree?"

She examined the tree, then nodded.

"Sure, if that's what you want to do."

"Yeah," he said, standing up, rising from the blanket.

"Then we'll go get sandwiches for lunch," she said. "In about fifteen minutes?"

He was off scrambling for the tree now.

"Tim . . ." she cried out.

He stopped and turned to look back at her.

"Be careful, honey," she told him.

"OK, Mom," he replied, and then he resumed his dash for the tree.

OK, Mom. It didn't sink in right away, but when it did, it struck her hard. It was a turning point. His tone had shifted. He had called her Mom before, but this was different. This time he said Mom naturally, without hesitation, without awkwardness or concentration or self-consciousness.

He was returning.

Nearby, the sunny sounds of Motown played on somebody's boombox. The wind rippled the grass. Anita felt a sudden, unexpected moment of transcendental calm. She soaked it in before it moved on. She had a good feeling that there would be more moments like this.

Today was another victory. Anita watched her son tackle the tree and begin to climb. He was fast and determined. Two of the smaller children watched with envy as Tim made his ascent.

He looked so grown-up right then. At ease with the world. Anita couldn't help but smile.

He's a magical boy, she thought to herself. He will endure. He's going to grow up strong, a survivor. Just like his mother.

THE CRIMINALIST
WILLIAM RELLING JR.

Detective Rachel Siegel is a twelve-year veteran of the San Patricio Sheriff's Department. But she's never seen anything like the handiwork of the Pied Piper, the vicious serial killer who's been terrifying that part of California for months. Because she's the best at what she does, it's now her job to catch this maniac—but she has very personal reasons, too, for wanting him stopped

Kenneth Bennett works for the Department of Neuropsychiatry at St. Louis's Washington University. There's something special about the Pied Piper case that draws Bennett almost against his will to the west coast. He has no choice but to help Siegel in her frantic search—even if it gets both of them killed in the process.

ANDREW HARPER

RED ANGEL

The Darden State Hospital for the Criminally Insane holds hundreds of dangerous criminals. Trey Campbell works in the psych wing of Ward D, home to the most violent murderers, where he finds a young man who is in communication with a serial killer who has just begun terrorizing Southern California—a killer known only as the Red Angel.

Campbell has 24 hours to find the Red Angel and face the terror at the heart of a human monster. To do so, he must trust the only one who can provide information—Michael Scoleri, a psychotic murderer himself, who may be the only link to the elusive and cunning Red Angel. Will it take a killer to catch a killer?

ISOLATION
CHRISTOPHER BELTON

It was specially designed to kill. It's a biologically engineered bacterium that at its onset produces symptoms similar to the flu. But this is no flu. This bacterium spreads a form of meningitis that is particularly contagious—and over 80% fatal within four days. Now the disease is spreading like wildfire. There is no known cure. Only death.

Peter Bryant is an American working at the Tokyo-based pharmaceutical company that developed the deadly bacterium. Bryant becomes caught between two governments and enmeshed in a web of secrecy and murder. With the Japanese government teetering on the brink of collapse and the lives of millions hanging in the balance, only Bryant can uncover the truth. But can he do it in time?

TARGET
ACQUIRED
JOEL NARLOCK

It's the perfect weapon. It's small, with a wingspan of less than two feet and weighing less than two pounds. It can go anywhere, flying silently past all defenses. It's controlled remotely, so no pilot is endangered in even the most hazardous mission. It has incredible accuracy, able to effectively strike any target at great distances. It's a UAV, or Unmanned Aerial Vehicle, sometimes called a drone. The U.S. government has been perfecting it as the latest tool of war. But now a prototype has fallen into the wrong hands . . . and it's aimed at Washington. The government and the military are racing to stop the threat, but are they already too late?
